"Spencer returned to the corridor. The second door led to the basement. He drew his gun and went silently down the stairs. A single wall lamp glowed dimly. He saw Ahmed and Denise in the wine cellar, and he heard her soft screams. He ran forward and fired one shot, almost surgically removing the top of the Arab's head.

"The jacket of her suit and her blouse had been ripped away from her chest and a rope was attached from her wrists to the metal base of wine racks. She lay on her side and he realized from the glazed look in her eyes that she was in shock.

" 'My shoulder,' she said, so quietly that the words were merely whispers on the air.

" 'Hang on,' Spencer said. He wedged the side of his hand into her mouth and with his free hand twisted her shoulder powerfully, until the bone in her arm slid back into its socket with a liquid, metallic sound and, as he did this, her teeth closed on his hand like tiny, powered spikes."

CAPRIFOIL

William P. McGivern

PYRAMID BOOKS
NEW YORK

CAPRIFOIL

A PYRAMID BOOK

Published by arrangement with Dodd, Mead & Company. Pyramid edition published September 1973.

ISBN 0-515-03153-4

Library of Congress Catalog Card Number: 72-727

Pyramid Books are published by Pyramid Communications, Inc. Its trademarks, consisting of the word "Pyramid" and the portrayal of a pyramid, are registered in the United States Patent Office.

Pyramid Communications, Inc., 919 Third Avenue, New York, New York 10022

To Megan Maureen McGivern, her own CDM

Caprifoil (Kæ'prifoil). 1578. (Ad. med. L. Caprifolium; cf. F. Chèvrefeuille) The Honeysuckle or Woodbine; also Eng. name for plants of the N.O. *Caprifoliaceæ*.

Chapter One

West Ireland
October 13
Monday
1700 hours

File One
To Analysis: Wash. D.C.

. . . fishing a stream on the west coast of Ireland a few miles above Galway. Place: not so far inland I couldn't see the oyster flats, the island, the fishing boats, the green-and-white swells.

I saw him just a few minutes before I hooked a trout. He came to the top of a ridge fifty or sixty yards above me, a big man with black hair, wearing a Bawneen, and carrying a rifle in the crook of his arm. He didn't have a dog with him, but he wouldn't be after rabbits anyway with a rifle; out of habit I moved downstream toward the cover of a stand of trees.

I caught the trout and thrust him flapping into my creel bag.

The first shot hit the water inches from my right knee. I was in the water and swimming when the second shot struck the bed of the creek and sent a spray of silt foaming up around my face. I had hoped for this, but hadn't counted on it; concealed by the muddy water, I made the opposite bank twenty yards down stream.

He didn't fire again. I didn't see him again, but heard someone scrambling up the ridge above the stream. A car started; the sound died fast.

I collected my gear and ran upstream on the bank to the motorcycle.

At the Twin Mares, a country pub, I drank a pint and explained to people I know casually that I'd slipped from a rock into the stream. I then phoned our cottage in Bally Vaughan, thirty kilometers from Clare.

Charlie was all right. She asked me if I'd caught a lot of fish.

Charlie is my nickname for Charity Finch, with whom I've lived the last ten months. I met her in London and brought her back here with me. She is twenty-five, red-haired, a fine sailor and skier. Rather than describe her as a great lay, I would call her a sensualist; by which I mean that she savors what is physical and intimate without guilt. I mention this because it suggests a contradiction to me. Her father is a Unitarian minister in Brewster, Massachusetts. Her mother is a lawyer. They are vocal liberals. Marchers, picketers, demonstrators. Does this equate with a mindless sensuality and hedonism? In any event: Charity was graduated from Bryn Mawr in 1967. This is all I know about Charity Finch. Whether her background is what she says it is, I don't know; but my guess, for what little any guess is worth in an evalua-

8

tion, is that she is not lying. She can be checked out in detail by her passport, No. 2190552.

The above will establish for Analysis the geography, the company I was in. I believe the substance of my report begins with the telephone conversation I had with Charlie that afternoon from the Twin Mares.

"Charlie, did I get a message?"

"Yes, and a queer one. A man named Harry Adams called from Paris. He told me to tell you that Caprifoil is missing."

"Nothing else? Charlie, listen: you must leave the cottage immediately. Drive to Dublin—"

She said: "This is crazy. I can't—"

"Take the road through Ballinsole and Athlone. I'll meet you in Dublin."

"I can't. I've got my hair in curlers. Just where the devil are you? Hang on. A car just pulled up outside."

"No. Charlie, listen. For God's sake!"

"There are three men," she said. "They're at the door."

"Tell them I destroyed the letter without reading it. The seal is in the fireplace."

"I'll be right back."

"Don't go yet!" But I was too late.

I heard her footsteps. I heard the door open. Then I heard what might have been a blow from a fist. It had that curious but unmistakable non-metallic sound; flesh against flesh. After a moment, I heard someone breathing into the phone.

At approximately 1800 hours, I arrived at our cottage. More time was lost checking the area behind it and the stretch of beach.

Charlie was hysterical, which was normal, but again this devoured time. There were three of them, not old, not young, that was all she could tell me, except that they had struck her and then had abused

9

her in more effective ways. She had told them what I had ordered her to, that I had destroyed the letter without reading it, and her confusion about all this must have seemed so genuine (which it was) that at last they accepted her word for it and departed.

With this established, I sat down and began to write this report, which I am identifying as File One. When it is complete, I will post it at Green Drop, Shannon.

"Aren't you going to tell me one damn thing?"

"Charlie, I can't. Not now."

"Who tried to kill us?"

"I don't know."

"What did that mean—'Caprifoil is missing'?"

I shook my head. She called me a liar. She was in a highly emotional state, which isn't like Charlie.

Four days ago, I received a letter from Andre Leroi. Inside its envelope was a smaller envelope, sealed with wax. Andre Leroi's letter, dated the tenth of this month, I will not paraphrase; a verbatim copy follows.

My dear friend,

I must ask you a favor. Since you know I am a serious person, it is probably redundant of me to beg you to consider my requests with the utmost seriousness. Nevertheless, I do beg you to do just that, old friend.

I am going off on a short trip. If I do not return to Paris by the thirteenth of this month, please open the sealed envelope enclosed in this missive and act upon its contents as your conscience and prudence dictate. I have dispatched identical requests to Harry Adams and Wyndom Ackerley, except that I have asked Harry Adams, since he is in Paris, to coordinate this affair. Therefore, if my gloomy fears are realized, you will hear from Harry Adams on the morning of the thirteenth. *On the morning of the thirteenth.*

If you do not hear from him at that time, please be so

good as to immediately destroy the enclosed, sealed letter.
As ever . . .

This letter, I repeat, arrived four days ago, on the tenth.

"Caprifoil" was the code name of Andre Leroi, a French agent who assisted me in a combined operation in Germany in the late sixties. Harry Adams, who called from Paris late this afternoon to say that Caprifoil, Andre Leroi, is missing, also worked with me in Germany. The remaining member of our group was a Britisher, Wyndom Ackerley. We were detached from our national agencies, except for certain administrative conventions, and had complete latitude in the exercise of our mission. Details of that operation are on file in your office.

Since Andre Leroi had not proscribed communications with Harry Adams and Wyndom Ackerley, I got in touch with them the same day the letter arrived. Our tentative conclusion then, with which we were in varying stages of agreement, was this: there has been a reaction from the German business we were all involved in. Some agency, official or unofficial, is now instituting reprisals. Andre, who is romantic, but isn't aware of it (his great weakness, by the way), may be attempting to settle matters by himself. It seems obvious that the sealed envelope contained information defining the threat which must still exist for me, Harry Adams, and Wyndom Ackerley.

The miscalculation I made may not be obvious to you; but it is obvious to me.

I destroyed the sealed letter from Andre Leroi at noon today. I obeyed Andre's injunction. I destroyed the sealed letter without reading it. I didn't expand or interpret Andre's injunctions. But it is necessary to admit that I failed to remember that Harry Adams truly believes that people miss planes. He gives every-

11

body a second chance, adding time buffers which may assure another's safety while endangering his own. For some reason, he did not call me when Andre said he would. Knowing Harry Adams, I should have waited another day before destroying Andre's letter.

I have used the phrase "the threat which must still exist for me, Harry Adams, and Wyndom Ackerley." It is obvious that Andre has failed to eliminate that threat.

These are the essential facts. I am not in need of sanctuary, official assistance or recognition. We will handle this matter discreetly, I can assure you. I am putting you in the picture because this information may be useful to you.

I will add my last conversation with Charlie, because it contains an admission I regret; but having made it, I must advise you of it. She said: "I've lived with you ten months, and all I know about you is that you like to fish, that you drink too much, and that you have nightmares."

"I was an agent in Germany. That may have something to do with what's happening now."

"That doesn't tell me anything."

"Well, just remember, there's always a war on, and some people fight it with guns and maybe a certain honor. But there's another kind of war that's fought in alleys, with bribes and lies, and no honor at all."

I told her I must leave, and suggested she proceed immediately to Dublin. She went into our bedroom and closed the door.

I will post this report at Green Drop, Shannon. I am carrying a Browning Automatic. I have a permit which was issued in Brussels but is also valid in France, courtesy of Theophile LeMaitre, the Suretè.

With a Green Drop priority, the file from West Ireland was delivered the following morning by jet and courier to Senior Evaluation Officer Maurice Stein, CIB. As with numerous other CIB staffers, Stein's budget for his section, plus Stein himself, were buried in the office of the Department of Wild Life. In consequence, Stein worked under the glassy-eyed surveillance of various stuffed birds and animals which had been collected by his predecessor, who had been, in fact, a legitimate old wild life hand.

On Stein's bookcase stood a ring-necked pheasant, three feet from beak to tail tip; in the corner an immense Goshawk with mildewing feathers and fierce red eyes gingerly held a faded gray squirrel in its yellow talons; even larger than the goshawk was the black swan filling yet another corner, the gift of Australian bird fanciers; on Stein's desk was the only animal he had any affinity for, an elf owl, six inches tall, with solemn yellow eyes set in saucers of soft white feathers, and a plump little breast precisely armored with soft, brown feathers.

Stein was not a whimsical man, nor was he given to self-conscious posturings, but it occasionally amused him to whisper secrets into the elf owl's ear, and then cross his arms and smile triumphantly at his little mounted friend, one owl-like conspirator to the other, sharing the horrors of the Saracen Vector, the Doomsday engines, and the other putatively unthinkable possibilities, which, in fact (as Stein well knew), people thought about all the time and seemed to be anticipating with almost pleasurable curiosity.

It was a highly dubious virtue, in Stein's judgment, that human beings had the capacity to adapt to horrors that were escalating at a cyclical rate of increase and intensity. As prospects of peace and security in the world constantly worsened people tended to look back on yesterday's crises with a sense of weary nostalgia. The Saracen Vector, for example: the top

13

officials who knew precisely what it was were probably yearning for the comparatively benign era of Arab hijackings and dynamitings, and the good old days when Hussein ceded his military powers to his chief of staff, General Mashour Haditha, and when the Arab guerilla chieftains were splintered by the divisions in Al Fatah and were still employing the relatively milder tactics of terror prescribed by Chairman Mao.

The burning of passenger planes, the attack on Jordan by Syria, and the civilian slaughter in Amman, all of these were projected in gentle pastel colors now, for—as with all other crises in the past—they had not, in fact, caused the destruction of the world.

But the knowledge of what might happen abruptly and finally to the world was like poison to Stein. He was literally and morbidly convinced it would one day kill him. His tolerance was declining, not increasing; he was no longer impervious to what he thought of as an over-kill of frightening news. And he took no consolation from the fact that this same over-kill was destroying the mental balance of people in jobs vastly more sensitive than his own. This fact only added to his anxieties; he had no wish to be the last sane person in Intelligence.

He realized with gloom that there was something rank and sick in his compulsion to unburden himself to his elf owl. But who else could he tell? He frequently was possessed by a frightening conviction that his short, thin body was simply a test tube into which some callous authority was constantly pouring dangerously volatile chemicals. It was all right so long as no one put a stopper in the test tube. That was how Maurice Stein felt. If they stoppered him, he would explode. He kept from being stoppered by playing his violin and by indulging constantly spiralling sexual fantasies and by talking to his little elf owl.

Stein stared at File One from Green Drop, Shannon. He read the report carefully before glancing at the name at the bottom of the last page. "August Spencer," he said, remembering things about the man. Sighing, he looked to the little elf owl for sympathy and consolation. "August Spencer," he said once again and added: "*Merde.*"

Stein sighed. Spencer's breed had served a purpose, which, to put it simply, was the readiness to commit murder for their country without the anodyne of flags and music and uniforms and slogans.

Stein reread Spencer's report carefully and reached for his telephone.

One of Stein's more important professional skills was simply the knowledge of how to go about collecting classified information from government files. It was essential to know the right people and the right data banks. While Stein had the authority to subpoena almost anything he wanted, he found it a waste of time to use it. Also, there was the chance of creating needless enmities. But sometimes there was no recourse. Anyone who filed a tax return, rented a car, collected Social Security or welfare, travelled by airplane, belonged to the American Civil Liberties Union or the NAACP, attended peace rallies or demonstrated for the poor—anyone engaged in that sort of activity automatically became an object of interest to the government. Surveillance was a constantly expanding and proliferating industry, because who could say how much was enough? The army, the FBI, the CIA and CIB all insisted on more computers and more data banks jammed with microfilm to protect and police the areas of their responsibility. Stein had no moral attitude to any of this. Keep the Commies out of the army, and the kooks off the campus. Or the other way around. It mattered little to Stein. But he did have a professional view of this constantly expanding peeping Tom-ism, and it was a sour one, since it tended to make his own work that much more difficult.

One irritating recent development was that many of the computers had been programmed to "borrow" from one another, but since they weren't always accurate and discriminating in this function, it frequently happened that credit data and criminal and educational data got jammed together into useless "master" files. Unscrambling these skeins of sensitive information could be boring and exasperating, and Stein hoped, as he waited for a connection, that he would have no problems of that sort with his Caprifoil file.

But his mood was not sanguine. He was fifteen minutes from his next cigarette and many hours from the relieving warmth of martinis and a luxuriant perusal of certain books he kept on locked shelves in his bachelor apartment. But that wasn't it, he decided. He disliked omens but he sensed an ironic portent in that word, Caprifoil. So full of subtle disturbing meanings ... Capri, capricious, cabri, the goat, and foil, to frustrate, to pierce, to destroy, to defeat. ... It meant the honeysuckle, the woodbine, lovely things but weak, damp and enveloping, with a tenuous, feminine persistence which would, in the gentle corrosions of time, bring down the healthiest of oaks, the strongest of walls.

Andre Leroi was French. That name had sharpened Stein's interest in August Spencer's report. An important man, Leroi. But was he the oak, the unbreachable wall, or the tenderly cruel, slowly coiling menace suggested in his code name? Stein enjoyed such speculation because he was aware that the unchosen seemingly innocent word could flood a sentence with illumination. He wondered what Spencer's code name had been. ...

Andre Leroi's career had flowed smoothly from espionage into government, and he presently enjoyed a post of respectable intimacy with President Barrault.

A voice sounded in Stein's ear, and he sighed with relief, for he knew he had got to the right person and the right data bank on his first try. Within the hour, Stein was studying the files on August Spencer, whose code name in that German business had been Wolfbane.

Chapter Two

G.N. Wyndom Ackerley, known to certain friends as "Bunny," cleared Customs at Orly in the late afternoon. An attaché case swinging negligently in his hand, he strolled through the crowded and echoing main concourse to the taxi ranks. There was something both elegant and military in the effortless ease with which he managed his body; it was the walk of a man who seemed to remember music from distant parade grounds, and to a knowledgeable observer, this leisurely controlled gait, this Guardsman's stride, would have identified Bunny Ackerley as convincingly as a fingerprint. He wore a trench coat, a blue blazer, flannel slacks, and Clark's desert boots. Ackerley was a large, fair man with curly blond hair; his manner, and his altar-boy eyes sparkling behind thick, horn-rimmed glasses, projected the sort of sunny well-being which invited confidences from strangers. At any hour of the day or night, Ackerley seemed to give the impression that he had just enjoyed eight hours of dreamless sleep and had breakfasted extravagantly on kippers and eggs and lashings of tea. But Ackerley's appearance of expansive good humor was not an accurate reflection of the three facts which were presently bothering him.

Fact number one was that his father had died the night before and that he, Ackerley, had no way of knowing if he could return to England for the funeral. Poor old boy, he thought. Fact number two was that now, as the titular head of the family, he must assume the responsibilities of that post, and set an example for his younger brothers and many nieces and nephews. Shoulders back, steady on, good lads. Fact number three was Spencer's chilling conviction that Andre Leroi had been murdered. And if Spencer were right (and he was always so bloody right), one needn't be a mind reader to guess that Spencer might be next. Or Harry Adams. Or good old Bunny Ackerley.

Someone tapped his arm. "You got the time?"

Ackerley stopped and smiled down at the man who had addressed him, a cheerful, balding, perspiring American, who wore a hat with an absurdly narrow brim, and instead of a proper tie, a "thing" (for the life of him, Ackerley couldn't think of a better word) made of leather thongs and metal loops. Alongside this man stood a young lad of perhaps twelve, who also smiled, and stared at Ackerley. The boy wore a wash-and-wear shirt and over this a zippered jacket made of shiny, almost phosphorescent material. On the front of the jacket were stitched in red thread the words: "Little Leaguers, Dayton, O."

"I make it half-past five," Ackerley said, after carefully studying his Patek-Phillipe.

"Thanks a lot. My name's Welles, Jim Welles. This is my son, Bobby." Somewhat to his surprise, Ackerley

19

found his hand being pumped up and down like a piston by Mr. Welles.

Ackerley smiled pleasantly.

"Sure thing. God, it's good to hear somebody speak English. We've been here a week and haven't heard anything but this yak, yak, yak."

"Yak, yak, yak," young Bobby Welles said.

Spencer had advised him to expect surveillance at the airport, but would they (whoever the devil "they" might be) intrust the job to such an improbable pair? Ackerley found that difficult to believe. But then again, why not? The American in Europe, puzzling over currencies, suspicious of the water, that creature, particularly if accompanied by a genuine little-league boy, was so numerous as to be practically invisible. But where was Mrs. Welles? Had they been professional, there would have been a Mrs. Welles, a young matron with those marvellous American legs.

Ackerley allowed his eyes to drift casually from the Welles to a cluster of people queuing up at a bank of telephone booths. Everyone else seemed in motion, rushing toward taxis and buses.

"Yak, yak, yak," young Bobby Welles said.

"It's like this, you see," Ackerley said in the kindest possible voice. "They speak French here, because, in point of fact, that is the language of France."

Ackerley spotted his man then. Dressed in a dark overcoat and a dark suit, he was partially concealed by the lines of people waiting to make phone calls. He was tall and slender, with black hair and the sort of complexion frequently defined as Irish; that is, there was a redness and puffiness in his cheeks which might result from too much golf or fishing in cold, moist winds, or too much drinking in rooms warmed unsatisfactorily by meager fires. The Irishman was watching Ackerley across the top of a newspaper.

"We don't understand any French, so it's confusing

20

for us," Mr. Welles said. Quite suddenly, his eyes became unnaturally bright. "The boy's mother, my wife, that is—" His voice trailed off and he turned away from Ackerley to stare at the hurrying crowds. "She died just a month ago, you see, and Bobby and I decided to take a little trip, just bum around Europe like a pair of bachelors."

"I'm dreadfully sorry to hear that," Ackerley said. "May I offer you my sympathy?"

"Sure, that's okay. Thanks."

"Do you plan to go to London?"

"That's part of the tour. We hit London next week."

In for a penny, in for a pound, Ackerley thought. He fished a business card from his pocket, scribbled rapidly on it. "In that event, this might amuse you. If you'd like to see an old British club, give this to the hall porter." He handed the card to Welles, who accepted it with what seemed to be reflexive suspicion. "They'll be pleased to show you around," Ackerley said. "The library is considered to be quite fine. I wouldn't know. But you can have lunch, look the place over."

Bobby Welles was regarding Ackerley with more respect, obviously savoring his dismissal of libraries. Mr. Welles smiled and looked at his son. "Well, what about it, Bobby? Shall we take up this nice man's offer?"

"I'd like to," Bobby Welles said. "Thank you, sir."

"One thing you won't have to worry about," Mr. Welles said to Ackerley. "I'll wear a tie."

Probably a very pleasant chap, Ackerley thought, as he proceeded to the taxi ranks.

Ackerley hailed a cab and gave the driver instructions in his ungrammatical but functional French. Glancing into the rear-vision mirror, he saw the man with the Irish complexion climbing into the cab directly behind his. There was nothing to do about it at the moment, so he let his thoughts drift to his personal problems.

The death of his father had stirred in him a mellow sadness, but not true grief. The old boy, after all, had passed seventy, and had probably taken all that any healthy, simple-minded man could reasonably expect to take from life. He had gone off with the hunt at dawn a week ago and fallen at the last fence before the open meadow and the easy canter to his stables. The broken hip was mending when pneumonia set in, and the old gentleman, while speaking to his man, Jeremy, was taken away in mid-sentence: "we drew our first fox at the copse before the mill pond and—"

All in all, as good a way to go as a man could hope for. Ackerley had loved his father and wouldn't have changed him in the slightest, had that indeed been possible. But he had always lived with a small and secret terror that he might not measure up to the example the old man had set as a father and a soldier. But it was, in truth, a small terror and he had lived with it comfortably.

Ackerley was a man given to memories rather than reflections; he recalled the good things in his life rather idly and without appraisal, as a child might turn the pages of an album of photographs, looking uncritically at old, familiar scenes and faces.

Although Ackerley's father had been a man of determined and frequently heroic action, Ackerley thought of him most fondly at ease and in repose: instructing the grooms in his severely genial manner, listening with fond, smiling interest to his pretty wife's tales of triumphs in the garden and nursery, or seated before the fire in the hall, tall and handsome in tweeds and boots, thrilling his five freshly bathed, ready-for-bed sons with the topography and terrors of the battles of the Somme. They had heard it again and again, but never tired of it. On the contrary, although every word of the splendid tale was engraved on their minds and hearts, they always waited for the climax with rapt and breathless attention.

(Ackerley's father had served in both world wars, marrying when he was in his late forties. He had found World War I a gentleman's affair; of World War II he had few good words.)

His father usually paused to drain his glass before uttering the words which to Ackerley were as satisfying and thrilling as flags straining in a swift breeze. "The 34th fell back, its flank enfiladed from Ovillers. But the XV Corps, our gallant lads, took the bastion of Fricourt village and woods."

Ackerley knew that if he himself were dying, and through some miracle were given a chance to relive one moment of his life, he would choose the exact instant when he had waited, shivering with excitement, to hear his father say: "... our gallant lads took the bastion of Fricourt village and woods."

The cab stopped with a jolt in the streams of traffic at the Alexandre Bridge.

Ackerley paid the driver and glanced through the rear window of the cab. The Irishman was still with him, leaving a cab parked halfway down the block. Ackerley crossed the bridge and started down moss-slick steps which led to the lower level, where Spencer was seated on a bench facing the Seine and reading a newspaper. Tourist boats churned up and down the river, their white wakes cresting on the cold green water. Old men in black overcoats were fishing along the banks. There was a blue haze on the air, the city still looked clean and white, thanks to Malraux's sand-blasting. Children on the tourist boats were throwing bread to circling birds.

Ackerley felt a thrill of pleasure at the sight of Spencer. He looked as big and formidable as ever, bulky in a gray duffle coat, with a cigarette plastered in the corner of his mouth, his head tilted to avoid the spiralling blue smoke, and wide shoulders hunched slightly against the cold wind off the river. He wore no hat, and his thick black hair was tousled by the breezes. Coming up behind him, Ackerley wondered momentarily if Spencer's reflexes were as alert as ever; but that thought was dispelled when Spencer, without turning, said, "Hello, Bunny. I'm very sorry about your father." They had talked the night before.

"Thank you." Ackerley sat down beside Spencer and fumbled in his pockets for a pipe and tobacco pouch.

"He was a good man."

"Yes, he was," Ackerley said.

When Spencer's parents died, he had been sent from Tennessee to live with an uncle, a sulky driver on the Midwest circuits. Spencer's boyhood had been spent with horses, at tracks and blacksmith shops and stables. His Uncle John had been a fierce, proud man whose most lasting injunction to Spencer had been: "When you say you're going to do something, then Goddamnit, go ahead and do it." Until he had met the colonel, that was about all Spencer had known, the dangerous sensitivity of his people in Tennessee, and the cool, proud anger of his Uncle John.

"He was riding straight to the end," Ackerley said.

"Well, if he could have planned it, that's the way he'd have wanted it."

Ackerley smiled at Spencer's hard profile, noting with a blend of affection and regret the first traces of gray at his temples. "You've kept in shape. How's that lovely bird of yours?"

"Charlie? She's fine."

"I thought her name was Charity something-or-other."

24

"You can't sleep with a girl and call her Charity. You might wind up getting just that."

"Now that's too deep for me."

Their words meant nothing now, they were merely sounds on the cold air, but the very pointlessness of the exchanges reflected their reluctance to get down to business, for they both knew from experience that the business ahead might be difficult and dangerous. One of their rules was not to make assumptions; another was not to know too much. Do your part of the job, and never mind what the others are doing, and don't ask why they're doing it. That was one prescription for staying alive and healthy.

But what worried Spencer now was the fact that he and Ackerley did know all about that mess in Germany, and a good deal about espionage in general, and it was the combination of the two that was frightening. In trying to save their lives, they might embarrass the Americans, and that could be fatal. Spencer knew, because he had been part of the team, that many sensitive military and diplomatic operations of the government were always conducted in secret, and ad hoc, by men who were not professional diplomats or soldiers. Spencer had seen the change in the last ten years, during which time the Pentagon and the Congress had yielded significant policy controls to the CIA and to the National Security Agency. Military operations had been launched by former Green Berets on CIA contracts, and no one in the Pentagon had known a thing about it. Members of the Secret Team operating under their powerful "need to know" orders could by-pass State, Defense and the Congress, despite the fact that the team was not a cohesive, over-all planning board, but simply a collection of security-cleared individuals ranging downward from the CIA and the NSA to civilians in the Pentagon and career professionals in the intelligence service. Policies were hacked out in piecemeal fashion, which inevitably resulted in contradictory directives.

One member of the team might decide to allow Spencer and Ackerley to do what was necessary to save their lives, while the man at the next desk could make the opposite decision; eliminate them before they embarrass us. There had been these confusions when the Mossadegh government was overthrown in Iran; when the CIA destroyed the Arbenz government in Guatemala; when the CIA elevated an obscure army captain named Ramon Magsaysay to the presidency of the Philippines.

And a series of escalating confusions when President Magsaysay had later been killed in a plane crash under somewhat curious circumstances.

Spencer knew he was returning to a world he distrusted and feared, and the irony was that, for a long time, he had believed he had escaped from it. He remembered with perhaps a therapeutic irrelevance that Clement Attlee, Prime Minister of Great Britain, had once written: "I certainly knew nothing about dropping the bomb, except that it was larger. We knew nothing whatever about the genetic effects of an atomic explosion. I knew nothing about fallout. As far as I knew, President Truman and Winston Churchill knew nothing of these things either."

Well, it was trite to say the world was crazy, he thought. But it was probably true. Ignorance of the effects hadn't deterred anyone. They had dropped it by design on Japan and Bikini and Eniwetok, and they had dropped it by accident on Spain and Greenland. The lichen in the Arctic land masses feed on the air. And the caribou eat the lichen in the winter, he had read somewhere, and now the Eskimos who eat the caribou are infecting themselves with dangerous levels of radioactive fallout.

Spencer looked down at the backs of his big hands,

and decided they had better get down to business. Paris was a good place to start over again, he thought, for he had also done some necessary work here for Benton, who was now very important in the CIA. They had burned the files of that work in the incinerator on top of the U.S. Embassy, and the rich tenants in apartments near Rue Honorè de Fauborg had complained much about the soft film of ash which had seeped into their lounges and salons.

"Where did you pick up the tail?" he asked Ackerley. "He's at the top of the stairs now."

"Looks Irish, doesn't he? Well, the Irishman, if that's what he is, was waiting for me when I cleared Customs."

Spencer was silent a moment. They could lose the Irishman easily enough, or eliminate him for that matter, but his presence worried Spencer because it tended to confirm his suspicion that their enemy was official rather than nonofficial; private individuals would hardly have the intelligence facilities and manpower to establish such thorough surveillance.

"Have you got in touch with Harry Adams?" Ackerley asked him.

"I called his flat twice. There was no answer."

"Does he still have that place near the Pont Mirabeau?"

"Yes."

"I think we should go around to Harry's," Ackerley said.

"There's no particular hurry. If Harry's dead, he's dead. Let's take time and add things up. I believe Andre is dead. Someone tried to kill me." Spencer turned and looked at Ackerley. "My conclusion hasn't changed; it's because of that German business."

"Yes, it's the only job the four of us worked on together," Ackerley said. They were silent for a time, and then Ackerley said casually, "Let's go around to Harry's."

"No, wait a minute. How are you fixed for cash?"

Ackerley looked surprised. "I've got plenty, as a matter of fact. Why?"

"The thing is this, Bunny. We've got two alternatives." Spencer was speaking slowly and quietly, with no particular emotion in his voice, but there was something in his eyes that reflected a weary resignation. "One, we can find whoever is trying to kill us, and prevent them from trying again."

"Well, that's quite obvious," Ackerley said.

"Or we can send a signal to Harry if he's still alive, and tell him we're running for it."

"London's going to be a bloody bore," Ackerley said. He smiled suddenly and pointed to an excited old man who had caught a fish. "First time I ever saw that—someone catching a fish here. Old boots, automobile tires, but never a fish. You see, with my father gone, I'll have to set a decent example for the nephews and nieces. If we decide to run for it, I rather like Morocco. Where would you go?"

"I'm not sure. I know a place in Tennessee," Spencer said.

Ackerley looked embarrassed then, and Spencer guessed why; he knew what Ackerley was about to say, and he knew that Ackerley was fumbling for words that would not sound theatrical. Ackerley said, "Well, I think I'll go around to Harry's."

The wind was rising coldly from the river. Spencer stood and looped the top button of his duffle coat. "You lose the Irishman, then go over to Harry's," he said. "I'll see what I can find out from Andre's wife. Call me at the Angleterre around eight. I'm registered as John Carpenter. We can go over to Billy's Relais and drink some vodka."

"Sounds excellent," Ackerley said. "Please give my very best to Michele."

They shook hands and walked off rapidly in opposite directions.

The Lerois lived in a massive but chic apartment building in the Sixteenth Arrondissement. Under careful observation from two doormen, Spencer phoned from the lobby, and Michele was waiting in the open door of her apartment when he stepped from the elevator. She ran to him and kissed him on both cheeks, and hugged him.

"My dear, what a marvellous surprise."

The sound of her voice told him nothing; it was as husky as he remembered it, threaded with laughter.

"But you, poor darling. You've missed Andre."

Spencer smiled and looked into her lovely gray eyes, for now he knew the lies were starting. "I guess I should have called," he said. "Where is Andre?"

"He's off skiing in Gstaad."

"Oh, damn!" Spencer said.

"I'll give you a number where you can reach him. He's probably on the slopes now, but you can call him at dinner. He'll be having cocktails in his room, feeling lonely and guilty, I hope."

"Was it a business trip?"

Michele had hooked an arm through his and they were strolling toward the open door of her apartment. Two heavy-set men in blue smocks, electricians apparently, were checking the wiring at the baseboard near the closed door of another apartment. Their tools were spread out on the floor, and they seemed to be working intelligently and industriously, but Spencer noticed the slight betraying bulge beneath their blue smocks, and surmised they were police.

Michele was saying, "Actually, it was business and pleasure. It's some Euro-Mart committee that President Barrault asked him to audit. Andre and his group will probably attend meetings till lunch, and then have a good time for themselves." Michele hugged Spencer's arm affectionately. "And so I have you all to myself. But at the risk of sounding like a wife, Andre does need a rest. The President demands so much of his time lately."

"Flattering but fatiguing," Spencer said.

"Exactly."

Spencer smiled at her, wondering if she were lying, or if she had been lied to. If this was an act, it was a damned good one. She was smiling up at him, seemingly happy and untroubled, slender and stylish, with long blond hair just touching her shoulders, and looking *très mode,* he thought, in a black suede skirt and a white shirtwaist cinched by a broad leather belt decorated with brass chains.

A damned good act, Spencer thought, except that the offer of Andre's phone number in Gstaad had come a bit too soon. That was intended to deflect him, but from what? Spencer knew very well that Andre was not in Gstaad.

"There's another dear friend I want you to meet," Michele said, as they entered her apartment.

The Leroi's drawing room was done in tones of white and gold. The walls and rugs were as blindingly white as popcorn, while the divans, chairs and draperies glowed warmly in citrus yellows and tawny bronzes.

Michele's friend stood at the fireplace, and his complexion and clothing blended handsomely with the tints and shades of the room. He wore a superbly cut dark-brown uniform, his hair gleamed like old silver in the flickering light from the log fire behind him, and his narrow patrician face was tanned the color of mahogany.

Spencer recognized him from newspaper pictures.

"General Mercier, August Spencer."

They shook hands, and the General smiled and studied Spencer with eyes that were as warm as the colors of the room. "Of course I have heard much about you, Mr. Spencer. From both Andre and Michele."

Spencer attempted to smile easily, but such deceptions were difficult for him; he hoped his expression didn't completely betray his cold and suspicious conviction that Michele and the general were playing a charade for his benefit.

He glanced at Michele. "When will Andre be back?"

"I'm not sure." Her smile was casually rueful. "The Euro-Mart thing is over at the end of the week, but he may take the opportunity to see some friends in Lausanne. You remember the Winklemans, don't you, August?"

"Yes, of course." It was all too casual and plausible for Spencer to swallow for a minute; they had obviously prepared an efficiently flexible timetable for Andre, and this puzzled and worried him. Had they known he would be stopping by? Or had they devised this covering story for someone else?

"Now, what will you have to drink?"

Spencer asked for a brandy, the general a vermouth cassis. While Michele busied herself at a narrow yellow-and-white bar, the general asked Spencer if he were in Paris on business or on pleasure. Spencer said a little bit of both, and the general said that was a civilized way to travel.

The general chatted on, urbanely and easily, commending new restaurants and galleries to Spencer's attention. Spencer listened with as much of a pretense of interest as he could manage, but he kept an eye discreetly on Michele, for his experience told him that, if anything were to be given away here, it would be by her and not by this quite remarkable man, General Mercier.

Had Spencer been conceited or vain, he might have been flattered by the performance being given (apparently) for his sole benefit. But being what he was, the play-acting only made him additionally wary.

("When people are lying to you, watch their eyes. They'll give them away every time." That's what the colonel had told him. The colonel believed everything was as simple as the flag and the Lord's Prayer. He believed that brave men looked brave. He believed that cowards and liars were betrayed by their shifting eyes, their trembling hands.)

He glanced at Michele, whose hands were swiftly and deftly making their drinks with no betraying tremors. Well, he thought, the colonel had been more right than wrong about the important things in life, and not many men could be summed up with a verdict like that. Spencer continued to listen with polite attention to General Mercier, who was now discussing politics in casual and knowledgeable terms. Meanwhile, Spencer flipped through his mental dossier on the general.

Jean Paul Mercier. Age fifty-nine. The product of an enormously wealthy family whose diversified holdings included cloth mills in Lille, vineyards in Bordeaux and oil deposits in the Sahara. He had been graduated as first cadet in his class at St. Cyr and had represented France in the Olympic Games at Rome in 1936. Fencing. Foils or saber, Spencer wasn't sure. General Mercier had fought with the Free French in World War II, had been an intimate of General de Gaulle and General LeClerc. He had been a vocal critic of the French government's decision to withdrew its armies from Morocco and Algeria, but he had not gone so far as the clique of generals who had been court-martialed and sent to prison for insubordination; General Mercier had been prudent enough to stop short of open mutiny. Since that time, General

Mercier had served with distinction as liaison officer to his country's ambassadors in London and Washington. His star had failed to rise during the de Gaulle years; the two men were in substantial agreement in many areas, but their soaring egos, it was rumored, made it impossible for them to work together. But General Mercier's star was now in full ascendancy; he was a ranking officer of the Comité Militaire Permanent, whose function it was to advise the President of the Republic, the titular head of the armed forces, on military affairs. Mercier's responsibilities also included various departments of Intelligence, and his select cadre of agents (whose numbers, it was rumored, were known only to the general) took orders only from him and reported only to him. In addition to all this, he was a close and favored advisor to President Barrault.

General Mercier's wife, Helene, one of the great beauties of her time, had been paralyzed in a riding accident and now reigned from a wheel chair over the Mercier estates in the south of France. Spencer had no information about the General's mistresses; if he took his pleasure in those areas, he managed it discreetly.

And that was about all Spencer knew of General Mercier, who was now saying, "We have our student uprisings, as you do in the States. But all in all, these are healthy signs." The general paused to sip his drink and smile at Michele. "Perfect, my dear."

"Mine, too," Spencer said.

"In any event, these disorders are similar to the squabbles in a normal family. In the case of your blacks, for example, they remained children for too long a time, ignorant, docile, but nonetheless cheerful."

Michele frowned and said, "Yes, but they were ignorant only because they were uneducated."

The general and Michele were trying too hard with

33

this casual chit-chat, Spencer thought; and attitudes and words were exactly right, of course, civilized and without heat, but neither of them could mask the obvious fact that they had no interest at all in the conversation.

"Precisely," the general said to Michele. "They were uneducated. Now they have reached the age of adolescence. They are demanding more freedom. And while this is commendable, freedom without judgment creates chaos."

The phone began to ring and Michele excused herself and hurried into the foyer to answer it. She returned in a matter of seconds and said to Spencer, "It's for you." And Spencer, as he walked past her into the foyer, noticed that she was looking at him oddly, a faint frown forming above her eyes.

Spencer picked up the phone and said, "Yes?"

"I'm at Harry Adams'." It was Ackerley. "Do you think Michele recognized my voice?"

Spencer noticed that General Mercier was sipping his drink and glancing casually at him over the rim of the glass. The general's silver hair and darkly tanned features were strangely camouflaged by the colors of the brilliant gold-and-white drawing room, and Spencer couldn't judge the expression on his face.

"Well, I'm not sure," Spencer said, and for the general's benefit, glanced casually at his watch.

"Your hunch was sound. Harry's dead."

Spencer managed a smile. "If that's your schedule, I guess it can't be helped. I can meet you at your office in about twenty minutes if I don't get tied up in traffic. Is that okay with you?"

"I'll wait here."

Spencer replaced the receiver in its gold-and-ivory cradle and returned to the drawing room. "The business end of my trip just caught up with me," he said. Spencer shook hands with the general and thanked
34

him for his briefing on the city's new and interesting restaurants and galleries. Michele came with him to the door. "Will I see you before you go back to Ireland?" she asked him.

"No, I'm sorry, I'm returning tonight. But would you give me the number where I can reach Andre? I'll at least say hello to him."

"Yes, of course. I'm glad you remembered."

She scribbled a number on a notebook beside the phone, folded the piece of paper and tucked it into the pocket of his shirt. And when she patted his chest with a gesture that was demurely coquettish, Spencer felt the delicate trembling of her fingers. Well, the colonel may have known what he was talking about after all, he thought. Watch their eyes, watch their hands. . . .

As they walked to the elevators, Michele linked her arm through his, and glanced up at him with an odd smile. "Was that Bunny Ackerley on the phone?"

"Why, no. That was a man I'm trying to buy a piece of land from in Ireland. Did you think his voice sounded like Bunny's?"

"Just for a second, yes."

"That's strange. I never noticed any similarity."

Spencer kissed her on the cheek and stepped into the elevator. She waved a hand to him in a small and somewhat childish gesture of farewell, and then the doors slid shut on her smiling lips and worried eyes.

Harry Adams had died hard. Spencer stood in the small, musty bedroom and looked down at the body of his old friend on the floor. Harry had been a handsome man with reddish hair, a light complexion, and friendly, humorous eyes. But he wasn't handsome now, of course, because no one with a blue face and a tongue sticking three inches out of his mouth could be called handsome. Ackerley had already searched the

35

apartment, but had found no letters from Andre Leroi. Spencer picked up a photograph album and glanced through it. Faces stared at him from fading black-and-white snapshots. An elderly couple seated on a porch swing, two young men in shirt sleeves holding bottles of beer in salutes to the photographer, and one of Harry Adams, a blurred figure in a group shot on the White House lawn with Secretary Rusk. Aunts, uncles, nieces, nephews, on elm-lined streets, in convertibles parked in front of frame houses in Midwestern towns.

There were no pictures of his wife, which was rather strange, he thought, for, regardless of the fact that she had reduced Harry Adams from a full man to a nonentity, he had never stopped loving her, hopelessly and abjectly. When she had completed the de-balling process on him with smiling, savage efficiency, she had left him for a padded, balding real-estate salesman named Pierre something-or-other—Vignon, that was it, Pierre Vignon. They lived in Paris. What was her name? Alice, yes. Harry Adams had stayed on in Paris, short of funds, in only fair health, hoping to catch a glimpse of her on the swarming sidewalks.

He returned to the small living room where Ackerley stood at the windows looking down at Pont Mirabeau and the dark river. Except for the address, which was 47 Avenue de Webbe, there was nothing very attractive about the apartment. Fifty dollars worth of furniture, a faded rug, and a table with a bottle of Vermouth and two wine glasses on it. A fly was crawling around the rim of one of the glasses.

"I was followed here," he said to Ackerley. "A black sedan, a Peugeot with two men in it. They parked on the avenue, across from the entrance to the building."

"Then strategy would indicate we leave by the rear

exit," Ackerley said. "I realize that's not a brilliant suggestion, but it's all that occurs to me. Did you notice a triangle of blue lights on the bonnet of the Peugeot?"

"Yes. That's Suretè, right?"

"In the last Table of Organization I looked at, they're listed as a complementary unit to the narcotics squad. They're designated as Force Three units, I believe. They're out in the open, and seem to supply plain old-fashioned muscle. But I've talked to people who should know about such matters, and they tell me the Force Three units report directly to General Mercier."

Spencer experienced an uncomfortable coldness in his stomach.

"What's the matter?" Ackerley asked him.

"I've just spent the last half-hour with General Mercier."

"What the devil is going on?" Ackerley said, in a suddenly worried voice. "Why would Mercier be interested in us? And who is trying to kill us off?"

"I still think it's that German business. But maybe we're overlooking something obvious. Tell me about your housekeeper again."

"Very well. I left for the country at approximately 9:00 A.M. Jenny was alone in the flat. At 9:30 there was a knock on the door, and she answered it, assuming I had forgotten something. There were three men in the hall. They overpowered her, and demanded the combination of my wall safe. She knew it, of course—"

Spencer interrupted him. "Why do you say 'of course'?"

"Well, I keep my checkbooks there, and when I'm in the country, it's sometimes necessary to make deposits or withdrawals. She handles those matters for me."

"All right, go on."

"They filled the tub with water and held her head under it, and after they did this several times, Jenny gave them the combination. They took Andre's sealed letter away with them, but didn't touch £300 in cash lying loose in the safe. She didn't get a decent look at the men. When I talked to her in the hospital she was shot full of dope. She was vague."

"Okay, let's try to get out of here," Spencer said. Then he stopped and looked thoughtfully about the shabby room. He was silent for a moment, while Ackerley watched him with mild curiosity.

"What is it, August?"

"I think we're acting like windy amateurs," Spencer said.

"That could be a highly intelligent reaction," Ackerley said. "Considering that General Mercier is one of the most powerful men in France. We wouldn't stand a chance against his Force Three units. We wouldn't be heard from again, until they decided to release us. ... And there's a chance we'd never be heard from again, period."

"But that's my point," Spencer said. "General Mercier, in collusion with Michele, gave me a bland story about Andre, handed me my hat. The Force Three units are playing wait-and-see. They could walk in here now and ask sticky questions about Harry Adams, and why we hadn't called the flics. My guess is they don't intend to."

"I'm not comfortable with guesses," Ackerley said, with a smile which didn't match his troubled voice.

"They may want us to walk away from this thing," Spencer said. "They're giving us that chance."

"It's not a very good one," Ackerley said.

"I agree. We're in too deep to depend on the patience of Mercier's private troops."

They were silent a moment, and then Ackerley

said: "Let's look at this thing closely. Obviously it was Andre's intention that we open those sealed letters if he disappeared."

"Then Harry Adams must have had the time and the opportunity to open his sealed letter. Which is why he was murdered." Spencer glanced about the room with fresh interest. "Is that what you're getting at, Bunny?"

"You've made a knight's move in thought," Ackerley said. "But that's about it."

"Then the question is, why didn't he get in touch with us, and tell us about the contents of that letter?"

"Well, to make an obvious guess, he was on the run. He didn't have time to make a phone call, couldn't shake whoever was tailing him."

Spencer began an inspection of the room, looking into ashtrays and behind pictures, checking under coasters and trays on the bar. Ackerley joined him.

"Harry *did* manage to get back to these digs," Ackerley said, while he poked his fingers into a can of stale tobacco. "The lock on the door was smashed when I got here. Harry had a few minutes alone."

"He had the letter with him or its contents memorized," Spencer said. "And so, knowing his silence would bring us to Paris and to him, he must have left us a signal."

They ripped the kitchen apart; they tipped the electric toaster upside down, shaking out scatterings of brittle crumbs, and they removed the paper linings from shelves and dug into containers of sugar and flour and tea. In Harry's bathroom they removed wrappers from bars of soap and unrolled the complete spool of toilet tissue in a fruitless search for a written message.

In the living room they found something interesting, a pair of sticky smudges on the cloudy mirror behind the bar, which looked as if they had been made

39

by some kind of adhesive tape. Spencer measured the distance between the smudges and found it to be a bit more than four inches.

"About the width of an envelope," Ackerley said.

"Yes, but if Harry left a message here, taped to the mirror, that raises another problem," Spencer said.

"You mean, why didn't he hide it?"

"Why, indeed," Spencer said, and there was a faint smile on his lips now, the reaction of a hunter to the first sign of his quarry. "They, whoever they are— Mercier's Force Three, German agents, official or otherwise—they knew Harry had examined the contents of Andre's sealed envelope. Otherwise, he wouldn't be running from them. It follows that they knew he would try to alert us. Leave a message."

Ackerley's eyes turned to the smudge spots on the cloudy bar mirror. "Harry left a message in an obvious place for them—" He looked at Spencer. "He left another one for us. Is that it?"

"I think so," Spencer said.

"Then it must be here."

They intensified their efforts, employing skills they had learned almost by osmosis in the tracking of men driven by guilt and fear to desperate ingenuities. They arbitrarily called the kitchen and bathroom clean and concentrated on the drab bed-sitting room.

Spencer took the photograph albums apart and shook out the books casually stacked on the bedside table. Ackerley checked a miscellany of bills and letters, shaking their contents onto the floor.

Spencer's tension increased with each passing moment, because he suspected that the Force Three units might be studying their watches closely now, and wondering why he and Ackerley were wasting precious time in Harry Adams' apartment. As professionals, they would be expected to take in the situation and its ramifications at a glance, estimate their own danger like computers, and then take discreet, evasive action toward safety.

Ackerley was flicking through a message pad which he had picked up from Harry Adams' desk. He turned the pad at an angle to a lamp in an effort to pick up any creases or indentations made by a pencil on a preceding page.

"Wait a minute," Spencer said, as Ackerley tossed the pad back on the desk. "What was the number we used? Nineteen, wasn't it?"

"Jesus, I am a clod," Ackerley said, and snatched up the pad and began counting off the pages. When he reached nineteen, he angled the pad against the light. "Here it is," he said. "Harry wrote something on page nineteen. I make out an impression on page twenty. How in Christ did I forget we always left messages twenty-deep in a pad?"

Spencer had already taken a pencil and notebook from his pocket. "Let me have it," he said.

Ackerley squinted at the page, angled the pad for a sharper reflection, and said, "Numeral two—stroke—numeral one—stroke—numeral three."

"Check," Spencer said, writing rapidly.

"Then a series of capital letters," Ackerley said. "In sequence they are: A—Z—U—C—A—D. . . ."

Spencer looked blankly at his notebook. "Azucad? Is that it? Azucad?"

"Seems to be. But wait. There's one more letter. It's either a capital O or a capital U."

Spencer frowned and pulled on the lobe of his ear. "Azucado? Azucadu? Ring a bell?"

"No." Ackerley turned and glanced at the front door of the apartment. Either he had heard a soft footfall or his nerves were playing tricks on him. "I think we've overstayed our welcome," he said.

"Right. Take the notebook. Let's go."

They went slowly down the rear staircase to a dark

41

hallway which was empty and smelled of cats. In the lane between the building and the river, there was a cold, rising wind that stirred leaves and refuse in the gutters and rattled the bare crowns of sycamore trees. Spencer touched Ackerley's arm and strolled to the front of Harry's building where it faced the Avenue de Webbe. Ackerley remained behind to cover him from the shadows.

Spencer watched the traffic speeding from the city, but saw no sign of the Peugeot which had trailed him from Michele's apartment. He raised a hand and Ackerley joined him. For a moment they stared at one another in a puzzled silence, and then Spencer shrugged and said, "Well, we might as well have dinner."

They chose a restaurant on the Left Bank which they knew wouldn't be crowded at this hour, and selected a table which put their backs to a wall and gave them a view of the doors opening on the street and on the kitchen.

"It's two down and two to go, apparently," Ackerley said. "Not much point in dieting." They ordered white wine and oysters, red wine and entrecôtes. Spencer left the table as Ackerley and an elderly waiter began to discuss the wines.

Madame sat at the cash register with a plump cat, and she was pleased to allow Spencer to use her telephone to call Gstaad. The desk clerk at the hotel in Gstaad told Spencer that M. Leroi was presently in the dining room, and that he would send a telephone to his table. A moment later, the desk clerk came back on the line, full of apologies, to explain (as Spencer had guessed he would) that M. Leroi had finished his dinner and gone out for the evening. Would there be any message? Spencer said no, and returned to his table. He sipped some wine which Ackerley assured him was excellent and told Ackerley of his call to Gstaad. "It could be a cover Andre established for himself," he said.

"In which case, Michele may not be lying," Ackerley said.

"Possibly. I think she suspects Andre is in trouble, but I can't believe she suspects he's dead."

Ackerley flicked the tiny dark kidney from each of his oysters, and waved off all sauces except for a few drops of lemon juice with which he made certain they were alive.

"Let's assume it's the German business," Spencer said. "Andre tried to settle matters by himself, but took out three insurance polices in the forms of letters to me, to you, and to Harry Adams. Then he went off, giving himself four days to finish the job. When and if he failed to return to Paris, we were expected to open the sealed letter, which probably informed us jointly that we were in serious trouble. Does that much hang together?"

"Too many assumptions," Ackerley said, and let an oyster slide down his throat.

"What else can we do?" Spencer said, with a touch of irritation in his voice. "I assume whoever grabbed Andre made him talk—with drugs or a dental drill against an exposed nerve. He told them about the letters and they had three days' grace to find us and find the letters."

Ackerley shook his head. "How could they have known about the letters? That part of it doesn't hang together."

"Yes," Spencer said. "You can give a man sodium pentothal but you've still got to know the right questions to ask him."

"You want to go to Germany, don't you?"

"I think I'd better."

Ackerley put down his fork and looked steadily at Spencer. For a moment, he was silent, and Spencer

43

couldn't judge his mood; the glasses Ackerley wore had a curious way of masking his expression.

"You insist it's the German business," Ackerley said, at last. "Do I take it you intend to go to Frankfurt?"

"I think it's necessary."

"I'm not sure it would be wise."

"Well, we're in the not exactly pleasant situation of not knowing what's wise until we've tried it," Spencer said. "While I'm gone, you can look up Alice Vignon, Harry's ex-wife, and a girl named Denise Morand, who was a close friend of Andre. Also, try to find out what Azucado means."

"I met Denise once," Ackerley said. "A dancer, wasn't she?"

"Yes."

Ackerley cleared his throat. After a moment, he deliberately removed his thick horn-rimmed glasses, and the effect of this gesture was quite astonishing, for removing the glasses was like removing a disguise, because with them disappeared the silly Englishman, the genial bumbling ass with bowler and stick, and in the place of this comical stereotype was a man whose eyes reflected a cold and dangerous confidence that no prudent man would be tempted to ignore. Ackerley's ability to pass himself off as a mildly ludicrous incompetent had kept him alive in many situations in many countries. A number of men had died with a last wondering thought about where the funny Englishman had disappeared to, and where the cold-eyed assassin had come from.

"Spencer, I know you have a son in Frankfurt," Ackerley said in a deceptively quiet voice. "You've pointed out, quite unnecessarily, that our necks are on the block. But I don't want my head lopped off because of what may be your irrelevant emotional considerations. Am I making myself clear?"

"You know damn well I've got to see Ilse," Spencer

said. "There's no other way to contact the people who may be trying to kill us. And if I see her, I will probably see my son. But that's not the reason I'm going to Frankfurt."

"Well, that's fair enough," Ackerley said, and replaced his glasses, and with them his air of complacent amiability. "How old is the boy now?"

"Almost six."

Ackerley hesitated, and then said tentatively, "You've never seen him?"

"No," Spencer said.

"Well, I imagine you'd like to see him. Perfectly natural curiosity. Why don't you bring some kind of stuffed whatnot?"

Spencer sighed faintly. "Figuratively speaking, Bunny, I wish you'd get rid of those goddamn glasses until we're home safe and free."

"As you know, I never feel comfortable without them," Ackerley said.

Spencer ate a few pieces of his steak. Several other tables filled up, and the restaurant became noisy. He knew they must get started. He was worried about General Mercier and Peugeots with three blue lights. If Mercier was involved in this business, it discredited Spencer's theory that the trouble stemmed from the work they had done in Germany. And they had already given Mercier one significant bit of information, which was that they weren't in Paris for casual reasons, but had come to look for Caprifoil. He put down his fork and glanced at Ackerley.

"We'll use Billy's Relais as a mail-and-phone drop. I'll file a report at Green Drop Fauborg before I go out to the airport. I want someone to know what we're up to."

"Yes, that's always useful," Ackerley said. He patted his lips with a snowy napkin and removed his glasses. "But one last thing, August. You'll explain to those people in Germany that we were operating under orders, and that there was nothing personal in what we did."

"I'll do my very best, Bunny. And, if I'm not successful, I may have to kill them all. That's what you wanted to hear, right?"

Ackerley replaced his glasses and said thoughtfully, "It seems drastic, but yes, that's what I wanted to hear." His mood changed; he smiled. "Denise Morand, she's quite lovely, as I recall. Is she—was she—Andre's mistress?"

"I think that's likely."

"I'm more interested in Harry's ex-wife," Ackerley said. "Harry failed to send us a signal on Andre's timetable. Maybe his ex-wife can tell us why."

"If he had any excuse at all, he'd go to her," Spencer said.

They finished their coffee, paid the bill, and separated outside the restaurant. Ackerley waited for a taxi and Spencer walked through the dark streets to his hotel in the Rue Jacob.

Spencer wrote a terse account of what had happened since he had arrived in Paris. Except for certain subtleties (such as Michele's and Mercier's role in this business), the only fact Spencer could supply Evaluation in Washington was that Harry Adams had been murdered. But he made no mention of the coded message they had found in Harry's apartment.

Chapter Three

It was late afternoon when Senior Evaluation Officer Stein completed his preliminary work on Spencer's files and the report which Spencer had filed at Green Drop Shannon. Stein cheerlessly stubbed out his cigarette. He had smoked his allotted two packs; he would not be eligible for another cigarette until he was at home with his first martini in hand. Stifling a twinge of self pity, he settled back in his chair, locked his hands behind his neck, and frowned at his elf owl. Spencer. . . .

One of Stein's functions was to attempt to gauge the emotional state of agents at the time they were writing their reports. He had to watch for (and try to correct for) indications of fatigue, hysteria, complacence, persecution complexes, vague feelings of not being appreciated, and so on. They were human after all, and were inclined to minimize their mistakes and maximize their successes. But the problem here was complicated by the fact that Spencer was no longer an agent of the government. He was a private citizen, with no more official significance than a retired postal worker, and this was one of the reasons that Stein found him such a bundle of confusing contradictions. Spencer's own image of himself, Stein was quite sure, was probably far from accurate. Spencer seemed to fancy himself a pragmatist, but he more than likely suffered the same flaw he had detected in Andre Leroi, which was a dangerously romantic view of the world.

Stein reread Spencer's report. After underlining several sentences which he felt were revealing, he proceeded to read them aloud to his circle of stuffed birds. Stein's voice was clear and pleasant, and he enjoyed a feeling for dramatic rendition. The fact that his audience was not only a captive one, but a dead one, did not bother him overly much any more; Stein had learned to embrace therapy where he found it.

"Rather than describe her as a great lay, I would call her a sensualist; by which I mean that she savors what is physical and intimate without guilt. I mention this because it suggests a contradiction to me. Her father is a Unitarian minister in Brewster, Massachusetts. Her mother is a lawyer. They are vocal liberals. Marchers, picketers, demonstrators. Does this equate with a mindless sensuality and hedonism?"

How old-fashioned, Stein thought, with mild surprise.

"Charlie was hysterical, but again this devoured time. . . . there were three of them . . . they had struck her and then had abused her in more effective ways."

Very cool and judicious. . . . Was Spencer telling us he cared nothing for this lovely sensualist with whom he had been sleeping for a year?

Stein pondered this. What was Spencer concealing? Was he attempting to convince them that his reaction had been cold, dispassionate, practical? And hence, to be approved?

"I am not in need of sanctuary, official assistance or recognition. We will handle this matter discreetly, I assure you."

How eager you are to get back into it, Stein thought. How boring that life in Ireland must have been for you. . . .

Stein was beginning to feel depressed, for he scented trouble. Trouble in terms of extra hours at his desk, and a much deeper backgrounding on Spencer and his friends Leroi, Ackerley and Adams, for he now had the uneasy feeling that Spencer had already misjudged his problems. Now go slow, he said to himself. He's on the scene. Why doubt his evaluation?

But something in the report supported Stein's intuition. He flipped through the pages until he found it. He read it again, nodding with satisfaction.

". . . there's always a war on, and some people fight it with guns and a certain honor. But there's another kind of war that's fought in dark alleys, with bribes and lies and no honor at all."

Yes, that was it . . . The love of those dark alleys might mar his judgment. It would have to. He read the last of Spencer's report, noting how unmistakable the contradictions appeared now, the lion snuggling up to the lamb

Stein turned his attention to the official files on Spencer. A letter from one Colonel Andrew Bradford had interested him; now he reread it carefully. The letter had been written as a character reference for August Spencer at the time Spencer had decided to transfer to Army Intelligence from the Infantry, in which he held the rank of Captain. The letter was dated July 6, 1962. Stein did some arithmetic and decided that Spencer was old for his rank. But it was difficult to judge with infantrymen; some of them savored the field, and refused the posts which led to associations with colonels and generals who influenced promotions.

The letter head read: "Andrew Bradford, Colonel U.S.A., Ret. The Blue Oaks, Chester County, Penna." The letter was handwritten on a paper of fine stock.

To Whom It May Concern:

As a soldier, it was my professional duty to evaluate and judge the character of the men in my command. Since I performed that task for the majority of my sixty-five years, I believe I am qualified to assess the moral and physical character of my foster son, August Spencer.

I first met August Spencer in the late fall in the year 1948. He was then twelve or thirteen. August was with his uncle, John Spencer, who had come to see me about an ad I had placed for an experienced groom.

I liked the looks of John Spencer. He was a big-boned, well-muscled man, with forthright and confident manners. He and his nephew, August, were simply dressed, but neatly and cleanly, and I was favorably impressed with them.

John Spencer worked for me for two years. In the winter of 1951, he contracted pneumonia, and died within days. Thereafter, my wife, Rosalie, and I raised August as our son. He was adopted legally by us in 1952. The papers are filed in the Chester Court House.

August grew up in a healthy country atmosphere. Our own two sons were respectively three and four years older than August at this time, and were proficient shots and riders. August needed no help from anyone where horses were concerned, but it was my pleasure to teach him to shoot, and he was soon an outstanding marksman.

But ours was not a family of exclusively outdoor pursuits. We were not all "jocks" as they say today. We instructed our boys by word and deed in love of, and service to, country. In those early years, I recall only one occasion when I was disappointed in August. A small thing, but I will make it part of the record, since I firmly believe

50

that such things (if not immediately and intelligently corrected) may lead to graver errors. He was attempting a joke, of course, but I overheard him saying to one of his young friends: "Mothers couldn't be everywhere, so they created God." I asked him to join me in my study, and I told him I favored the correct phrasing of that pleasant old aphorism, which, of course, is, "*God* couldn't be everywhere, so he created mothers."

To his credit, August understood that his attempt at humor had been wide of the mark. . . .

Stein began to yawn. The reaction was partially a customary withdrawal from nicotine, but he felt he had a picture of the colonel which this Chinese-torture flow of addenda would only obscure rather than illuminate. Stein began skipping. Spencer had attended the University of Pennsylvania . . . the colonel was closer to his adopted son, August, than he was to his natural sons . . . in drawing to a close, the colonel listed certain manly mottoes he had felt it worthwhile to drill into his sons. . . .

There was Grant on the art of war. "The art of war is simple enough. Find out where your enemy is. Get at him as soon as you can. Strike at him as hard as you can and as often as you can, and keep moving on."

I slept and dreamed that life was beauty.
I woke—and found that life was duty.

Stein didn't recognize that one. But he knew the next: ". . . a patriotism in the context of our times? . . . a patriotism which is not short, frenzied outbursts of emotion, but the tranquil and steady dedication of a lifetime . . . a mighty assignment. For it is often easier to fight for principles than to live up to them."

That was familiar to Stein, in thought and cadence. Adlai Stevenson. . . .

Again the colonel rambled. Bits and pieces about country life. Spencer's army medals. The letter concluded, rather touchingly, Stein thought, with the simple statement that Spencer would serve his country in any way he was asked to, with honor and courage.

The letter was signed "Andrew Bradford, Col., U.S.A., Ret."

Stein glanced at another note in Spencer's file: the colonel had died in 1965, and his estate had been distributed equally among August Spencer and Theodore and Jonathan Bradford of New York City, the natural sons of Colonel Bradford. Theodore Bradford was a broker, his younger brother, Jonathan, a lawyer. They had chosen (with Spencer's approval) to sell the Blue Oaks horse farm in Chester County, Pennsylvania, to a real-estate and development company in Newark, New Jersey. The amount paid to each owner after taxes and commissions had come to $185,000.

That answered one of Stein's questions—where Spencer had got the funds to retire from the CIA and establish himself as a gentleman of leisure devoted to trout fishing and sampling the ales and spirits of Ireland. But Spencer's resignation didn't sound like that of a man galloping off to the fleshpots. He had written simply but bitterly to Benton: "Request my application for resignation be acted upon firmly and speedily. I am not, and will never be, of much further use to you."

Well, Spencer was one more rara avis, Stein thought, glancing with some fondness at the exotic stuffed birds that decorated his office.

Stein dialed a number and to his pleasant surprise hit the right person and the right data bank for the second consecutive time within twenty-four hours. When a voice answered curtly, "Graham," Stein said, "Maurice Stein, Jim. I need more information on August Spencer. I also need files on—better take this down—Andre Leroi, G.N. Wyndom Ackerley and Harry Adams. They worked together in a German apparatus in 1964 and 1965."

There was a pause. Then Graham said: "Those files aren't available."

"They've been reclassified?"

"I don't know. They're just not available."

Stein felt a pleasurable stir of anger. He was not important, and he knew it. Sometimes he wondered if his exhaustively researched, and exhaustingly accurate and extensive reports were even read by his immediate chief, a smooth and plausible member of the Wasp establishment named Arthur Fennaday.

Fennaday, as an evaluation chief, lived his working hours in the rarified atmosphere of top government. In meetings with State, Defense, or the Pentagon, he dealt with the secretaries or the joint chiefs. But Fennaday seldom gave Stein the satisfaction of replying to his reports or commenting on their conclusions one way or the other. This had embittered Stein over the years, because he knew that his judgments and evaluations were the raw material which Fennaday used when he briefed the Cabinet and the White House. If the reports were praised, Stein never heard it. Fennaday was a quirky, bantering man, with a half-smile which suggested an amused, mildly eccentric view of the world. He was also given to tic-y behavior, such as always carrying an umbrella, but never opening it when it rained, and giving parties on odd occasions, such as St. Bartholomew's Eve or the date on which Roger Maris broke Babe Ruth's home-run record. Stein enjoyed reflecting on his chief's eccentricities, for it supported his conviction that Fennaday was quite likely approaching crack-up time. ("I want hunches, guesses, innuendoes," was one of Fennaday's familiar remarks. "But"—then came the crinkling smile, the familiar cock of the head, the leisurely drawl—"I want those things supported by *tons* of facts.")

It was the compulsion for facts more than anything else that convinced Stein that Fennaday was showing cracks. Facts and more facts, until every mind and filing cabinet and data bank was suffocating from a steadily rising, steadily proliferating accumulation of facts, in all shapes and sizes, most in duplicate, many in triplicate, and the seams of all their containers, human or mechanical, bulging. Fennaday couldn't get enough facts. He had lost faith in his ability to detect the two or three significant facts in a given problem; to camouflage his apostasy, he had taken to multiplying his options so that failure became not only plausible but inevitable.

Stein looked with smiling anticipation at the phone in his hand. He knew he would never make more than his present $21,000 a year; he knew that no chauffeur-driven limousine with flags flying at its fenders would ever carry him to and from work; he knew he would never dine with the important congressmen; but there was one thing with which Stein managed to sustain his ego, and that was the simple but heady knowledge that very few officials in the government could deny him the right to inspect confidential and top secret files. As an evaluation officer, Stein functioned with a "need to know" clearance, and this gave him an authority that was awesome in its all-embracing vagueness.

"I need to know certain things about the backgrounds of these men I mentioned to you," Stein said. Nothing in his voice betrayed his pleasantly simmering emotional state; on the contrary, his tone was one of mild but cordial surprise. "I'm completing an evaluation, and at the risk of being obvious, I can't finish the job without those files."

"I'm sorry. They're not available."

"If you make me take this matter to Burns, you may regret it."

"That's where you'll have to take it. I'll connect you."

There was a click, a pause, then another miniature voice sounded into Stein's ear. "Burns here. What do you want, Stein?"

"Thank you. What I need are files on—better take this down—Andre Leroi, Harry Adams, and G.N. Wyndom Ackerley. They worked in a German—"

"You can't have those files."

"Now you listen to me—"

"Don't bother raising your voice, Maurice. Stop wasting your breath and your time. Those files have been pulled by the White House."

The phone clicked in Stein's ear. A little chill went down his spine. He tried to dismiss his curiosity. Over the years, he had acquired a talent for selective forgetting. And what he had just learned from Graham and Burns was nothing to remember, nothing to speculate on. It was none of Stein's business why the White House was clamping a security lid on what was obstensibly some cops-and-robbers stuff going on over in Ireland and France.

Stein rang for a courier to deliver his incomplete evaluation on Spencer to his chief, Arthur Fennaday.

Stein put on his muffler, his overcoat and hat, and bade a cheerless goodnight to the rows of stuffed birds, whose glassy eyes now reflected the gleaming and shifting patterns traced on the ceiling by the headlights of the city's thickening, homeward-bound traffic. A cold sleety rain was driven against the windows by sharply rising winds. Water formed and ran down the panes in slow waves. Stein thought with keen relish of his warm apartment, his cigarettes and martinis. He snapped out the lights and went home.

Arthur Fennaday had a cold which he had been

trying to shake for the past week or so, and the day's raw wetness had done little to improve it. He parked his Buick in the breezeway which separated his colonial home from a three-car garage, and when he cut the motor, the sound of the rain drummed against the steamy windows of the car. Only his wife's Chevrolet was in the garage; his son's Porsche and his daughter's Camaro were gone. Fennaday got out of the car, briefcase in one hand, tightly rolled umbrella in the other, and hesitated for a second or so under the roof of the breezeway. The rain seemed to be coming down harder now, making a noisy metallic rattle in the bare branches of the big maples which stood like impoverished sentinels along the wide street. Damn, he thought, and ran along a flagstoned path that led to the entrance of his home while the rain pounded with what seemed to him a gleeful enthusiasm on the crown of his hat and the shoulders of his topcoat.

The foyer of the Fennaday home was warm and spacious and cheerfully lighted. Fennaday stripped off his damp topcoat and dropped it on a maplewood chest, which served as a repository for their children's ice skates and hockey sticks in the winter, and scuba gear and tennis rackets in the summer. As he placed his hat and unopened umbrella on top of his coat, Fennaday thought of his children, and what he thought was, they'll soon be gone for good, and then came the chilling, weakening conviction which he had not yet made the doctor understand: we'll all be gone, all of us, everywhere. He called for his wife, and she came from the kitchen through the dining room and gave him a smile and a hug and a kiss on the cheek.

"How was your day?"

"So-so," he said. "The usual."

Fennaday's wife, Eileen, was a plain woman with graying hair, but people frequently thought she was beautiful because she had an excellent clothes sense, and a slim body which she took sedulous care of. But more importantly, there was usually an expression of warmth and animation on her face, and when she met people casually at dinner and cocktail parties, they usually attributed that expression to an intelligent interest in what they were talking about. Fennaday noted with mild dismay that she was dressed a bit more festively than usual, in a shocking-pink pants suit with a black ribbon in her hair.

"Are we going out?"

"No, why? Would you like to?"

"Good God, no. But you're pretty fancy for an evening at home. Where are the kids?"

"Tim drove up to the Poconos with the Nelsons. Shirley is spending the night with Ruthie Brennan. I thought we'd have dinner in the study."

"Can you hold things for about half-an-hour? I've still got a few reports to look at."

She hugged him again, and said, "When you retire, I'm going to burn that briefcase of yours right out on the front lawn."

She went back to the kitchen for ice, and Fennaday looked into the serenely shining living room with the eyes of a stranger. He was fortunate to have this home, this understanding wife, and a son and daughter who were excellent students and not only seriously motivated, but damn fine company for him on their occasional week-end fishing or camping trips. But why, Fennaday wondered unhappily, did he have these attacks of loneliness and anxiety?

He turned and walked down the hall to his study, a tall man with an ambling stride, who bore a marked resemblance to Gregory Peck. When people commented on this, Fennaday usually smiled and said, "A very old Gregory Peck, I'm afraid." But he was flattered by his likeness to the film star, and quite unconsciously he had adopted several mannerisms which heightened the resemblance; he affected what he thought of as a "quizzical" smile, and he allowed a lock of his dark hair to fall across his forehead, and he lowered his speaking voice a tone or two and infused it with a warmth which he believed roughly approximated that of the actor's.

Fennaday made himself a stiff scotch and water in his study. He settled down in a black leather chair with his briefcase on his knees, and stared for a moment or so at his faint reflection in the dark screen of the television set. He looked tired and gloomy. People worried because they didn't know how to think; that was one element in his syndrome of gloomy depression. He couldn't think about problems with his customary clarity and logic anymore. Instead, he worried. . . .

Fennaday finished half his drink, and then read Stein's report on August Spencer's file from Green Drop Shannon.

He couldn't see any significance in it. Someone had tried to kill Spencer. Spencer thought it was a reprisal for something he and the others had done in Germany several years back. Well? Maybe it was. Maybe it wasn't. "Caprifoil was missing. . . ." What did that mean?

Fennaday felt a dizzying stab of exasperation as he noted the surmises and guesswork in Stein's evaluation. While he seldom communicated with Stein, he felt impelled to do so now. He scribbled a note: "Stein. Please remember that for every *guess*, I want a *ton* of facts."

Fennaday knew from scuttlebutt that Stein felt he was developing a neurotic dependence on facts. That did happen to people in Evaluation, of course; as long as they could demand facts, and still more facts, they could forestall making judgments. But Fennaday knew better than Stein that all branches of Intelligence were in an endless competition for every conceivably relevant scrap of information, with the result that, to secure "scoops," agents frequently lied to their opposite numbers in other bureaus, and attempted to discredit their contracts, thus making a farce of the popularly held opinion that they were all working for the same country with the same goals in mind.

No, Stein didn't know anything about that. Stein didn't realize that the "facts" differed widely from agent to agent, from problem to problem, and that you couldn't arrive at even an approximation of the truth unless you got all the facts everywhere and pieced them into a pattern . . . perspective, he thought, perspective first, then patterns. Fennaday felt his pulse; it was racing. Stein was a smart-ass, that's what he was, a typically over-educated New York type, with all kinds of degrees in sociology and psychology, but without the rock-hard common sense that could analyze problems . . . Fennaday frowned faintly, searching for a word. Perspective, that was it. Analyze problems with perspective.

Stein thought masses of facts were plebeian. He thought that theorizing was more elegant than digging up weighable and measurable facts. Well, let him, Fennaday thought, with a flash of pleasurable anger.

Stein didn't know that Defense was continuing its attempts to make Middle Eastern policy, despite the fact that State was threatening to make it an "either-or" issue with the President. But I know that, Fennaday thought. Nor did Stein know of that air-conditioned and antiseptic building near the Tansonnhut Air Base at Saigon, with its families of blinking computers, and its billions of facts about our enemies throughout the Far East. . . .

Jesus Christ, what's wrong with me? Fennaday

thought anxiously. He finished his drink and sat down and picked up another report. I'm not in an information contest with Stein. In fact, the old saw, the less you know the better, was truer than ever these days. Stop worrying about Stein. There was enough to worry about in the reports that crossed his desk every hour.

... Al Fatah, east of Jordan, with Soviet guns ... Israeli reprisals against Syria ... Armed Forces political activity in Bonn ... the Saracen Vector ... the murder of Russian émigrés in Munich . . . the assassination of Lin Tung in Peking ... the riots in Rawalpindi . . . the military coup in Pakistan . . . the power vacuum in Egypt. ...

The raw material was stacked mile-high. All it needed was a spark. His phone rang twice, then stopped, and he knew Eileen had taken the call in the living room. A few seconds later she opened the study door and pointed at his phone. Her expression told him it was top priority.

"It's the White House," she said. "General Rose."

Fennaday quickly made a note of the time, and said to his wife, "Get me a cup of black coffee." The drink had started a buzzing in his ears.

"Yes, sir."

"I've sent a car for you, Fennaday," General Rose said. There was a curious edge to his voice; it was tension, or excitement, or what? Hostility? "It should be there in a few minutes. You have an incomplete evaluation from Maurice Stein on a report filed by an ex-CIA agent, August Spencer. I—"

"I've read it, sir, but—" Fennaday began to say, but General Rose didn't stop talking.

"—want that report right away. We have Stein's copy. Don't let yours out of your hands until you get to my office. And use the rear entrance."

The phone clicked in Fennaday's ear before he could say "Yes, sir."

His cheeks were burning. No explanation, no token apology. "Sorry to trouble you—" "Hope this doesn't interfere with your plans for this evening—" Just barked orders, a four-star general to a private.

But in spite of his resentment, Fennaday felt stirred by excitement and curiosity. What was there in Spencer's report to cause such a flap?

Lieutenant-General Theodore Rose reported directly to the President in areas embracing intelligence and national security, and was therefore, by any odds, one of the most important and influential men in the government. He had a reputation for fairness and toughness, and an unswerving loyalty to the President, and while there were certain Washington observers (New York newspapermen, for the most part) who intimated that he owned far less than a first-class mind, there were few of his detractors who would go so far as to say that General Rose was not a seasoned and knowledgeable veteran in the areas of information he was accountable for.

As the black Cadillac turned into West Executive Avenue, Fennaday looked out at the White House and thought again about the edge of hostility in General Rose's voice. The chauffeur, a middle-aged man who had been silent since picking up Fennaday, spoke into his dashboard phone. "Limousine 146, one passenger."

Perhaps it hadn't been hostility, Fennaday thought, perhaps it was simply tension or exasperation. After all, he'd done nothing to incur General Rose's hostility. As far as he knew . . . as far as anyone knew anything in this town.

He began to experience the familiar out-of-focus disorientation, the symptom which had first sent him for help to Dr. Benedict. When he displayed his White House pass to uniformed guards at the gate, and then to the Secret Service detail at the rear entrance of the White House, Fennaday was conscious of the lights' becoming unnaturally bright, and he was aware of the sudden loudness of the car door slamming, and of his own footsteps on the stairs leading down to the warren of tiny offices in the basement of the West Wing. Everything was intensified, sharpened, articulated; while at the same time, the edges of his vision blurred into confusing patterns, and sounds lost all meaning in accelerating volume.

Fennaday braced himself against a wall with his hand. Secretaries hurried by him, snatches of chatter trailing in their wake. "'Five copies in a ringed folder,' he said, and I told him. . . ." "If we work overtime till eighty-thirty, we get chauffeured home, so say a prayer. . . ." "He had dinner at his desk, they said. . . ."

Dr. Benedict had explained to Fennaday that his symptoms were the result of anxiety. Clinical anxiety. The out-of-focus vision, the difficulty in breathing, the jello-like condition of his knees, the abrupt and treacherous loss of balance—they were rather like advance warnings, Dr. Benedict said, of conditions which Fennaday fully expected to obtain in the future. But this sense of impending doom, this conviction the world would one day destroy itself, and that all human values as we have known them would be obliterated—this, Dr. Benedict said, was—in an old-fashioned, non-psychiatrically oriented phrase—just plain pessimism. It bothered lots of people. Nothing unique about it. Because, in plain fact, such things happened. Look at Rome, Greece, Carthage, the Incas, the British Empire, for that matter. "They were all destroyed, the world smashed to bits about their heads. But these things right themselves later on." Dr.

Benedict was a roly-poly man with old-fashioned glasses and a heavy gold watch chain stretched tightly across his vest, and he earned (it was estimated) a quarter of a million a year by advising those who could afford him that since the past was marked by disasters, so must be the present, and the only sensible thing to do was trust our leaders and the future, and hope for the best, and so forth. ...

Fennaday shook his head to clear it, and looked about. The corridors were noisy with people hurrying this way and that, most of them with files in their hands. There were secretaries, communications people, and a brace of long-striding presidential aides, who nodded to Fennaday as they went by him. They had looked at him with curiosity, he thought with some satisfaction. They don't know why I'm in on this, whatever "this" turned out to be. He noted that the White House Staff Mess was still open and doing business, which was strange, since the mess usually closed after serving Group Two at 2:30 P.M. There was something in the air, he realized, and he knew what it was, for he had sensed it on other occasions; it was the almost pleasurable human reaction to crisis, a chemical intoxication that stemmed from pepped-up endocrines and the bracing tonic of surging adrenalin.

Crisis managers called it Bay Of Pigs Number Five.

Fennaday steadied himself with an effort, and drew several deep breaths which slowly cleared his head and brought the sights around him back into focus.

General Rose glanced up quickly when his aide, Major Gunning, opened the door. "Mr. Fennaday, sir," the major said.

"Get him in here."

General Rose's tall, wide-shouldered frame had the whale-bone look of cavalry. His hair was white, cut short, and his face was so deeply tanned that his dark-blue eyes looked almost black. He came around his desk in springy strides and shook hands with Fennaday, but without taking his eyes from Fennaday's attaché case.

"It's right here," Fennaday said, and took Stein's report from his case and gave it to General Rose. "I've come to only one conclusion about it so far."

This invitation to discussion was declined by General Rose, who stood frowning in a preoccupied silence at Stein's report.

Fennaday tried a direct approach. "The fact is, General Rose, I've read that report. Obviously, you would have preferred I hadn't. But we can't help that now. It seems apparent that some of our former agents are in trouble. The question is, do we abandon them, or do we take them off the hook, officially or unofficially?"

General Rose turned and looked steadily at Fennaday. His eyes were black, Fennaday thought; he had never noticed this before, but it was true; the general's eyes were like globes of ebony neatly emplaced in his lined, deeply tanned face. After a moment of deliberation, General Rose said, "I must ask you to forget this report, and everything it contains. Do you understand me?"

"Yes, sir."

"We have placed a stop on Green Drop reports, so you won't hear anymore from August Spencer." Almost as an after-thought, he added, "This is no reflection on your section, or on your own ability or discretion. Naturally."

Fennaday lacked Stein's ability to dismiss curiosity with an act of will, but experience told him that speculation would be pointless, for he knew the matter was now and forever out of his hands. He would in all probability never know what trouble Spencer was

64

in, or what Caprifoil meant. A bit pointlessly he thanked General Rose, and left.

General Rose punched a button on his phone console that put him in direct contact with Douglas Benton of CIA. When the connection was completed, he said, "Benton, we've got the last of them. Fennaday just brought it in. Do your people have contact with Spencer?"

"Not yet."

"You'll do what's necessary?" It was a question, and yet it wasn't.

"Yes," Benton said. "Now this just came in. Do you have it? Harry Adams is dead."

"We have that signal," General Rose said, and felt a stir of disgust at himself for the note of satisfaction he was not able to keep from his voice.

Chapter Four

"... espionage is one of the human activities where truth and fiction are most closely interwoven. ..."

Spencer reread the sentence, then put the magazine aside to accept a drink from a stewardess in the first-class cabin of Lufthansa's Flight 906 to Frankfurt. They were at 20,000 feet and the night was so clear that he could see the lights of Bonn below them. Above, there were stars. Spencer sipped his drink and the magazine slipped from his lap to the floor, but he didn't bother to pick it up. The article he had been reading was by a reporter who contended that guess-work and speculation were the essence of espionage. Because, the writer argued, weren't there many truths? And many degrees of truth? And, therefore, why should the "official versions" have more validity than the vague hunches and suspicions of the average man in the street?

True enough, Spencer thought, and believing that let you sleep comfortably. But you never knew whether you believed it to get to sleep or whether you believed it because it was true.

With enough "facts" you could prove anything you wanted to. Perhaps you were allowed a glimpse of one "truth" to prove that another "truth" was a deception. But the deception may have been the functional "truth" after all. Lies were security, and whatever "truths" you were told might be moats and drawbridges to protect desperately necessary pretenses.

Spencer's speculations were not idle. He was thinking in terms of self-preservation. If not the German business, then the source of danger to him and Ackerley might be rooted in the top levels of the French or American governments. A judgment against them on those levels, would result in an irreversible sentence ... Somehow, Spencer knew he must make his "truth" match their "truth."

He had met Andre Leroi in Frankfort for the first time. Spencer had worked with both Harry Adams and Bunny Ackerley on several other occasions. The job they had been given to do had its roots in the distant past. ...

When World War II ended, Meinz Felfe, a dedicated Nazi, was chief of the Gestapo in Salzburg, Austria. Felfe was captured by the Russians and with no apparent soul-searching promptly became a dedicated Communist. The Russians placed Felfe and as many others of the Gestapo they could find into the East German Secret Police, STB. After eleven dedicated years, Felfe "defected" to the West, and with a cabal of his former Salzburg Gestapo agents gradually infiltrated the Federal German Intelligence Service, specifically the section embraced by the Counter-Intelligence Department, 3-F. Felfe operated for Moscow for another period of eleven years as a top-ranking intelligence agent in the West German Intelligence Service, BND. In that time, with his customary dedication, Meinz Felfe handed over to the Russian Secret Service, KGB, more than 15,000 intelligence photographs vital to the security of NATO and to the Free World.

In addition, he supplied Moscow with hundreds of rolls of microfilm of naval installations, airfields, prototype aircrafts and weapons; in short, everything in Western Europe that might be useful to the Kremlin.

Meinz Felfe was exposed as a double agent in 1963. Felfe and his Salzburg cohorts were apprehended and plucked from their positions of sensitive security in department 3-F. Some were tried and imprisoned; some, like Meinz Felfe himself, were traded back to the Russian KGB Secret Police.

But the job of rooting out the double agents in 3-F had not been done with ruthless, surgical precision. The leaks continued, and by 1965 the microfilm and photographs were flowing once more to the Kremlin and to the STB offices in East Berlin.

Obviously, a final solution was required; and Spencer and his team were sent to Frankfurt to provide it.

They had been detached from their national agencies except for a certain logistical dependence, and it had been explicitly understood among them that the success of their mission would demand a suspension of certain moral and ethical conventions.

Fifteen officers worked in the German Counter-Intelligence Department 3-F. In a period of three months, Andre Leroi and Harry Adams had exposed four of them as double agents, and Spencer and Ackerley had rooted out five others, two who were double agents, and three who were simply greedy and foolish enough to sell classified information to the highest bidder, the bidders in this case being August Spencer and Wyndom Ackerley.

Spencer's team could find no proof of complicity or conspiracy in the backgrounds and behavior of the remaining six officers; that, however, was irrelevant, for they were operating under "do what is necessary" orders and they had decided to destroy the innocent with the guilty to achieve maximum security. In the end, as so frequently happens, the innocence of the innocents was not absolute; after all, if a man has never taken a bribe, it may be only because he was never offered one. This was a cruel and vicious pressure to exert on human beings, but the stakes were high enough to justify it. Losing a battle to the Soviets at that time might have imposed cruel and vicious pressures on the Free World. Everyone believed that. They believed it so implicitly and effortlessly that they didn't think about it.

And so Spencer did his job. Every man has his capacity for indiscretion, his price, his breaking point; it was Spencer's task to analyze suspected frailties of mind or body and to test them with appropriate pressures.

In the case of Waldo Mueller, the appropriate pressure had been a slim, blond youth from Bavaria with homosexual tendencies and no compunction about being photographed in Waldo's beefy embrace.

Hans Maas had been compromised by his religion, in a sense. A deeply philosophical man, he was disturbed by the nature of his work, its secrets, its dangers. Doctor Maas semantically examined and inconclusively speculated on the true nature of treason. If God was universal, and national boundaries finite, then in destroying them, was not the traitor doing God's work? Spencer's team had learned of this when Doctor Maas confessed himself to someone he believed to be his parish priest.

Karl Weber had been discredited for accepting a bribe, and that had been the worst of it for Spencer, the climacteric of his career, if not his life.

Benton had offered him three months of R&R, and a desk job at headquarters in Virginia. But Spencer had tacked it up, had quit cold. Benton, with the attitude of the faithful toward any apostasy, hadn't forgiven him for it.

The "no smoking" and "seat belt" signs flashed on and Lufthansa's Flight 906 banked toward its letdown pattern above Frankfurt.

Many more buildings of steel and glass had been put up since the last time Spencer had been there. He took the airport bus to the railway station in the middle of the city and from there, a cab to the Frankfurter Hof. He ordered a bottle of Black Label and a bottle of Perrier water and made himself a drink. He sat in a deep chair facing the door, sipping the drink slowly, the weight of the Browning comfortable against his shoulder. More from habit than necessity, he checked the gun, then replaced it in the holster. After an hour or so, he made himself a second drink, stronger this time, and settled back more comfortably in the chair, feeling a pleasurable weariness as some of the tensions flowed from him.

Spencer was quite certain he had been followed from Paris. But he had no visitors that night, and at dawn he allowed himself to sleep.

The following afternoon, Spencer took a cab through the crowded city to an address on Mainzersstrasse. The driver, an old man wrapped to the eyes in a red muffler, was separated from Spencer by a thick slab of reinforced glass, beneath which were metal receptacles for the payment of fares and the making of change: Western Germany's crime rate was one of the higher in Europe. In a voice muffled by the wool scarf across his mouth the driver told him they would pass Goethe's house. "Look out the right side when we turn the next corner. You must go to the zoo," he said, as he turned into the Mainzersstrasse. "They have snow machines for the penguins. It is on television every Sunday."

When the cab drove away, Spencer stood on the sidewalk and looked up and down the street. Nothing had changed very much. There were rows of modest town houses, some of them centuries old, others rebuilt or replaced since the bombings; they all gleamed with fresh paint and shining brass door trims. There were children playing down the block, kicking a soccer ball. Their voices were happy and their faces were flushed with the bracing cold. Pale sunlight fell through the bare trees and made patterns of copper and gold among the children. The scene, with its simple and healthy beauty, filled Spencer with a weariness he did not quite understand. He went up the stairs and rang the bell of Ilse's home.

Her hair was no longer as bright and blond as he had remembered it, like a field of wheat in the sunlight; its gold was streaked with silver at her temples.

The pleasant, inquiring smile froze on her lips. She tried to close the door, but Spencer put his hand against it. "Will you listen to me for a minute?"

"I don't want to talk to you," Ilse said. "There is nothing you can say I want to hear."

"Please. I don't use that word very often, you know."

"And you're so damn proud of it," Ilse said. "Oh, hell. Come in."

She glanced at the boys playing on the sidewalk and then closed the door and led Spencer into the living room off the hallway.

Ilse picked up a package of cigarettes and a book of matches from a coffee table, and lighted a cigarette with a quick flurry of gestures. Shaking the flame from the match, she dropped it in an ashtray and walked tensely to the windows facing the street, her left hand hugging her right elbow in a curiously defensive posture. She wouldn't make it easy for him, of course. Even when they had been lovers, there was that brittle core of independence, that reserve of spirit, which defined them as separate, never fused, entities. She had been thin when he knew her, and the planes of her face were sharp under the wheat-colored hair. Now she had more curves than angles, but there was still a suggestion of girlishness in her slim arms and legs. He had been wrong about her hair; in the afternoon light he had thought the fine blond-wheat color was something lost to time, but now he realized that it had been shaded by artifice, softened to match a new maturity in her eyes and features.

She had money, then. He didn't send her enough for beauty salons and the pale-blue knit dress she was wearing, which even to Spencer's eyes reflected a deceptive expensive simplicity. The room was not as he remembered it; there were new pieces, chests and highboys, and a white wool rug decorated with tufts of beige wool. There were several lamps of beaten brass, with shades of silky, almost transparent leather. Spencer had seen them in Morocco.

The silence was as hostile as the rigidity of her back and shoulders. At last he said: "Did I see him? Was he playing out front?"

"No. Karl is at school." She turned and faced him then, a derisive smile smoothing her full lips. "Did you come back to see your son?"

"No," Spencer said. He could still hurt her, he realized, with some surprise, for a betraying tide of color rose in her pale cheeks. "I'd like to see Karl, if you don't mind. But I didn't come here for that."

72

"Why did you come back? No one here wants to see you or talk with you."

"I can understand that," he said. He was silent until a faint frown began to shadow her cool blue eyes. Then he said, "Someone is trying to kill me. Do you remember Harry Adams and Andre Leroi?"

"Oh yes, how could I forget them?" She locked her thin hands together and pressed them against her breasts, and he saw the effort she was making to control her anger. "The men who worked for you, who sat here in this room and drank coffee before the fire on cold nights. While they helped you play your dirty little games with my father."

"You'll be pleased to know they're dead then," he said.

"You still like to set traps, don't you, August?" She made a dismissing gesture with her shoulders. "I'm not pleased they're dead. Relieved perhaps, but not pleased. The world needs men to guard their own honor, not just their neighbor's."

"That's a good sentiment, and in a good world, it would make some sense," Spencer said. "I came here to talk to your father. I want you to arrange it."

"My God, you can't be serious!" Ilse sat down in a chair, and turned her face from him. She pounded her fist weakly on the arm of the chair. "After you destroyed him, lied to him, you want to meet and talk about the good old days over some steins of beer?"

"It was my job to have money offered to your father," Spencer said. "That's what I did, Ilse. Your father accepted the money. That's what he did."

"You've got it all memorized, like multiplication tables," she said, and there was a sudden fierce anger and scorn in her voice. "You know that's not all you did. Goddamnit, you know it. My father refused your filthy bribes again and again, and reported every contact to his superiors. But you offered the bribes again

73

and again. You knew the trouble we were in, and you blocked his credit and his bank account until he was like a man being forced to the edge of a cliff by a ring of bayonets. And when he fell, was that altogether his fault? Or would you blame the smiling men with the bayonets?"

Spencer said, without conviction, "How can you divide guilt in nice, equal slices?"

Ilse hugged her arms across her breasts, tightly and convulsively, as if she had suddenly been exposed to a draft of bitterly cold air. "And you did that to him while we were lovers," she said, in a dull and listless voice. "While I carried your child." She turned away from him and walked to the windows and looked into the street. The sustaining anger seemed to drain slowly from her body; her shoulders sagged wearily, and there was something helpless and forlorn in the way her pale hands hung limply at her sides. After what seemed an interminable silence, she turned and looked at him. "I'm sorry, I thought I had got over it. Sometimes months go by and I never think of you." She smiled ruefully and walked past him into the hallway. "I must go and collect Karl now." She took a heather-blue tweed coat from a wall rack and slung it over her shoulders.

"Would you mind if I came with you?"

"What would be the point of it?"

"He's my son, and I've never seen him. You told me to stay away from him, and I did. But if you insist on that, it will hurt you as much as it does me."

"In a technical sense Karl is your son. But you are not his father."

"Is someone else playing that part?"

"Yes, a pleasant man who works in the export business. He travels two weeks each month in Morocco, buying things. When he is home, he spends two evenings a week with us. He is extremely fond of Karl.

74

The other nights he is husband and father to his wife and children."

"I loved you." Spencer spoke with an effort. "You don't have to call me a liar, a traitor, a moral spastic. I've used those words so often to myself that they hardly hurt anymore. But I did love you."

Ilse came closer to him and unexpectedly touched his cheek with the back of her fingers. "No, August. You loved the idea of loving honor more." There was a sense of finality and weariness in her smile as she hooked an arm through his, and said, "Come, you can look at Karl. What difference can it make?"

They picked him out of a queue of seemingly identical children at his school and took him to a café near the zoo. He drank cocoa and ate marzipan with unaffected relish and talked animatedly to Spencer of a football match he had seen a month before in the Stadtwald. He had rosy cheeks and blue eyes and dark hair. He was at a stage of epicene beauty. Only the sturdy uniform and short hair defined him as a boy; in other trappings, he would have looked like an entrancing little girl.

"How old are you?" Spencer asked him.

"I am five-and-a-half, sir. I will be six on May the fourteenth."

In the thin cold sunlight Ilse was beautiful, he thought. And the little boy was beautiful too. It was strange to watch him licking the marzipan from his fingers, and to think back to the time when he had been conceived. Spencer remembered the trip down the Rhine with Ilse in the late fall, more than six years ago. The excursion boat had red-and-white awnings. Accordion players in blue jackets with gold braid wandered the decks playing marches and waltzes, and at night the heavy woods lining the river rose up beside the ship like steep black walls.

Something stirred in him as he looked at his son. He is mine, Spencer thought, and the guilt and betrayal didn't affect that. They were linked by permanent bonds; the fact that they were accidental bonds didn't matter either. His face must have betrayed him, for Ilse asked, "What are you thinking about?"

"I was thinking about the accordions," he said.

"They were noisy enough," Ilse said. She collected her purse and gloves and smiled at the little boy. "Come, we must be going now." She looked away and frowned, as if she were trying to remember something, but when she turned back to Spencer, the little frown faded away and her eyes seemed to leap at him like arrows. "Where are you staying?"

Spencer returned to his hotel. It was almost dark and a wet snow was falling on the crowds hurrying along the sidewalks. The snow melted on unbroken expanses of umbrellas and ran in dirty streams in the gutter.

Spencer's room was luxuriously warm. He opened the window and a cold wind blew in. He could see the railroad station and the long lighted columns of coaches snaking under its vaulted glass dome. The wind gusted and a haze of snowflakes swirled into the room.

The Black Label was almost gone. He called room service and ordered another bottle, and more Perrier and three glasses. Neatness was a compulsion with him, so he fussed around putting the room into order. He removed the Browning and a robe and slippers from his leather flight bag, and from one of the outside pockets of the same handy rig, clean linen and toilet articles. Spencer put the Browning in the pocket of the robe, and hung the robe in an immense wooden chest that stood against the wall beside a writing desk. He arranged the toilet articles in rows on the glass shelf below the medicine cabinet.

Spencer undressed and went into the bathroom with underwear and a pair of gray slacks. The water from the shower was so hot, it quickly filled the room with swirling steam. Spencer rubbed the clouded surface of the mirror and lathered his face with shaving cream.

A knock sounded on the door. "Come in," Spencer called, and began shaving.

The waiter put the tray of whiskey and Perrier and glasses on the writing desk and told Spencer he could sign for them later.

Spencer thanked him and waited until he heard the door close before stepping into the shower-stall and savoring the needle-sharp burst of hot water against his chest and shoulders. After showering, he rubbed himself down with a warm, rough towel. The steam from the shower had eddied into the bedroom, and the objects there, the bed, the writing desk, the immense wooden chest, seemed shifting and unsubstantial, like cliffs seen through a heavy fog. Spencer put on his slacks and walked into the bedroom, feeling the cold draft from the window and seeing snowflakes like pearls drifting through the steam. And he heard what he had been almost sure he would hear, a quiet, confident voice which said: "Mr. Spencer, would you please turn around slowly?"

"I ordered a drink for you," Spencer said. "Whiskey, all right?"

"They told me you were observant."

The steam drifted toward the ceiling, clearing the air, and Spencer turned and looked at the large young man who stood just inside the room, holding a gun in a hand so big it dwarfed the weapon. And the gun was no toy, Spencer noticed; it was a Beretta

Brigadier, with respectable stopping power in its cartridges, which were nine mm. (Luger) Parabellum.

He was young, about twenty-seven or twenty-eight, Spencer guessed, with a short blond crew-cut, a thickly corded neck and wide, bulky shoulders. He looked like he might have played football in the Big Ten, at fullback or perhaps in the defensive line, with much weight-lifting during the off-season. There was something amusing about his size; Spencer could imagine parents wondering with fond surprise where the devil all that bulk had come from. But there was nothing amusing about the young man's eyes, which were cool and blue, with a faint light shimmering behind them.

Spencer, who was a fair judge of eyes, managed a careful, easy smile. He might have been lulled by the athletic and typically American height and bulk, or the tweed jacket, the Brooks Brothers shirt and ties, and the charcoal-gray slacks and shining Basque moccasins. All of this was almost comically proper, and might easily have fooled a casual observer. But Spencer wasn't fooled by the man's eyes.

"What do you want?" he asked him.

"Where did you pick me up?"

"On the flight from Orly," Spencer said. "When you're tailing a man in first-class, I'd advise you to travel first-class yourself. People in the same compartment look one another over, take a reading on one another, it's very normal. But you were the only person in second-class interested in me. Do you want that drink?"

"No, thank you. I don't drink." He smiled pleasantly enough, and glanced toward the tray on the writing desk. "But if you need one, go right ahead."

Spencer thanked him with a nod, and made himself a double whiskey with Perrier, and drank it without ice, with deliberate relish. He put down the glass and said, "Well, you've got the gun. That entitles you to talk, I guess."

"My name is Cord, Richard Cord. I work for the same people you once did, and on about the same basis."

"Then you have considerable latitude."

"Yes. My instructions are to take you to the American Embassy in Bonn. I've got a car and driver waiting downstairs."

"But there are people I have to see here in Frankfurt," Spencer said.

"That's impossible."

"Why?"

"Because we have a report from Interpol that you murdered someone in Paris named Harry Adams."

"That's a lie, and I imagine you know it."

"You mean it's a lie that we have a report at Interpol? Or is it a lie that you killed Harry Adams?"

"I didn't kill Harry Adams."

Cord looked pained. "Mr. Spencer, that's not important. The report says you did, and that report is completely in order, with all the proper initials and endorsements."

Spencer thought about it. He was trapped and he didn't like it. His business was, in fact, staying alive, and he knew he was better at it than they were. But that wasn't what bothered him.

"Let me ask you one question," he said. "Do your orders include a British agent, G.N. Wyndom Ackerley?"

"I've just one job to do," Cord said, with a puzzled smile. "To take you to Bonn, or to leave you here. I thought you understood?"

"Is there any leeway for a deal? I'd like to go to Paris first, and get a signal to Ackerley."

"That doesn't interest me," Cord said.

"You're not the one they're trying to kill."

"Right." Cord said, with an easy smile. He pushed the Beretta under the waistband of his trousers, and buttoned his jacket to conceal it.

"What you're doing may cause Ackerley's death," Spencer said.

"Maybe, maybe not," Cord said.

Spencer threw his flight bag on the bed and opened the door of the tall wooden chest, and removed his paisley dressing robe and slipped his arms into it. When he turned around, the muzzle of his Browning was pointing squarely at Cord's stomach.

"Jesus you are stupid," Cord said. "You know what I've got to do, Mr. Spencer, and you know what you've got to do."

"That's right, stay alive," Spencer said.

Spencer ripped the Beretta from Cord's waistband, and rammed the muzzle of his Browning with all his strength into Cord's stomach. Cord chopped a right hand at Spencer, but the blow lacked speed and consequently force, because he was having trouble breathing; and that trouble was accelerated when Spencer slammed the edge of his left palm down against the straining muscles of Cord's throat. The blow sent Cord to his knees. He braced himself with one hand on the floor, and labored to squeeze air into his straining lungs.

Spencer collected a towel from the bathroom, wrapped it around the butt of his Browning and slugged Cord with merciful efficiency across the base of his skull. He eased Cord onto the floor, then put the Beretta away under the mattress. Cord's I.D. was not illuminating: according to a business card in his wallet, he travelled in a line of home-and-office furniture for a company in Springfield, Massachusetts. There were Diners Club and Carte Blanche cards, a driver's license, and a permit for the Beretta issued in Rome. Spencer thought a minute. Then he turned Cord's limp, sagging body over, and removed the holster from his left shoulder. On the back of the holster he found a pair of tiny screws, which innocently held the carrying strap in place. Removing the screws with the tips of his pen knife, Spencer put them aside and tugged gently at the carrying strap. An inch-square section of leather fell back, revealing a tiny compartment in which there were several tightly rolled pieces of paper. Spencer examined them; they were CIA, CIB and Interpol I.D.

Spencer took everything from Cord's wallet except several hundred dollars in various currencies. After looking through the cards of his own wallet, Spencer selected several and placed them in Cord's wallet. He put the holster under the mattress with the Beretta and flushed the Intelligence I.D. and the permit for the Beretta down the toilet. Then he applied whiskey judiciously to Cord's jacket and shirt and called the desk and asked for the manager of the hotel.

"You have not seen this man before, Herr Spencer?"

The hotel manager, Herr Maganer, had arrived at his middle years with a comfortably padded body and shrewd but lively blue eyes. He stared at Cord's sprawled body with professional disinterest.

Spencer had affected a slangy, vernacular manner in his first explanations to Herr Maganer, and he continued now in that vein, saying: "It beats the hell out of me! Never saw him before in my life. He knocked on the door, and when I opened it, he began talking about some convention or other he was supposed to be at. I think that's what he said, because he'd been drinking, and I don't think he could have hit the ground with his hat."

With experienced deftness, Herr Maganer fished a wallet from the inside pocket of Cord's jacket. He put on his glasses, tilted his head back, and examined var-

81

ious cards. "His name, it appears, is John Baker. Manager of an electronics firm in Zurich. There are no traveler's checks, but a good amount of cash. To drink is one thing. To drink this way is altogether another."

"Well, he goes wandering around a strange city in this condition, no telling what might happen. Maybe the police would put him up for the night."

And it was so arranged by Herr Maganer. Three men from the hotel's baggage rooms carried "Mr. Baker" down a rear entrance to a loading ramp, from which he was put into the firmly respectful hands of the Frankfurt police. . . .

Ilse didn't drink whiskey. "It's like you not to remember," she said. "Why is the room so cold?"

"I opened the window for a while."

She sat on the edge of the bed and looked at him with a friendly smile. "Did you like Karl?"

"He's fine. You've got to admit he looks a little bit like me."

"Oh sure. He's got your dark hair and eyes. I think he'll be big like you. He's quite strong."

She wore short black boots and a beige wool suit that matched the wheat-blond of her hair.

"I can get you anything you like from room service," Spencer said.

"No, never mind." She removed a chain and locket from her throat and let them trickle from her fingers into a little pool of gold on the bedside table.

"How about a sandwich? Or some wine?"

"You talk like a businessman who picked me up in the lobby. Rubbing your hands together, promising me goodies. Afterward, you'll want to show me pictures of your children." She kicked off her small black boots and pushed her nylons down until they fell in loops about her ankles. "I didn't come here to drink wine. You know that. Help me with my brassiere."

82

Spencer turned out the lamp on the bedside table. From somewhere across the street a flashing neon sign created a pulsing glow in the room, and the light fell across the bed as rhythmically as a heart beat. Spencer knelt and moved his hands up the backs of her slim cool legs, and then held her waist tightly and buried his face against her breasts.

She laughed and said, "You liked our little Karl, then?"

"I told you, he's wonderful."

She laughed again, and Spencer wondered why. He knew her strong but controlled streak of sadism, but he had never particularly minded that in Ilse, or in any other woman, for that matter. It didn't justify things when he left them, he was too honest to contend that; but it did ease things.

If passion at its most exhilarating could still be calculating, that was the kind of love-making they enjoyed that night. There was pleasure without joy, involvement without abandon, patience without kindness, laughter without smiles. They were on guard, and wary, clinging with all their strength to an indifference which made them invulnerable. Even when all the nerves of pleasure were laid bare for sweetness and agony, they were clinical in their attentions, holding back everything that might lead to a surrender of self and being. Once when she shuddered from the depths of her body and screamed softly, he held her close and whispered that it was all right. And she struck him then in the face with her fist, and in a raging voice, said, "Of course it is, goddamnit, what else did you think? Why else do you think I'm here?"

The bargaining tone of their love-making seemed to intensify with the first glimmering lights on the horizon.

But at first they had talked like lovers, holding one another warmly and securely in the darkness.

"Do you have a girl?" she asked him.

"Well, I did have. I'm not sure I still do."

"What is she like?"

"She's a redhead, interested in the world, very liberal, you know the kind."

"Come on, I don't care about all that. How old is she?"

"Twenty-four."

"Please tell me she has a horrible American voice."

"No, she spent her last two years of college in Florence. You'd probably think she was Swiss."

"And she's beautiful, of course, slim and stylish, and all the rest of it."

"I have no complaints."

She laughed. "Christ, you're smug. Don't you think you're lucky?"

"Well, I've never felt lucky." For a moment, he was honest with her. "That's the truth. I've never felt lucky."

She laughed again, and touched him. "Doesn't that make you feel lucky?"

Later, they talked like amiable partners in a commercial enterprise.

"I called my father," she said. "He agreed to see you."

"Just like that?"

"What?"

Sometimes she missed the oblique in English. "What did he think of meeting me? Did he like the idea?"

"He hated it. Before he agreed, he demanded a favor of me. He expects you at his home at nine in the morning."

"That's no good," Spencer said. "I won't meet him there."

"Christ, you want everything. You think you have some rights now, some privileges?" She was angry. "He didn't want to see you. He loathes you, and loathes the past. He's only doing this for me. Isn't that good enough for you?"

Spencer rose on an elbow, found his cigarettes and gave one to Ilse and put another between his lips. In the small spurting flame of the match, he saw the sullen anger in her mouth and eyes. "Of course it's not good enough," he said. "I'd be a fool to meet him where he wants. I'll tell you where and when I'll meet your father."

"I will ask him. I don't know if he will agree."

"He will," Spencer said drily. "As a favor to you."

"You're clever." She turned and looked at him, and her expression was one of mild surprise. "But I forgot, you always were."

"No, I'm just a pessimist. It usually amounts to the same thing."

"Then you'll understand why he's doing me a favor. You can guess what his terms are."

"Yes, I can guess." Spencer understood now why she had laughed at him. She had asked him if he liked Karl, and she had watched his eyes and listened to the tone of his voice when he had answered her, and she had realized there was a way to hurt him, after all. It was a little bit too much, he thought, but he was already resigned to it. It was always a little bit too much lately. There was Ilse in the past, warm and loving, while his orders were to destroy her father. There was Charlie and the mists off the Aran Islands and trout breaking from green water into sunlight against their will, and whiskies in front of a fire with the storms outside and Charlie in his arms. He had wanted, or believed he wanted, all that, but he couldn't have it. Instead, he had to look for the men who were trying to kill him. He might have been better off with the horse farm. He could have made a life out of riding and gunning, buying and selling horses, he might even have learned to play golf and talk about crops and weather and politics in the locker room of the country club on weekends. But in his heart, he knew that wouldn't have satisfied him. He had been molded and pounded and shaped into something that would never fit into any of life's comfortable pigeonholes. He had been programmed for activities with capital letters—Country, Duty, Obedience. The colonel had told him to make sure he was a good man, a man with strength and character, and then to put his trust in guns. "A gun is no better and no worse than the man who uses it," the colonel had told him one day when they were out gunning for pheasants. The day had been brilliant and Spencer had never forgotten it. Maples and sycamores blazed red and yellow, and the thin pale sunlight sparkled like diamonds in the turning leaves. Their gun dog, a big and powerful Irish setter bitch, coursed back and forth in front of them, seeming to appear and disappear almost magically, lost against the thorn bushes one instant, her red coat dissolving into the crimson berries, and the next instant exploding beautifully and dramatically into sight when she crossed into stands of vivid green fir trees. Spencer had never forgotten any of that, nor had he forgotten what the colonel told him that day. "Remember this, son. If you're going to be a professional soldier, make yourself into a good man, a man of virtue and character. And then you can always trust your gun."

He was brought back from that faraway and strangely unreal time by Ilse's voice.

"You know what my father wants," she said.

Spencer turned on the bedside lamp and sat on the side of the bed with his back to Ilse.

"Tell me," he said.

"He will meet and talk with you if you promise me

never to come back here," she said. "You can never see me or Karl again."

"Well, I can promise," he said. "But suppose I don't keep my word?"

"I have a feeling he would enjoy that," Ilse said. "He would enjoy knowing you didn't have that much honor."

"Then he wins," Spencer said. "Either way, he wins."

"Do you promise?"

"Tell me what *you* want."

She was silent a moment, and he turned and looked at her. She smiled at him; under a strand of her wheat-blond hair her eyes were cool and distant. "I don't want you to come back," she said slowly. "I don't want you ever to come back."

He nodded and stood up. "All right, I won't. Call your father and tell him. I'll shower and shave."

"I'll be gone when you're through."

And she was. There was nothing left but the slim impression of her body on the bed, and the faint lemon tang of her perfume.

The morning was raw and ugly and thin rain misted the windows of his cab. When they stopped at the south entrance to the Stadtswald and Spencer climbed from the cab after paying the driver, the rain almost extinguished the cigarette plastered to his lips. He threw it aside, and, after returning the driver's smiling salute, walked through the Stadtswald and the archery ranges toward the soccer stadium which loomed like a big animal against the dirty gray sky. Spencer had told Ilse to tell her father he would meet him here, in the stands on the northern side of the playing field. It was a place where he could not easily be surprised; in the expanses of empty seats, another person would be immediately evident.

Spencer walked down a ramp which led to the southern side of the playing field. He stopped in the shadows of the mouth of the ramp and looked across to the steeply pitched rows of seats on the north side of the stadium. The rain fell in a slow, misting drizzle, and it distorted his vision, but after scanning the seats on the opposite side for a moment, he finally made out Ilse's father seated in the middle of the stands, his head and shoulders no larger than those of a child at this distance.

Spencer moved out from the protection of the ramp, and cautiously studied the tiers of seats on the southern side of the stadium. As nearly as he could tell, he and Herr Weber were the only persons present at this cold and desolate hour. Spencer walked across this playing field, his Wellingtons making a sucking sound on the ice-crusted mud and grass. The wind was capricious within the confines of the vast bowl; some areas were like the eye of a cyclone, still and eerily silent, while in other places gales spiralled about him wildly as they rushed after thermals toward the sky. Spencer held the collars of his duffel coat tightly against his throat and ascended a ramp that led him to the seats on the northern side of the stadium. He went down an aisle past row after row of empty seats and sat down beside Herr Karl Weber. The old man didn't look at him. Spencer lit a cigarette and offered the pack to Herr Weber.

"No. Thank you," Herr Weber said.

Spencer studied the old man's profile and realized with bitter resignation that his trip to Germany had been a waste of precious time. A necessary waste of time, of course, he thought, and then knew with a tiny stir of panic that he was relying on the old maxims that he had been taught to trust blindly. He was seeking some strength and security in the flinty precepts which had until now so comfortably ordered his life. Negative information was as valuable in its own way as positive information. . . . A "no" might point the way toward a "yes." . . . Never make any assumption without the additional assumption that your first assumption was wrong. . . . Never mind the big picture. Just fill in your part of it. . . .

He was in desperate need, Spencer realized, for some bedrock truths to use as armor against his present confusion and anxiety.

When Spencer had seen him last, six or seven years ago, Herr Weber had been in his late forties, a vigorous, lusty, powerful man, with the eyes of an adventurer, and a full head of the shining blond hair which he had bequeathed to Ilse. But now, seated in the swirling rain beside Spencer was only the faded memory of that man. Herr Weber wore a black overcoat and crushed black felt hat, and the hair at his temples was white. His face was pale and lined with worrisome tensions, and he couldn't control the nervous flutter of his eyelids or a rhythmic tremor at the corner of his mouth, which was like the reflex of someone prepared to smile hastily at rebuffs. The weight of his old hat seemed to be pressing his head deeply into the folds of his overcoat.

"I believe Andre Leroi is dead," Spencer said. "I know Harry Adams is dead. That's why I'm here."

The rain was falling more heavily now, and Spencer threw away his sodden cigarette. Herr Weber had begun to laugh and the sound of it sent a little chill down Spencer's spine, for it was a sound like the claws of a furred creature scratching vainly at a wall for freedom.

"My Ilse told me they are dead," Herr Weber said. With what seemed an immense effort, he swivelled his head around and peered up from under his hat brim at Spencer. "You think I killed them?"

"What can you tell me about Waldo Mueller and Hans Maas?"

"Waldo died two months ago. He moved to Augsburg when he got out of prison. But he had very bad lungs, you remember that, don't you? Poor Waldo always smoked too much. He was never without that cigarette in the corner of his mouth. Well, he died two months ago. Who else did you say?"

"Hans Maas, Dr. Hans Maas."

"Ah, Dr. Maas. Dr. Hans Maas. Well, he went to Cologne after the prison term. Everyone wanted to go away, you see, because there was such shame. I stayed only for my Ilse. Hans lives with his sister in Cologne. You remember he used to have a philosophical—" The old man sighed wearily. "What is the word? Bent, yes bent. He used to have a philosophical bent, that's what Hans had. Always struggling with Kant and Hume and the others. You remember the questions he used to ask? How much is a man responsible for? Which is higher, the human conscience or the state?"

The old man's voice had become threaded with dry humor as he looked back at an area of his past which seemed to be without pain for him.

"You remember, he was fond of quoting Pascal: 'I have discovered that all human evil stems from this, man's being unable to sit still in a room.' You remember, August?"

"Yes, I heard him say that."

"Well, you would be surprised at Hans now. Truly surprised, August. He reads very little, and he has no more bent for philosophy. I found a nice little Bible one day in the book shop, and I sent it to Hans for his birthday, but he sent it back with a note saying he didn't like the way it began. Think of that! A man with such reverence and intelligence to say that to me. I think Hans became irreverent after he went to church to confess to the priest his vague theories about treason. Yes, I think so. When he found out later that it was an agent of yours in the confessional, well, that caused him to become irreverent." Once again, Herr Weber turned and peered from under his hat brim into Spencer's face. "What do you think, August? Or do you think about any of these matters at all?"

"I'll try to give you an answer," Spencer said. He thought for a moment, and Herr Weber watched him alertly. "The victims think about such things more than anyone else," Spencer said. "The only luxury they can afford is righteousness."

"Ah, that's very good," Herr Weber said. "Dr. Maas would be proud of such a deep thought. But let me tell you one thing, August. I don't feel righteous. I don't waste my time feeling sorry for myself. You will never come back here, and you will never see your son again. That is what I am thinking about, and it gives me a good feeling. And how do you feel knowing someone has orders to kill you? As you had orders to destroy me and my friends?"

The wind and rain seemed suddenly colder. Spencer pulled the collar of his coat closer about his throat. It was the Americans who wanted them out of the way. But had they killed Harry Adams? And the French were after them too, he thought, remembering the Peugeots with the blue lights, the Force Three units that reported to General Mercier. It was a lonely and frightening feeling to know you could be caught and crushed between such powerful agencies.

"You have no deep thoughts about this?" Herr Weber smiled faintly and the tic at the corner of his mouth gave his expression a suggestion of slyness and conspiratorialness. It was as if his lips were winking at Spencer. "Somewhere they gave orders to kill you. The men with the guns won't examine the orders, you know. They won't say this is a bad thing to do and therefore we will not do it. Or, what do you think? That the men ordered to kill you will follow their conscience?"

"You know the answer to that," Spencer said.

"Of course, I do. My only wish is that they do not find you quickly and kill you quickly. If they take a reasonable time at their task, you can enjoy deep thoughts about it."

"I may disappoint you."

"But it isn't likely. No, August?"

"No, it's not likely."

Spencer thanked the old man for seeing him and talking with him, but it was like attempting to communicate with the stump of a tree. Herr Weber was staring out at the playing field and the eddies of rain sweeping across it, and while his lips were twisting in a slow labored manner, Spencer couldn't hear what he was saying.

Spencer left him like that, apparently talking to the rain and to his memories, and walked down the aisle to cross the playing field. He would be in Paris sometime this afternoon, and he had no plans beyond finding out if Bunny Ackerley were still alive; but he realized now that his first instincts had been sound, and he should have trusted them—they ought to have started running while there was still time.

But there was more to it than that. Like a goddamn amateur he had assumed where the trouble was rooted, and had assumed it would be useful to put the Americans into the picture. All his Green Drop reports had accomplished was to make it easier for them to find him. Spencer knew he could drop out of sight, go to ground in Paris, but it was his resigned conviction that it was now too late to correct the mistakes he had already made.

On the way to the airport a young cab driver told

him there was serious trouble awaiting Germany in the World Soccer Cup trials.

The airport was hot. Spencer spotted agents at the counters of a half-dozen carriers. He turned slowly and bought a newspaper at a kiosk. Scanning the headlines with apparent interest, he strolled back to the cabs and caught a ride into the city. In a cafe, behind steaming windows, surrounded with the mellow aromas of beer and spiced sausages, he phoned Billy's Relais in Paris. Billy, himself, answered in his sprightly cockney voice. Spencer asked if there were any messages from Plumrose.

"How's that? Who might this be?"

"This is Wolfbane, Billy."

"No messages but a phone number. Hold on, I'll give it to you."

When spencer had the number, he thanked Billy and dialed Paris again. Within seconds, to his enormous relief, he was speaking to Ackerley.

"It's probably not necessary to tell you, but they've got this area staked out," Spencer said.

"Quite unnecessary," Ackerley said. "I seem to draw a crowd wherever I go."

"Who are they? Americans?"

"No, Mercier's people, and some bloody Moroccans."

Christ, Spencer thought, and smiled with a reflexive gallows humor. What the hell were *they* doing in it? "I'll take a train and find a hotel outside town. I'll meet you at Billy's tonight."

"Listen, old man, I unscrambled that coded message we found in Foxglove's apartment. Remember Theophile LeMaitre?"

"Get with it, Bunny. Of course I remember him."

"I checked out Denise Morand at Interpol, courtesy LeMaitre. I tried him on *azucado*. We got it straight away. The numeral *two* means two *languages*. The numerals *one* and *three* mean that *one* letter has been dropped *three* times. Once we had that, we just ran down the alphabet until the word made sense."

"*Azul*," Spencer said. "What's the rest of it?"

"*Azul, clad*. Add the third *l* to the last letter, which is *o*, and you get 'azul clad *lo*.'"

"Blue clad," Spencer said. "I think I've got it."

"Right. Blue clad, blue gown. . . ." Bunny hummed a bar of "My Sweet Little Alice Blue Gown." "Harry's sweet little Alice has the letter. *Lo*, of course, means—"

"Yes," Spencer said. "The word *has* is understood. Alice has it. . . ."

"But I haven't got through to her yet," Ackerley said. "I talked to her husband, Pierre Something-or-other—Vignon, that's it—and I think he surmises some loot's involved."

"Bunny, for Christ's sake, be careful."

Ackerley assured him he would do just that. Spencer drank a beer which did not meld well with the Black Label of the night before and then joined the traffic in the crowded streets. Their gray and rain-soaked anonymity provided him protective cover to the train station.

Chapter Five

It seemed to Ackerley that in the decades since the war the rosy-pink complexion of Paris (which was how he remembered the city) had been dimmed by the dusty shades of American Negroes and Arabs from Metropolitan France.

Ackerley thought about this as he glanced about through layers of smoke in Le Saloon, which was a new and popular bar on the Left Bank and which was consequently crowded and noisy and expensive. There were about a dozen tables in the low-ceilinged room, and at least half were occupied by portly Arabs in black suits and red fezzes. A few American Negroes sat about with French girls, seemingly very much at home with the music and with their girls and the waiters, with whom they chattered in slangy, street-smart French.

The music blasting from electrically amplified guitars was giving Ackerley a headache. The sound leaped from wall to wall, from floor to ceiling, doubling back on itself like a trapped and frantic animal, and Ackerley found himself wishing that the four mop-headed musicians might somehow manage to electrocute themselves.

The small dance floor in front of the musicians was presently occupied by a pair of Arab jugglers who were shuttling bowling pins from one to the other with bewildering speed. They were slim young men with flashing smiles and oiled and muscular bodies. They wore sandals and short red sashes about their waists, and the soft lights flickered like quicksilver on their bare chests and supple limbs. Whether they were wearing anything under the red sashes, Ackerley couldn't be sure; but from the breathless attention of several of the Arabs, he decided they weren't.

The door on the street opened and Harry Adams' ex-wife, Alice, came in. Ackerley waved to her and she smiled and threaded her way through the crowded room to his table.

"Isn't this fun?" she asked, after he had ordered her drink, a Pernod with distilled water.

"Yes. Great fun." He had to shout above the music to be heard.

"I knew you'd like it. I adore it. It's the "in"-est possible place right now."

"Well, it was good of you to share it with me. The *in-est,* you say?"

She smiled and patted his large hand. "I know you don't like me, Bunny. You never did, but that's all right. I don't want to go to bed with you, and I think you feel the same way about me."

"It seems drastic to be so final about it."

She smiled and did something with her eyes which Ackerley thought of as "crinkling." Yes. She "crinkled" her eyes at him, no doubt of it.

"Maybe I've underestimated you," she said. "Did you actually have a yen for me?"

Ackerley smiled. "I think I've always been too, well, proper to have anything but respect for a married woman."

"You're a lovely liar."

Harry Adams had made a fool of himself over Alice. He had worshipped her, he had idolized her, and with the memory of that relationship always handy to prop up her ego Alice was convinced that no normal man could be near her for very long without being driven into a state of sexual frenzy.

She was only moderately attractive, in Ackerley's view. A slim woman of thirty-odd, with vividly blond hair and a sluttish style in her clothes, there was nothing distinguished about Alice except her cheery, surprised smile, which lent a suggestion of awkward innocence to her expression. Ackerley knew that Alice's smile had nothing to do with what she was thinking about. It simply looked good on her, like a bracelet or a ring, and that was the reason she wore it. Her problem basically, Ackerley thought, was that she hadn't been given enough vitamins and orange juice as a child. He had no evidence to support this; it was a purely subjective evaluation based on his mild distaste for the woman. But he was quite sure her bones were soft, that her teeth weren't good.

"It was so sad about Harry," she said. "Poor guy never seemed to get it all together. I had to leave him, you know that, Bunny, but he never got over it."

"Well, that's understandable."

"It was pathetic, really. But, oh Bunny, it was unfair that I had to be responsible for how much he loved me. That's a terrible responsibility, to realize you're just as important to someone as the air he breathes. I mean, that's not fair. I'm really not the eighth wonder of the world, you know."

97

"That's all very well for you to say," Ackerley said, with what seemed to him commendable ambiguity. He squeezed her hand lightly and imagined he felt her bones giving way under his touch. "Now, love, tell me about Harry's call."

"Well, naturally, I thought he wanted to talk about the child-support money. He was late again, you see. We didn't need it, not that we're rich, but we are comfortably situated. I mean, we own our flat here, and we have the beach lot at St. Tropez, and Pierre would buy me a car, but he says, and he's so right, what's the point of having two cars in the city? He's more than willing to support my son, Harry's and my son, that is, but I thought it was good for Harry to have that monthly responsibility because—"

Ackerley interrupted her smoothly. "Stiffens the spine, I'm sure. Now, Alice, about Harry's call?"

"Well, it was in the afternoon, and he said he had to see me right away. Well! Pierre is insanely jealous, you know, he'd never let me go to a masseur or a male hairdresser, the poor baby doesn't believe they're all faggykins, but Harry sounded so desperate that I told him to come right over. He told me he'd called August Spencer in Ireland that afternoon and called you in London. Well, about August Spencer, I thought, big deal, because I never liked him. Harry thought he was wonderful, and tried to live up to him. But he'd have been better off picking a nice, stable guy like you to look up to."

"Yes. And Harry, why did he want to see you?"

"He said you weren't in London, and that he wanted to leave something with me. Poor Harry was in such a state! He said his apartment wasn't safe, and when I asked him what he meant, he said it was something he couldn't talk about."

"He gave you a letter?"

"Aren't you smart!" Alice said. "He wanted me to

keep it for him." She beamed her cheery, surprised smile directly into his eyes. "Naturally, I was glad to."

"Have you read the letter?"

"No, it's in a sealed envelope."

Her reply was too prompt and practiced, he thought; despite her wide eyes and incurious smile, Ackerley knew she was lying.

"Love, I need that letter. It may save a pair of lives, one of which is very precious to me, since it's my own."

"Well, I certainly don't want to get mixed up in any of your business. I'm terrified of it." She looked at him anxiously, and wet her lips. A good act, Ackerley thought, and nothing for it but to let her finish it. "I'm really upset, Bunny," she said, and took his hand in an impulsive gesture. "I'd like to get away from Paris for a while. Maybe just to London to look at the shops. You know how Frenchmen are, and Pierre's no different, though I wouldn't change him for the world. They all have that security thing, they're always worrying about tomorrow, and investing every franc they don't need to actually live on. Pierre makes lots of money, but it all goes for old coins and stamps and silver and antiques, and our flat looks like the flea market half the time. He plans to hang onto them until they double their value, which is just fine, but it doesn't leave much for fun and games, if you know what I mean."

Ackerley smiled sympathetically, and waited for her to run down; he knew what was coming. She hadn't had a real vacation in three years, she told him, and Pierre didn't like the new clothes and wouldn't buy her any, although that was just an excuse to save the money, and there was no full-time maid, just a sullen peasant girl who came mornings twice a week, . . .

Ackerley contained his impatience. The music

seemed even more deafening and the lissom and
lf-naked young Arab jugglers were doing a spectac-
ar turn with dozens of brightly painted plates.

Spencer was probably arriving somewhere in the
city about now, he thought, after a discreet glance at
his watch. He had probably taken a train to Stuttgart
and flown out later in the day to Orleans, where he
could catch a bus into Paris. It was the long way
around, but if the Frankfurt airport had looked hot to
Spencer, then it was an odds-on-wager that it was under surveillance; Spencer's perception of danger was
damn near uncanny, Ackerley knew. But the knowledge that if danger existed, it existed equally for both
of them, did little to cheer him up.

"—the new Correges boots Pierre says are too expensive, even though he's got a kinky thing about
them. I know because he almost drools when he sees
a girl wearing them, but even so—"

"Alice, how much do you want for that letter?"

"Well, you don't have to act as if I'm trying to sell it
to you. I just want to get away from Paris, because
Harry got me mixed up in this business. That's fair,
isn't it? I thought about £300." She winked and
punched his arm lightly, gestures which Ackerley decided were meant to suggest a roguish good-fellow-
ship. "You're getting a bargain, Bunny."

Of course she had read it. "Very well," Ackerley
said. "Where is the letter?"

"At the apartment."

A dozen plates were spinning high in the air from
the hands of the jugglers, and the electric guitars
pounded to an ear-splitting climax.

Ackerley put money for their drinks on the table.
"Let's go," he said.

At that instant, the lights went out. Someone
screamed, but the sound of it was almost immediately
smothered in bellows of consternation from jugglers.

As the music died away in metallic grunts, the plates began to strike the floor, so rapidly that each splintering crash sounded like an echo of the one preceding it. Waiters shouted for silence and someone appeared with a flashlight.

If this was a practical joke, it was a good one, Ackerley thought, for putting an end to the awful music and the silly bare-assed jugglers with just the flick of a switch was a stroke of genius.

He stood and reached to take Alice by the arm. But Alice's arm wasn't where he expected it to be; it was hanging straight down toward the floor, and her head and shoulders were resting on the table. One Pernod wouldn't account for this, he thought, unless she'd been drinking before she came. But then he remembered that Alice drank very little as a rule. Like most deceitful people, she was afraid of what she might reveal. And it was as these thoughts drifted through his mind that Ackerley's hand encountered the shaft of metal protruding from between Alice's shoulder blades. It was like accidentally touching a live wire. Ackerley stiffened and moved to the opposite side of the table in one long stride. He scooped up the glass he had used and wiped it hastily with the end of his tie and put it back on the table.

At the front door a disturbance was going on, and he surmised from the angry shouts that some customers were trying to leave without paying their checks. Ackerley moved toward the rear of the club. When he collided with someone, he said, "There's gas coming from somewhere. Better get the hell out of here."

A woman near him began to scream. The struggle near the front became more violent. Ackerley raised his voice, and said, "Keep your hands off me, you goddamn fag," and shoved a man near him to the floor. In the ensuing uproar, which was punctuated with shouted profanities, Ackerley slipped into a cor-

101

ridor which was acrid with the stench of toilet drains. At the end of the corridor was a locked door, but knowing French dram-shop regulations, Ackerley guessed the key would be in the lock. It was, and in seconds he was strolling off into the shadows of the alley which ran behind Le Saloon.

August Spencer paid off his cab in front of Billy's Relais in the Rue Jacob. He had left his bus at the Place General LeClerc and, after calling the Relais and speaking briefly to Ackerley, had walked almost a mile before hailing a taxi.

Harry's wife, Alice, had been knifed to death. Sweet little Alice Blue Gown had had the letter, and sweet little Alice's blood had been spilled because of it. Spencer had told Ackerley to send Billy around to the Vignon's apartment, to check the action there. . . .

The street and sidewalks were empty and the wind was gusting and cold. A woman turned into the Rue Jacob from a street leading to the river and tottered toward Spencer in high-heeled white vinyl boots which were laced up almost to her bony knees. She wore a black fur coat, tightly belted at the waist, and a red scarf knotted about her throat. She stopped and gave Spencer a hard, intimate smile, but did not seem surprised when he shook his head. Shrugging, she asked him for a cigarette. Spencer gave her several and she laughed like a happy, surprised child and went off down the street with a new and confident swing to her hips. The sign in the window of the Relais read "Closed," in English and in French, but when Spencer rapped on the door it was opened almost immediately by a tall, wiry man with a golden smile and tufts of pure white hair sprouting from his ears like cotton candy.

"August, come in, come in," he said, the street

lights gleaming on his famous gold teeth and shining bald head. "It's been too long."

Billy closed and locked the door and led Spencer through the dark restaurant toward his office. There was just enough light for Spencer to see that the dozen or so tables were already set for tomorrow's lunch, glasses and silverware and napkins arranged neatly on snowy tablecloths. The fresh flowers would not be put out until noon tomorrow, Spencer knew; he had been a friend of Billy's and a patron of the Relais for years.

Billy Allen and the Relais had been fixtures in Paris for two generations, and like the Adlon in Berlin before it was bombed out, like the Hotel Aletti in Algiers and the Althaus in Trieste, Billy's Relais was a watering hole for journalists, French government officials and diplomats of all nationalities. The food and wines were startlingly good, even for Paris, and the prices were startlingly high, even for Paris; but the main attraction of Billy's Relais was Billy himself, and Billy's special charm included personality, a love of conspiracy and a deep conviction that his friends and customers were the finest people in the world. Billy had one other great talent, which was a love of secrets and the knack of keeping them.

"I did what Bunny told me to," he said, as they turned into a short corridor that led to his office. "I went around to that place where that guy lives. What's his name? Pierre Vignon. Cops all over the place. I stood about in the street with the neighbors. Seems somebody gave unlucky Pierre a bash on the head and ripped the bejesus out of his flat."

"Police make any arrests?"

"No. Whoever did it vanished like smoke." Billy reached for the doorknob and flashed a smile at Spencer. "It's just like the old days."

"Unfortunately, you're right," Spencer said, and

walked past Billy into a small office where Ackerley lay on a leather couch, a forearm across his eyes to shield them from the glare of the goosenecked lamp on a roll-topped desk.

Billy said, "I'll fix you lads a snack" and closed the door. When his footsteps had faded away in the direction of the kitchen, Spencer removed his duffle coat and sat down wearily and gratefully in a deep leather chair. He lit a cigarette and said to Ackerley, "Stupid question, perhaps, but did anyone get a good look at you?"

"Someone always gets a good look at you, August. I didn't do anything conspicuous like singing along with the band, but someone will remember me."

"Well, you did leave a dead female at your table."

"Yes, that was conspicuous. Now if it's not the Germans, who's trying to kill us?"

"Did you talk to Denise Morand?"

"No."

"She lives out near Versailles. But Theophile Le-Maitre gave me a private dossier on her."

"How long has LeMaitre been in Paris?"

"Someone in London, I forget who, told me Interpol sent him here from Corsica a couple of years ago. He's still grateful for that Naples business."

Ackerley sat up and took a bulky folder from the pocket of his trench coat, and handed it to Spencer.

"Bear in mind, this has no official existence," Ackerley said. "Every scrap of paper relating to Denise Morand was pulled by the Quai D'Orsay when Andre Leroi became close to Barrault."

"Then who prepared this file?"

"As you'll see, there's no signature. Just initials. Also, it's not dated, it's not classified, and it's not authorized by any particular department. My guess is that those details could be added later if anyone wanted to embarrass Andre or the Barrault regime." Ack-

104

erley smiled at Spencer. "She's a kissy devil. Did you know her?"

Spencer nodded and opened the file on Denise Morand.

There were four snapshots of her taken against a background of docks and ships, others in a garden or lawn facing a white frame house. There were several eight-by-ten glossies of Denise in ballet costume at an exercise bar. She was smiling radiantly at whoever had taken the picture, her red hair tied back with a black ribbon and her long and fantastically symmetrical legs creating the illusion that she was much taller than she actually was. She was about five-four barefoot, Spencer knew. He went quickly through her file. Born after World War II, she was in her late twenties. Her father was a painting contractor in Lyons. Emil Morand. Resistance with de Gaulle in Africa; later served as liaison with Patton's Third. Preparatory school, Convent of the Sacred Heart. Music lessons, ballet lessons, trips to Switzerland, Belgium, etc. Intimate with Robert Jordan. Intimate with Georges Clivet. Intimate with Roger Boucher.

"Who in hell are all these guys?" Spencer asked Ackerley.

"LeMaitre thinks they're fakes. But whether they're real people or not is moot. You'll come across more of them, and by the logic of numbers, the public could be led to believe Andre's mistress is a tramp."

Billy came in with a tray of sandwiches and wine. The sandwiches were made of rye bread and butter and thin pink ham and the wine was a red from the Rhone Valley. Spencer thought he wasn't hungry, but he was wrong; he was famished. The sandwiches and wine made him feel almost cheerful, but he was honest enough to admit to himself that it was the pictures of Denise rather than the food and drink which had raised his spirits.

Billy turned on the television set perched on top of the roll-top desk, and after the inevitable interval of snow and herring bones and static, the face of President Barrault, which was like that of a rich, suspicious peasant, filled the screen. When Billy left the office, Spencer stood and turned down the volume of the television set, so that President Barrault, with his swelling and collapsing mouth and cheeks, looked like an aged actor silently exercising away his wrinkles. One would have guessed, Spencer thought, that the last years of the de Gaulle regime would serve as a reminder to France that a man like Henri Barrault might not serve her best interests; and yet nations, like people, always seemed to choose the same kind of troubles.

Henri Barrault was in his late seventies and seemed to care more about his nation's past than he did about its future. In his regime, statues of France's immortals were commissioned by the hundreds. Boulevards were renamed to honor his country's writers and statesmen and soldiers, and men the Nazis had martyred were elevated to sainthood and the sites of their sacrifices commemorated with plaques and officially designated as places of veneration. No one paid any particular attention to these senile and somewhat romantic views of French history, but there were increasingly sharp critics of Barrault's foreign policy, which had alienated Great Britain and America by capriciously closing all French harbors and airports to much foreign military traffic.

Spencer had never been a professional France-watcher, but friends of his whose business it was to study France had told him that what Barrault's enemies feared at the present was that his wrath at the Saracen Vector might lead him to provoke all-out war on Egypt and Algeria. Barrault had never reconciled himself to the loss of France's colonies and he

106

despised with neurotic virulence the strident national-
ism of the Saracen Vector, that loose and secret feder-
ation of the so-called Fedayeen whose goal was the
destruction of Israel, and whose leaders had vowed
they would not lower their arms or their guidons until
they had reached the Israeli shores of the Mediterranean. It wasn't that Barrault was pro-Israel so much
as that he was anti-everyone who now occupied and
enjoyed the lands in Africa which he believed God
had created solely for the greater honor and glory of
France.

Spencer went back to the Denise Morand file. She
had joined the Paris Ballet in her late teens, danced
with the company for several years. Intimate with
Francois Charriere. Travelled to Russia with the Paris
Ballet on three occasions. Unknown whether Denise
Morand acted as courier for A. Leroi. This was
followed by a physical description, which Spencer
skipped. The evaluation concluded with a sentence
which Spencer thought was rather remarkable: "Subject is beautiful and possesses an arrogant sexuality
which has been known to make men slavishly de-
pendent on her."

Spencer stared at the image of President Barrault
on the television screen and began making calcula-
tions. Almost as if divining his thought, Ackerley nodded at the television set, and said, "Barrault went
down to his country place at Foix on the fourth. I've
checked back issues of *Figaro*. Andre Leroi was in the
presidential convoy. They drove down by car because, as you know, Barrault doesn't fly. It's not that
he's afraid, it's just that he doesn't like to be that far
from the beloved soil of France."

"And Barrault and his group returned from Foix to
Paris on the thirteenth," Spencer said.

"But Andre Leroi did not," Ackerley said. He

smoothed his wavy blond hair with his hands. He looked refreshed and alert.

"I'm no use to us in Paris for the moment," Ackerley said. "If I'm caught mucking around here by the police, I'll have to explain why I left sweet Alice with a knife in her back. I'd better go down to Foix. Not that I'll find Andre there."

Spencer knew what he meant. "But you'll find out who's interested in tailing you to Foix."

"Of course," Ackerley said. "I do have the odd, brilliant notion."

"Let's try to use our heads," Spencer said. "There's an international flap brewing. I can smell it. In some fashion it's tied to those sealed letters Andre sent us. Whatever accusations he made, whatever information he wanted to release obviously is top-secret dynamite. But now all three of those sealed letters have been recovered, and presumably destroyed or locked up. If that much is true, does it follow that you or I are out of it?"

Ackerley finished off a ham sandwich and drank some wine. Then he shook his head thoughtfully and said, "I shouldn't think so, August."

"I was afraid you'd say that," Spencer said.

"Well, it's clear enough. They, whoever *they* are, can't assume we didn't ignore Andre's injunction and take a peak at those letters."

"Yes, of course," Spencer said.

"That's why I'd better go down to Foix," Ackerley said. "If they're going to kill us, I'd prefer to be a moving target."

"Then I'll look up Denise Morand."

Spencer gave the Morand dossier to Billy and told him to put it in his safe. Then, with Billy's "Godspeeds" sounding pleasantly behind them, they went through the dark restaurant and into the night.

Chapter Six

The report which Spencer had written in Paris and consigned to Green Drop Faubourg had caused General Rose a spasm of anger and frustration. Spencer's trip to Frankfurt was not dangerous in itself; in fact, it was quite the opposite, a pointless and time-consuming escapade which would serve only to focus Spencer's attention on irrelevancies. But what worried General Rose was that Spencer had not been taken into custody by the CIA and was presently striking off in other directions to find Andre Leroi. Rose was exasperated by the pressures on him. In ten minutes, he must report to the President, and he had nothing encouraging or optimistic to tell him. General Rose picked up the phone which put him in direct contact with Douglas Benton of the CIA. When the connection was made, he said: "I'm accepting your recommendation vis-à-vis Arthur Fennaday and Maurice Stein and will so inform the President. For the time being, let them function normally. Can you tell me anything about August Spencer?"

"Nothing, except that he proved uncooperative in Frankfurt. Our man there only managed to extricate himself from jail a few hours ago. Spencer had destroyed his I.D."

"I wish to God you people would stop hiring amateurs."

"The agent was no amateur, General, and may I suggest we remain relevant. I'd like to remind you that men like Spencer are experienced and formidable. They are used to taking care of themselves and feel they can do it better than we can, and God knows I wouldn't argue with them on that score. We established surveillance in Frankfurt, but Spencer slipped through it. However, if you're short of good news for the President, here's something to tell him; we've established surveillance and security on Charity Finch and her parents. Charity Finch arrived from Dublin twenty-four hours ago on TWA Flight 150. We followed her from the airport to her home in Brewster, Massachusetts. It's too early to say the lid is on, but we're making progress. Do you have the signal on Harry Adams' former wife?"

"Alice Vignon, yes. We know she was murdered and was last seen with Wyndom Ackerley." General Rose glanced at his watch and stood abruptly. "Excuse me, Doug. I've got to go upstairs. I'll call you after our meeting."

General Rose left his desk and strode through the traffic of secretaries and aides to the stairs leading to the Oval Office. He did not give the impression of being in any particular hurry and he even managed a smile for some of the prettier girls.

The countryside north of Washington had been deadened by an early frost; pasture lands, flat from
110

the last haying, had been frozen into shades of brown and gray, and stiff, cold winds had stripped the leaves from the maples and sycamores. Herds of Holsteins stood like felt cut-outs against the gray sky, their black-and-white coloring complementing the drab tones of approaching winter.

Arthur Fennaday's wife was studying a map spread out on her yellow tweed skirt. They had turned off Highway One and were driving on a dirt road running between stands of bare locust trees.

"We should be coming to the Newhall turn-off in about a mile," Eileen Fennaday said.

"I don't know why you insisted we drive sixty miles to a party on Sunday afternoon. Even if we split early, we won't be home till midnight."

"Come on, relax and enjoy the view. It's actually rather pretty, in a kind of bleak way."

Fennaday made an unsuccessful effort to control a mounting nervousness and exasperation. He swore and hit the brakes as a brilliant golden-brown cock pheasant exploded from a tight coil of honeysuckle at the side of the road and flew in front of the car, wings pounding like drums against the heavy air.

"You're making me nervous," Eileen said, looking at his tense profile.

"Sorry," Fennaday said. "I haven't started to wind down yet. It was that kind of week." Fennaday patted her hand and gave her the smile which friends had told him resembled that of the actor Gregory Peck.

"You belong to Washington Monday through Friday. You deserve an odd weekend for us."

Close the door of your office, and forget about the folders in the locked drawers of your desk, forget about their implications and go home to chat with your wife and children about skiing and school grades, the defection of yet another maid, neighbor-

111

hood problems, marketing problems, school problems ... it was the sensible thing to do, of course, a way to keep your sanity, but so much easier said than done.

The facts that Fennaday could not currently put from his mind were four in number, the first an announcement by the Mexican Foreign Minister that the remains of a radioactive cobalt head of an Athena missile had been found in northern Mexico. The missile had been fired from Green River, Utah, had overshot the White Sands Missile Range in New Mexico, and had landed north of the San Ignacio Hill, eighteen kilometers from Carrillo, Chihuahua, near the state border of Durango. This was the fourth U.S. missile that had been fired into Mexican territory, and for the first time the word "coincidence" was being used with a question mark after it.

Item two: Belkakem Krim, aged forty-seven, one of the original Algerian revolutionary leaders, had been assassinated in Frankfurt, Germany. Krim had been garroted to death. Krim had been one of the first Algerian leaders to break with the Boumedienne government. The garrote, Fennaday thought, precluded the action of a fanatic; to garrote a man, you needed accomplices, a taut rope or wire and a thick wooden peg, and uninterrupted time in some isolated cellar. And this led to his third source of anxiety, the fact that such Arab guerillas and revolutionary leaders were now being hailed as the new and romantic heroes of the U.S. radical Left. Palestinian Commandos were taking their places in the hearts and minds of the young leftists, who now gave them the adulation which they had recently accorded Che Guevara and Mao Tse-tung. All of which made it explosively difficult to deal with the Saracen Vector, whose leaders were becoming the heroes of parodoxically anti-Israeli and pro-Leftist groups in the Western world. And there was the business of August Spencer and Caprifoil which bothered Fennaday because he had been so abruptly excluded from it by General Rose. He might have helped, but he had been told bluntly to keep out of it.

Fennaday had been to see his doctor Friday afternoon, but he hadn't told Eileen about it. All he had got from Doctor Benedict were some soothing words and another bottle of red pills, which so far had done nothing to relieve Fennaday's tensions. But what was eroding his self-esteem most unbearably was the feeling of shame and guilt produced by his depression. Too shaky and fragile to stand the pressure of the job, so let him retire early and go on down to Florida ... that's what they would say. ...

"It's the next turn, darling," Eileen said. "Just past the silo."

George Newhall was in the Justice Department in a job paying $26,000 a year, but his wife, Pris, was the only daughter of a wealthy cheese processor in Wisconsin, and as a result the Newhalls lived in stylish luxury here at their country place and in a similar manner at an exclusive apartment in Washington. In a burst of unbecoming and uncharacteristic whimsy, they had named their country place "Cheese-it, the Copse."

When the Fennadays arrived, more than a dozen guests were having drinks in the long living room whose bay windows provided a spectacular view of an artificial lake and open meadows. Fennaday and his wife knew everyone present; they were government people for the most part, a predictable, conservative group, which was leavened by the presence of U.S. Senator Christopher Laird, and to a considerably lesser extent by Calvin Hilsinger, the editor and only full-time employee of the Keystone Wire Service.

It was an attractive, privileged group in an attractive, privileged setting, and the exchange of greetings and murmurs of conversations were reassuringly casual and good-humored. The men wore sports jackets and slacks with cashmere sweaters and weskits, while the women, in clusters against the fireplace and bay windows, brightened the fall day with colorful pants suits and tweeds.

Fennaday glanced about the room. His wife joined their hostess, Pris Newhall, at the Irish butler which served as a bar. George Newhall was talking to some people from Commerce. Senator Laird was with Calvin Hilsinger. The Senator towered over the reporter and, in fact, at six-five, Senator Laird towered over everyone in the room. He was a striking figure, not only because of his height, but because of his thick black hair, his ruddy complexion and the Edwardian clothes he fancied, the narrow black trousers, the gleaming, ankle-high boots and the fingertip-length dark gray jacket trimmed with beige felt at collar and cuffs. Senator Laird had a flair for drama and the apt phrase, and his only serious failings, at least according to his critics, were a bullying ruthlessness when his temper was roused, and a stubbornness which sometimes made it difficult for him to negotiate differences with his colleagues.

Calvin Hilsinger was a young man with reasonably good looks and reasonably attractive manners who had inherited the Keystone Wire Service from his father, who had founded the agency after World War II. Keystone serviced thirty-odd small town newspapers in southern and central Pennsylvania, and while Keystone's coverage was not significant, there were a number of Congressmen, including Senator Laird, who realized that Hilsinger had a touch of the Mencken in him; it wasn't what he said, but how he said it that caused his paragraphs to be picked up occasionally by *Time* and *Newsweek* and the national

114

wire services. As a result Hilsinger was becoming increasingly important beyond the domains of the local papers he covered Washington for. Fennaday joined Senator Laird and Hilsinger, and the Senator turned to him with a welcoming smile which was flattering in its directness and warmth: "Hello, Art. Where's your good lady?"

Fennaday felt a surge of affection for Senator Laird. To be greeted in this fashion, with such unmistakable sincerity, reaffirmed his flawed sense of personal worth and significance.

"Eileen is getting me a drink," Fennaday said, and shook hands with Laird and Hilsinger. Hilsinger introduced him to the girl beside him, Rita Lindhoff, a slim, youthful brunette who worked at Keystone as Hilsinger's secretary. To Fennaday's relief, his tension and nervousness seemed to be easing in the presence of Senator Laird.

Senator Laird smiled at Fennaday and Hilsinger, but the poised confidence of his manner stretched out to embrace the room.

"This may interest you, Art," he said. "Hilsinger and I were having a discussion, no, let's be honest, we were having an argument over the appropriate response of our field agents in the CIA."

Hilsinger smiled. "I submit we weren't even having an argument. You were making a speech. I was listening, sir."

"I'm sorry if I gave that impression. But let me say again; I distinguish between excessive force used by an American policeman against an American citizen, and the kind of force it may be necessary for a CIA agent in the field to use against our enemies anywhere in the world."

"Well, are you suggesting that CIA agents be authorized to commit murder when, in their sole, unsupported judgment, it becomes necessary?"

Everyone in the room was listening to them now.

"These agents are playing a game without rules," Senator Laird said. He frowned thoughtfully and rubbed his jaw, as if weighing with an almost physical effort each word he was about to use. "Sometimes they must make them up as need dictates. Try to remember one thing, Hilsinger, before you sit in judgment on them. Our agents are front-line soldiers in a war for peace. And they are facing enemies, the KGB of Russia and the STB of East Germany, who are governed by no code of behavior or ethics whatsoever." The senator's voice rose slowly and steadily in volume, and Fennaday realized that its strident, metallic tone reminded him very much of the late Senator Joseph McCarthy of Wisconsin. "Now, let me ask you a couple of questions," Senator Laird said, with the impression he was restraining his anger with a commendable effort. "Do we let them slaughter our agents? Or do we give our people the means and authority to protect themselves? Because that's what it comes down to. When an American agent's life is in jeopardy, he must eliminate the threat to his life with an appropriate response, and if that means blowing someone's head off, I say fine."

At the bar Pris Newhall called out, "Hear! Hear!" and there was a sudden brisk patter of applause throughout the room.

Senator Laird smiled and shrugged lightly, gestures which let it be understood that while he was declining the personal approval of the group, he was at the same time accepting their approval as a sensible tribute to his convictions. It was a delicate tightrope to walk, but the senator managed it expertly. Although he was keenly concerned about his own image, he was shrewd enough and experienced enough to know that charisma was usually secondary to the championship of emotionally popular issues.

116

Being for the right thing at the right time, that was the trick. And now—and it had happened several times lately—he sensed that he had struck a nerve. Which interested him very much, because at this cool and weary time in history, bombast was either frowned on or yawned at; yet this fairly knowledgeable group had savored his intensity and his simulated anger, and he thought he knew why.

Senator Laird believed that the people were weary of impotent old Uncle Sam. It wouldn't matter so much if this impotence were not so painfully and maddeningly expensive. But people were getting sick of the very names of the extravagantly costly hardware which could never, under any circumstances, be used. He had noticed this on his last trip home. Usually, the Senate or the House could get what they wanted in the way of appropriations by scaring the customers. Someone supposedly in the know pointed off to Cienfuegos and declared the Russians were building an underwater rocket base there, and that was usually enough to get the extra funds the Pentagon was always in need of. But the scare tactics weren't working anymore. What the hell good is all that hardware if we can't use it? That's what the tax-payers were asking of Laird in mutinous accents. They knew it was an even match-up between the super powers of the world and they were weary of being had. The ICBMs, the sea-launched ballistic missiles, the MRVs and multiple independently targeted re-entry vehicles, all of this acronymic gadgetry seemed to have lost its appeal to the public. They paid for it, but deep in their bones and in their empty pocketbooks, they were beginning to suspect their money was being wasted. But, Senator Laird was thinking, this group had cheered the notion of an American agent blowing the head off an enemy agent. It was economical, true; you could kill someone for

117

the price of a bullet. To give full rein to undercover agents was quite possibly an emotional compensation for the nuclear weaponry you couldn't use at all; one man authorized to kill the enemy might just serve as a surrogate for the expensive hardware that was never going to kill anyone.

Someone took his arm with surprising strength.

"Senator, I must talk to you," Fennaday said. "Please, it's most important."

Senator Laird was about to beg off, gracefully and regretfully, since he had dinner plans in Washington that evening, but there was an urgency and tension in Fennaday's expression that changed his mind. "Of course, Art. Let me freshen my drink."

They found privacy in a study done in leather furniture and hunting prints. Senator Laird looked appraisingly at Fennaday, who stood perfectly still, a curiously soft smile on his lips.

"Are you all right, Art?"

"I feel fine, Senator." And it was true, Fennaday realized. From the instant he had decided to unburden himself to Senator Laird, Fennaday's tensions and anxieties had begun to fade away; it was like the breaking of a fever. "You made the issue perfectly clear, Senator, when you told Hilsinger there were only two choices: to protect and save our agents, or to let them be killed. To any person of honor, that means there is only one choice."

Senator Laird studied Fennaday with the eyes of a trained lawyer, analyzing and estimating his intelligence and credibility. At last he said: "Just what is it you want to talk to me about, Art?"

And Fennaday, with a sense of relief beyond measure, told Senator Laird of August Spencer's file from Ireland, and Maurice Stein's evaluation of it; and he told him that Caprifoil was missing. . . .

118

Several of the Newhall guests were leaving, and a woman in the driveway was calling out, "Cheese-it, the Cops!" in a wavering, falsetto voice. Calvin Hilsinger and Rita Lindhoff stood at the bay windows looking out at the meadows which were now so dark that they could see the reflection of the moon in the artificial lake at the edge of the forest. "You shouldn't argue with senators," Rita Lindhoff said, in her coldest voice.

She was truly angry, Hilsinger thought with some surprise; he could tell by the rigidity of her back and shoulders. He said, "They don't listen, so what difference does it make? They just like to project a down-to-earth relationship with the little people. Finding eternal truth in the mumblings of the noble but illiterate grape-pickers."

"Well, that's precisely why you shouldn't argue with them. You should report what they do and say, in writing, impersonally and fairly. But, Christ, don't get into this ego thing. Confiding to your diary that the big man talked to you."

Hilsinger smiled affectionately at her; she amused and excited him when she worked herself up to these intense peaks of feeling. He understood her strong emotions. She didn't enjoy these Wasp cocktail parties and she wasn't comfortable at them. But she couldn't admit this, and as a consequence she let her feelings fly off in other directions. Hilsinger didn't mind serving as an irrelevant lightning rod for her pent-up bolts.

Hilsinger saw Senator Laird coming toward them. The Senator was on a fence-mending mission, Hilsinger surmised. His guess proved correct, for the senator took his arm, smiled warmly at him and Rita and said, "Now, Cal, you realize there was nothing personal in our discussion. You asked a pertinent question, and I answered it as honestly as I could, but

119

perhaps with more heat than the occasion called for. I think you're pretty smart, Hilsinger, so let me ask you a question. Why do you think this room broke into applause at what I told you?"

From his great height, Senator Laird smiled down at Rita Lindhoff. "And you, young lady, can you tell me why such bloodthirsty sentiments are suddenly popular?"

Rita smiled demurely; Hilsinger felt like kicking her. "I really don't understand politics," she said.

The warmth left the Senator's eyes. "You think I'm kind of a horse's ass, don't you?"

Rita was still smiling. " 'Cry Havoc! and let slip the dogs of war' has always been a popular notion, Senator. The quotation is from Shakespeare."

"Why didn't you say so from the start? Mind if I guess? You've got that egg head notion you can get contaminated talking to politicians."

Rita began to moisten her lips; she couldn't bear direct and angry arguments. "I'm sorry, I didn't really think you cared what I thought."

"Of course I care," Senator Laird said. "Don't ever think I don't, young lady. And I care most when you're in that voting booth."

The senator smiled down on her. "Now, young lady, that quote you used was from Julius Caesar, I believe. Act Three, right?"

Rita appraised the pleasurable malice in the senator's smile, and said, "I wasn't even sure it was Shakespeare. I guessed."

Unexpectedly, the senator laughed. "Hilsinger, you got yourself a smart-ass. That's great."

Chapter Seven

August Spencer, a glass of brandy in his hand, paced restlessly in the softly lighted salon of Denise Morand's town house. The salon faced the Avenue de Versailles. Spencer could hear the rumble of rush-hour traffic and see the erratic play of headlights on the drawn shades and lemon-pale ceilings. He had traced Denise down at a mutual friend's and she had promised to meet him here at 6:30. She had told him where to find an emergency key, which was beside the finial on a carriage lamp at the entrance to the servants' quarters.

She had done well for herself, he decided, with the blend of fondness and amusement which always accompanied his thoughts of her. Not like a tidy, cautious little cat, but like some charming tawny animal that took what it wanted from a kill and scattered what was left for anyone who might care for it.

The salon reflected her tastes and resources; it was

prodigal and gaudy. The room was done in furs and hides, suede-skin sofas, zebra rugs, many tiny fat pillows of mink and sable. Surprisingly all of these blended harmoniously with her antiques, the winged chairs, the rosewood lowboys which held her collections of miniature soldiers.

Spencer looked at himself in the clouded mirror above the mantlepiece, and was largely satisfied with his appearance. His dark solid features did not betray his tensions; he needed a shave, but that was fine. Most tourists did.

His thoughts churned on one question: what was causing the flap? Why were the French and American governments reacting so swiftly and massively to the disappearance of Andre Leroi, who was, after all, only an auxiliary official in the Barrault administration? Spencer freshened his drink and attempted to sort out and analyze the facts he was reasonably certain of. And with the assistance of the remarkable card index in his memory, he tried to add some new dimension or significance to them. The effort seemed only to lead him up blind paths to stone walls. Then he examined certain current international problems to which Andre Leroi's disappearance might conceivably be linked.

Brazil. The government had appropriated millions in American industrial properties (as Castro had done earlier), but Brazil had avoided a showdown with the United States by an adroit financial maneuver, which had been created and proposed by someone with a deliberately low profile in the Treasury Department. In effect, the United States had loaned Brazil the money to pay off the American firms. Pure blackmail. . . . Cuba. The CIA's hard line contended that the Castro regime was so mired in Maoism that another armed invasion was imperative. Peru. Expropriation of the International Petroleum Company, a subsidiary of Standard Oil of New Jersey, gave its military government wide support and incited other South American governments to similar take-overs. The Middle East. The Rand Corporation (and Spencer regretted knowing this) had recommended "demonstration" nuclear attacks against selected Egyptian targets, and there were groups in the government and in Intelligence to whom this suggestion was pure catnip.

But did the disappearance of Andre Leroi fit into any of these simmering problems?

Spencer heard a car door slam. He walked rapidly to the windows facing the Avenue de Versailles and pulled the shade a half-inch with his fingertip.

Denise Morand stood on the sidewalk giving instructions to her chauffeur, a smiling young Arab in a gray whipcord uniform and polished leather puttees. The car was a cream-and-brown Jaguar sedan. Denise's chauffeur touched his fingers to his visored cap and added a smiling salaam to his salute before climbing into the car and driving off. Denise stood smiling with what seemed to be casual pleasure at the copper-colored leaves still clinging to the branches of the chestnut trees. A cool act, he thought, probably learned from Andre. There was no concern in her manner; if she were under surveillance, nothing could be learned or inferred from her leisurely enjoyment of the pleasant street scene.

Some children darted past her on the sidewalk, but none of them seemed any younger than Denise, he thought. This air of youthfulness was made of many things, he realized; her clothes, now an antelope suede suit and slim black boots, were always almost comically chic, but more than that, it was the grace which animated her dancer's body. The brilliant red hair which had been like an exuberant torch when she danced was a shade darker now, muted to a

123

golden brown, but the clean lines of her face and the strangely gentle excitement in her eyes hadn't changed with the years. She had always been an impulsive, willful creature, but these drives had been counterbalanced by a streak of peasant prudence, and when she had stopped dancing, she had invested her money in good sound stocks (suggested by Andre, Spencer guessed) and had moved on to a secure and queenly life in the suburbs of Paris.

"—but I never did any work for Andre, darling." They were seated together on the sofa in front of the fireplace, and he could see anxiety deepening in the frown that shadowed her eyes.

"You might have worked with him without realizing it," Spencer said. "You saw him a couple of weeks ago. Can you remember the exact date?"

"Well, let me think. It was about the twenty-first, the twenty-second. I know because I had been in the country until Sunday. Andre wanted to buy me some violets and a cup of tea and we met in the afternoon in the Bois de Bologne."

"What did you talk about?"

She shrugged and smiled. "He'd read something in a magazine he thought I'd enjoy. He told me the new Hamlet was dreadful. We're just friends, you see. We aren't lovers anymore, so our conversation wasn't very exciting." Denise touched his cheek with the back of her hand, "You're worried, aren't you, August?"

Spencer put a finger to his lips, and walked to the door. After listening a moment, he opened the door and stepped into a dim and silent corridor which ran the length of the house, from the entrance on the Avenue de Versailles to the servants quarters. Spencer walked down a short flight of steps to the foyer, which faced a glass-paneled door through which he could see cars flashing by on the avenue. He tried the handle of the door, but it was locked. He returned to the salon and sat down again beside Denise, wondering if his nerves were giving out on him.

"Where did you send your chauffeur?"

"Ahmed? To buy some records for me. Beatles, Joan Baez, a couple of Bartoks. He'll be gone for hours. What did you think you heard?"

Spencer shook his head, "I don't know. I don't know what panic sounds like." He frowned at the backs of his hands, hesitant to tell her what would only alarm her. "Andre may be in trouble. He left Paris four days ago, and I can't find out where he is."

"But won't Michele tell you?"

"I talked to Michele and she lied to me. She told me Andre was off skiing in Gstaad."

"And that's not true." It wasn't a question.

"That's not true," Spencer said.

"August, are you in some kind of trouble?"

"Yes. Someone is trying to kill me and Bunny Ackerley. We're mixed up with something heavy and we haven't a clue what it is. Let me ask you a couple of questions, okay?"

"Of course. Can I give you some more brandy?"

"No." He hesitated a few seconds, and then looked straight into her clear and anxious eyes. "I don't want to get you involved in this, Denise. But if you're truthful with me, you may get involved. You understand that?"

She said, with a trace of uncharacteristic irritation, "Oh, for Christ's sake, I don't expect the Croix de Guerre for helping an old friend!"

"Okay. When you went to Moscow and Leningrad with the ballet, did you ever deliver anything to anyone for Andre?"

"No. Nothing."

"Not so fast. Think about it for a minute. It could have been something casual, a box of cigars for a

125

friend of his at the embassy, or some Scotch, or a carton of Pears soap."

"None of those things, August."

"Then how about books? Or albums of music?"

"Do you think Andre would use me as a courier without telling me?"

"Yes, if Andre had needed you, he would use you," he said. "I probably would too. Did you ever buy any gifts for Andre in Russia? Gloves? Vodka? Anything at all?"

"Yes, I bought him a fur hat once," she said.

"Where did you buy it?"

"In Moscow. It was in a shop in a street named after Stalin, but I suppose they've changed that now."

"Did Andre tell you to buy the hat at this particular shop?"

"No."

"You're quite sure?"

"Yes."

Spencer decided he needed a drink. He walked to the bar and added a half-inch of brandy to what was left in his glass. Denise rose and came across the room to him and looked up into his troubled eyes.

"You want me to do something for you, August. Is that it?"

"I've go no one else to ask," he said.

"Then tell me what it is. If it's something inconvenient, I'll simply say no."

"I hope you mean that," Spencer said.

"Just try me. I'm at heart extremely cautious and selfish. And I'm easily frightened, remember that."

"All right. I want you to call Michele and ask her to meet you somewhere for a drink. She'll try to put you off. You have to be insistent; suggest you've heard from Andre. When you see her, you can pretend she misunderstood you. But you must get Michele to come and meet you."

"Well, that doesn't sound too difficult," Denise said. "I'm a rather good actress, and Michele is rather stupid. That's not just the bitch in me. It's what Andre says."

"Michele won't be alone. She'll have someone with her whom she'll probably introduce as a casual friend. But no matter how genteel or civilized he appears, he will be, in fact, one of General Mercier's people."

Her face sobered. "Pour me a little drink, please. Tell me the rest of it."

"You've got to manage a moment alone with Michele."

"I can try. There's always the powder room." She looked at him thoughtfully. "August, I've worked hard all my life, and I managed to get most of the things I wanted. I don't want to risk them in some adventure of yours and Andre's."

Spencer shrugged. "You can get hit by a car walking across the street. If you do what I ask you to, I'm reasonably sure there's no danger in it. But I can't promise that. When you've done this favor for me, then forget about me and everything we've talked about."

"Well, you're honest about it." She smiled. "What shall I tell Michele in the powder room?"

That night on the Boulevard St. Germaine the air was cold and the shadows from high street lamps were splintered by the bare branches of chestnut trees. Through this chiaroscuro effect flowed the traffic of Paris, students, workers and prostitutes, and occasional priests on bicycles holding their broad-brimmed black hats in place with the handles of umbrellas. In the glassed-in terraces of the Deux Magots and the Reine Blanche students sat reading, or scribbling on pads, the silence broken only by the occasional clatter of saucers or the hissing of isinglass stoves.

The official but unmarked sedan stopped beside the Deux Magots near the entrance to the cathedral of St. Germaine. A chauffeur opened the rear door and a pale man in a dark suit stepped out and gave his arm to Michele Leroi, who regarded him with an expression of smiling, tolerant impatience, while he removed a gold watch from his vest pocket and inspected it.

"A few Hail Marys for my mother, Claude," she said, and sighed. "It's the anniversary of her funeral."

The man with Michele was Claude Weismann. He was slender and tall and properly dressed in a dark suit and overcoat, and he wore a gold wedding ring. His manners were courteous to the point of superciliousness, but he had a habit of blinking his eyes rapidly which lent him a redeeming air of shyness and uncertainty. His forehead was high, and his eyes crinkled warmly on those occasions when he found anything to smile at. At the moment, he wasn't smiling.

"You realize, it's quite late."

"But you've enjoyed yourself, you can't deny that."

"Of course. It was a great pleasure to meet Denise Morand. I've seen her dance several times. And you'll admit I agreed to let you shop for handkerchiefs at Printemps." Weismann frowned again at his watch. "General Mercier requested us to return at seven-thirty."

"Then we'll be a few minutes late." She walked toward the church, and when Weismann made other vague, clucking sounds of protest, she looked over her shoulder at him and said sharply, "I have as much stake in this matter as he does. A candle and a few Hail Marys won't matter."

Inside the church of St. Germaine the coldness of centuries was trapped in the old stones. The scent of flowers was like silvered icicles in her nostrils. Michele wore a tweed suit and a dark cape with a dramatic red wool lining, but the coldness of the

128

church pierced through them to her very bones, and she felt little shivers of goose flesh on her arms and legs. The effort to be casual with Claude Weismann required a physical as well as a mental act of control; it was one thing to direct your body and hands not to tremble, and to command your lips to smile, but once these orders were given, it was up to the terrified flesh to execute them, and this was what frightened her, the effort of holding herself together and the fear of what might happen if her will failed and she cracked into a thousand pieces. It had been easier when they had been with Denise at the American bar in the Prince de Galles.

She knelt at the communion rail and prayed with stiff lips to the Presence behind the golden doors of the tabernacle. Dear God, give me strength, protect and defend him. . . .

Then she moved into the ring wing of the transept and deposited a franc in the cylinder that flanked the rows of votive candles. She lighted a candle with a taper and the flame rose slowly within the thick red glass. When she returned to the communion rail and knelt to pray for her mother, she knew that Claude Weismann was almost directly behind her in the first pew, his eyes anxiously checking the gold watch he held in his hand.

The old frozen wood hurt her knees. It felt icy and rough through her nylons. She wondered how she looked from behind to Claude Weismann. Probably fetching. The tips of her tiny suede pumps resting on the stone floor, her bowed head gleaming in soft yellow candlelight, a figure of chic and worldly submission, a woman on her knees, a barbarous and atavistic symbol. Men savored it. But who in God's name knew? A whore had told her that. Denise would know. Her thoughts skittered about in her head like frightened mice. She was grateful for the cold pain in

129

her knees, the eyes of Claude Weismann staring (she surmised) at her. Like a child squeezing its eyes shut against darkness, she was trying to hide from thinking of what she must do. . . .

Michele crossed herself and rose from the communion rail, and when she started down the left-hand aisle Claude Weismann stood and joined her. Hand-carved wooden confessionals lined the wall to the baptistery of the church, and above several of these glowed soft red lights, indicating the presence of a priest.

In the gloom ahead, Michele saw the figure of a slim woman who wore a widow's veil which concealed her face. The woman knelt near the aisle, her head bent in prayer. Michele's heart beat faster; her step faltered, and Claude Weismann caught her arm in a strong hand. No, no dear God, she thought, this would end it all. She said quietly, "I'm all right. Please." Claude Weismann released her arm, and murmured something Michele barely heard, and certainly didn't understand, for she was staring into the eyes of Denise Morand, who had parted the widow's veil to reveal features starkly white in the gathering gloom of the church.

"Excuse me," Michele said to Claude Weismann, and turned gracefully but swiftly toward the confessional to which she had been directed by a single flick of Denise's eyes.

Claude Weismann put out a hand to stop her. But he hesitated for an instant, confused by the sovereign and reasonable nature of her action, and by that time it was too late; the heavy door of the confessional was already swinging shut on Michele.

Claude Weismann glanced about uneasily. A woman in a dark suit and a widow's veil was walking away from him toward the nave of the church. Something in the way she moved, something in her graceful carriage, seemed familiar to him, but he couldn't recall where he might have seen her. Claude Weismann took a pew near the confessional Michele had entered and once again took out his watch and looked at it.

In the confessional the priest's panel slid back with a whispering sound which suggested centuries of muted conspiracy between those who sinned and those who forgave. Michele stared through the gloom at August Spencer's hard profile, and, in a voice which threatened at any instant to rise in terror, said: "General Mercier told me to lie to you."

"Then stop lying now," Spencer said. "Unless you want two more deaths on your hands. Where is Andre? And for Christ's sake, keep your voice down."

"Andre is in Algeria. With President Barrault." The words came in a thick, straining rush; it was as if a strangler's hands were about her throat. "There was a breakdown in security, no one was supposed to know the President had left France, but some messages weren't sent, or maybe they were, God only knows, but the President's party was taken by the Saracen Vector, and President Barrault is being held as a hostage."

Spencer considered himself a calm and practical man; in assaying reactions, his own and those of other persons, he had made it a rule to avoid metaphors, and what he thought of as "the wheels of if;" that is, he always attempted to define his emotions in a one-to-one relationship with reality rather than depending on the removes and buffers of figures of speech. The wheels of if was his simple phrase to describe the irrelevant considerations of what might have been, or what ought to have been. But now, in trying to analyze the information given him by Michele, he realized that the complacent calmness with which he had

131

always credited himself was indeed a myth; for there was a thunder of blood in his ears as he thought of the repercussions that would be caused by the fact that a leader of one of the mightiest nations of the world was being held captive by a para-national group of adventurers somewhere in Algeria. This was a ticking bomb as big as the world itself. And he, and Bunny Ackerley, should have kept their stupid hands away from it.

Michele whispered other things to him which he absorbed like a man in a trance, and then she was gone, and there was a tentative tapping on the closed panel on the other side of the confessional. Acting helplessly, reflexively, Spencer pushed the panel back and saw the dim outline of a man's face arranged in neat squares by the grill work which separated them.

"Do you speak English, Father?"

"I can't hear your confession. There are other priests."

"Please, Father. It took me a long time to work up my nerve." Spencer thought, if you could squeeze guilt out of a soft tube, that's what it would sound like.

"There is a young boy at the hotel I'm staying at, he's about sixteen, he works there, he carries luggage, brings trays up, but he's the nephew of the owner. And they've made him do terrible things with some of the guests, if you know what I mean."

Spencer knew he had to find Ackerley now. They would kill Ackerley, they would kill him, if they could get their hands on them.

"He came to my room tonight. He was lonely, he was crying. They wanted him to stay with an old man and he didn't want to and I told him he could stay with me."

Spencer tried to use his knowledge and brains. The fact that the security of a head of state had been

132

breached, that Barrault could be held by force in a foreign country, suggested a revolutionary potential of almost infinite proportions within France. Eradicating the prominent conspirators (Mercier?) wouldn't guarantee that other echelons of traitors didn't still exist in the armed forces and the government.

"He was so frightened, and he seemed so alone that I gave him a little wine, and we talked for a while."

Until the president of France was declared dead or was returned safely to Paris, any unclassified person who knew that he was missing might wittingly or unwittingly jeopardize the objectives of France, America, and any other nations which had been put in the picture. Those nations, with their monies and markets facing an international crisis, and their global security threatened, were now probably alerted to a war-readiness state, and their agents would have been given green lights to eliminate anyone who might escalate the danger of the situation. Therefore, Spencer decided, he had no options; he must go to Foix and find Ackerley. After that, they could maintain the lowest of profiles until the abduction of President Barrault exploded into headlines.

"I was only trying to comfort the boy, I swear to God that's all it was, but something got hold of me, something outside of me, because I'm married, Father, and I've got grown daughters in college, so it had to be something like insanity, or some kind of hypnotism. God, I don't know. But I took the boy, Father, and I didn't mean to. But what started as something friendly turned sick and ugly."

Spencer removed the neatly folded white handkerchief which he had placed over his collar and tie. He opened the priest's door of the confessional and looked out. The pews near the confessional were empty. Spencer rose to leave.

"Can you forgive me, Father? I can never forgive myself. But can you, Father?"

Why not, Spencer thought.

In this curious and dangerous voyage into his past, he had met Ilse and his son, and Ilse's father whom he had betrayed, and Michele and Denise, both of whom he had used and compromised, not because there were no other choices available, but because he had relished the freedom which belongs to anyone who chooses to live in a moral labyrinth. Why not forgive everybody?

"Ego tu absolve," Spencer said, and left the confessional and the church.

When he turned into the Rue Jacob, the sidewalks were crowded and hotel and shop windows were bright against the darkness. Two men were inspecting a tire on a Citroen opposite the entrance to his hotel, the Angleterre. Both men wore black overcoats and were squatting down beside the car, apparently discussing the condition of the tire.

Spencer stopped and looked into the window of a book store. Then he went into the shop and asked the young clerk if he might use the telephone. She said yes and pointed out the instrument. Spencer called the Angleterre.

"This is August Spencer," he told the desk clerk. "I've got to return to Ireland today. Would you pack—" Spencer then heard a distinctive sound which was the faint echoing effect caused when another telephone joined the connection.

"—my things and keep them at the hotel till next month. I can take care of the bill by mail, if that's all right. You have my address in Ireland."

"That will be quite satisfactory, Mr. Spencer. I wish you a pleasant trip." After an unnaturally long pause, the clerk said, "Are you at the airport now, Mr. Spencer?"

"Yes. My flight's in forty-five minutes."

Spencer bought a book on French cathedrals from the young girl tending the shop and leafed through it. Glancing up he saw two men come out of the Hotel Angleterre and hurry toward the men squatting beside the Citroen. One of the men said something, and all four men climbed into the car. The man at the wheel put a telephone to his lips, and was speaking into it as the Citroen passed the book shop.

Spencer turned a page of his book, and glanced absently at the majestic rose window above the altars of the cathedral at Chartres and wondered how he might gain some time and space in which to maneuver. The police of two countries, and perhaps more, were after him and Ackerley, but that wasn't what worried Spencer. It was intelligence agents, and the free-lancers employed by them, all functioning under "do what's necessary" orders, who knew so well the one best way to silence people. He could go to ground, of course, for there were a number of places in the city where no one would be likely to find him. Priest-holes for the damned. . . . But that might sign Bunny Ackerley's death warrant.

Spencer hurried from the shop and thrust the cathedral book into the surprised hands of an old man selling roasted chestnuts.

Somehow, Spencer thought, he must leave a cold trail for the police. Then somehow he must get down to Foix and warn Ackerley.

Chapter Eight

On Pennsylvania Avenue groups of pickets huddled together against the cold and speculated about the lights in the White House, while icy winds banged noisily against their cardboard placards, which variously demanded an end to poverty, an end to discrimination, an end to foreign involvement, an end to foreign noninvolvement, and an end to any and all pusillanimous half-measures in achieving these goals.

In the White House, without formal announcement, but in some unspoken, collusive fashion, all official schedules had been suspended; reporters had lingered in the press room after the more-or-less official 6:00 P.M. deadline for White House releases, and on the third floor of the West Wing, where the offices of many Presidential advisors were located, secretaries and staffers smoked nervously and watched their silent phones and speculated in quiet voices on why

President Montrose was meeting with the French and British ambassadors at this hour of the night.

The minute-by-minute character of the White House and its currents of gossip and rumor were determined inevitably by the whereabouts and functions of the President; if he walked his dog or swam before cocktails the mood of departing staffers would generally be one of casual relief and relaxation, but a late or skipped dinner, or the unexpected arrival of Cabinet ministers, or any heightened activity of the Secret Service details could cause an uneasy tremor in the normally charged atmosphere of this large white goldfish bowl that housed the President of the United States and his family.

Even resilient and experienced reporters, who trailed boredom and cynicism like proud pennants, fell victim to the subtle gradations of tension created by unanticipated changes in the Presidential schedule.

"Where is he?"

"They called down, he's in the elevator."

"Guess who got bounced off his afternoon appointment?"

"The Secretary?"

Such fragments and equally fragmentary responses nourished the almost pleasurable anxiety which seemed to be the only appropriate reaction to being one of the handful of people close to the most powerful man in the world.

Night went and dawn came. The lights of the city winked out, then on, and the empty approaches to the Capitol gradually thickened with cars whose headlights cut like yellow lances through the drifting fog. But the peaceful and inevitable progression from night to day seemed only to heighten the tensions in the White House. At 9:22 A.M., Presidential aide Judson Murphy, whose responsibilities centered on appointments, received a call from a top intelligence aide, Lieutenant General Rose.

"Jud, I need five minutes with the President."

"No way, General. He's got Secretary Hoopes and Secretary Post with him now and everybody, but everybody, else has been ripped off."

"I know the score and you know goddamn well I wouldn't ask if it wasn't something he's got to be briefed on."

"Put it in a memo, General," Jud Murphy said. "I'll try to get it on his desk before ice time. But that's no promise."

"Jud, I don't want to by-pass you and use my private line. But I'll do just that, if you don't get me five minutes right now."

"Goddamnit, aren't you listening? I told you—"

General Rose interrupted him and said: "There's been a security break on Caprifoil. Senator Laird's got wind of it, somehow. He's scheduled a press conference this morning. The scam is he's going to break what we know on Spencer and Wyndom Ackerley and Harry Adams."

"Jesus. I'll see if I can get to him. He said no calls, and he meant it. I'll try Mary."

Mary Donovan, a Presidential staff secretary, had a face as fresh and wholesome as a healthily frosted apple, and this suggestion of invigorating youth was accentuated rather than diminished by her silver-white hair and severely tailored red wool suit. She had been at her desk outside the Oval Office almost continuously since she had first scented the Bay of Pigs Number 5 on the wind, but her only concession to fatigue was a certain mild exasperation in her voice as she said to Judson Murphy, "I'll take care of it, Jud."

"You're a doll, Mary. I don't want to go in there. I've got a wife and small children."

138

"Well, I like chalking up firsts. And this is the first time I've ever interrupted the President in a meeting with the Secretary of State *and* the Secretary of Defense. It's you and General Rose, for five minutes. Right?"

"No, there will be one other person, Arthur Fennaday, a section chief in Intelligence."

"Jesus, Mary and Joseph, I hope you know what you're doing."

Mary Donovan replaced the phone, squared her shoulders in what was a completely unnecessary correction, and then stood and walked to the door that connected her office to the Oval Office. She knocked lightly, waited a moment and went inside.

The office which President Montrose tended to regard as an escape valve from the Oval Office was located on the second floor of the West Wing, and its three windows overlooked the helicopter landing pad and the winter-brown lawn stretching toward the iron fences on Pennsylvania Avenue. The furniture and decor of the room were somber; gray wallpaper, beige carpeting, green leather chairs and sofas. The only touch of color was a flattering caricature of the President fashioned of coral and presented to him by a delegation from the Ladies' Auxiliary of a Rotary Club in Hawaii. The air seemed close, and President Montrose tried to open a window. It wasn't locked, but it wouldn't give. As he tugged a second time, a tall young Secret Service detail appeared at the half-open door. Radar, the President thought.

"May I help you with that, Mr. President?"

"No, you may not, John." The President braced himself and exerted his full strength. The window shot upward and drafts of cold, foggy air swept into the room. The President rubbed his hands together in a satisfied manner and glanced at the Secret Service

139

detail. "There's nothing to it, John. It simply requires a knowledge of engineering stresses and incredible strength."

"Yes, sir. Anything else, Mr. President?"

The President shook his head and the Secret Service detail returned to his post in the corridor. President Montrose sat down in a deep chair and loosened the knot of his tie. He rubbed the tips of his fingers in a rotary motion against his temples, and breathed slowly and deeply and willed himself to think of nothing at all until the familiar therapies of massage and cold fresh air eased the pain that was like an iron bar pressing cruelly against his forehead. He was worried neither about the pain nor about his general health; he was big but not soft and he played handball three times a week despite the worried headshakes of his doctor, Admiral Brennan, who insisted that any man who played singles at handball after fifty-five was either a show-off, a fool or both. President Montrose was fifty-seven. He had explained to the Admiral that no one had heart attacks playing handball. Heart attacks always occurred on putting greens, on mild summer afternoons. The admiral didn't think that was funny. And the young Secret Service detail, President Montrose thought, didn't think the taradiddle about engineering and incredible strength was funny either.

He glanced down at a tiny dragon which hung from his watch chain. It was a flashy little object with ruby eyes and a body and tail made of gold and silver. President Montrose had worn it since his first months in office as a reminder to curb his propensity for droll comment. At his second press conference, he had told newsmen and a national television audience, in answer to a question on China, that while he addressed himself thoughtfully and assiduously to all problems stemming from that spectacularly industrialized land mass, nonetheless, Chinese problems seemed very much like Chinese food. No matter how hard he studied them, after a few hours he couldn't remember what they were. It was while leafing through the next morning's editorial pages that he decided he'd better buy himself the little dragon.

President Montrose heard footsteps in the corridor and glanced at the paper Mary Donovan had given him. On it were three names: Rose, Murphy, Arthur Fennaday. After Fennaday's name were the abbreviations Sec. Chf. Intel.

The Secret Service detail opened the door and stepped aside. "Mr. President, General Rose, Mr. Murphy and Mr. Fennaday."

"Ask them to come in, John."

Jud Murphy and General Rose entered the office and introduced Arthur Fennaday to President Montrose.

"I think we've met before," the President said. "Some reception or other. I remember, because you remind me of that actor—what's his name? Gregory Peck."

"A very old Gregory Peck," Fennaday said, and attempted a smile.

He was looking at an emotionally exhausted man, the President realized; the man was trying to hang onto his nerves, but he wasn't doing a very good job of it. Fennaday's smile was a shaky effort and he looked as if he hadn't slept well in months.

General Rose said abruptly, "Mr. President, Mr. Fennaday has read August Spencer's report filed from Green Drop, Shannon."

"It wasn't classified, Mr. President," Fennaday said, and smiled pointlessly.

General Rose continued: "Mr. Fennaday divulged the contents of the Spencer report to Senator Laird yesterday afternoon at a cocktail party."

141

"I should have asked for sick leave," Fennaday said, still attempting to reach the President's eyes and heart with his desperate smile. "I know that's no excuse, but things have been piling up on me, it's not anything specific, Mr. President, but I have a terrible feeling I've been told too many things. Too many things I can't do anything about. And I thought Senator Laird could help me." There were tears in Fennaday's eyes. "I needed someone, Mr. President, and I didn't realize until this morning what a dreadful breach of security I may have committed, and how shamefully I had betrayed my country's trust in me. When I realized all that, Mr. President, I came straight to General Rose—"

The President interrupted him smoothly. "I'm grateful that you did, Mr. Fennaday. Would you like some coffee?"

"No, thank you, Mr. President, I just want to try to undo any damage I've done."

General Rose said: "The point is, Mr. President, Senator Laird is holding a press conference in exactly one-half hour to discuss certain phases of the Spencer report, or all of it."

President Montrose nodded thoughtfully and glanced at his appointments aide, Judson Murphy.

"Jud, will you see to it that Mr. Fennaday is taken home? Once again, Mr. Fennaday, I want to express my gratitude to you for coming to General Rose about this matter. I don't want you to worry about this business any more. Jud, will you make sure that Mr. Fennaday isn't disturbed by anything or anybody?" This last was, in effect, a Presidential order that would keep Arthur Fennaday under the tightest possible security for as long as deemed necessary.

When Murphy and Fennaday had departed, President Montrose picked up one of the half-dozen phones in the office. "Get me Senator Laird," he said, and replaced the receiver. He glanced at General Rose and pointed to the half-open door. General Rose walked over and closed it. When the phone rang, President Montrose answered it. "Senator Laird? Good. Senator, I want you to do three things and I'd appreciate it if you don't ask any questions. Cancel your press conference and get over to my office immediately. And don't mention this call to anyone." The President frowned irritably at the receiver. At last he said sharply, "Goddamnit, Senator, you don't have to understand. In army vernacular, will you get your ass over here?"

The President put the phone down and looked at General Rose. "General, get me what you've got on the Saracen Vector."

"Good morning, Senator," Mary Donovan said. "You're looking well."

Senator Laird smiled and with a pretense of skepticism examined the jacket of his suit, which was cut from a pepper-and-salt tweed, whose shadings nicely complemented his luxuriant black hair. The collar of the jacket was very high, and was linked by a brass chain. Still smiling, the senator put his hands on Mary Donovan's desk, and fixed her with his warm, bright eyes.

"I'll tell you a secret, Mary, if you'll carry it to your grave. I'm the vainest bastard in the Senate."

Mary Donovan pressed a button on her desk. She didn't relish jokes, intimacies or implied conspiracies with the Senator, whom she considered a fool. "Are you expecting any calls, Senator?"

"No, ma'am, I'm all his."

The Senator went into the Oval Office. President Montrose and General Rose were present. The President came from behind his desk and shook hands

143

with him. "Thanks for coming right over, Senator. You know General Rose, of course."

The two men nodded and shook hands. "Senator, I suggest you sit down," President Montrose said. "I was standing when I got the news I'm going to pass on to you. Believe me, it's easier to take sitting down. Arthur Fennaday told me just fifteen minutes ago that he had discussed with you the contents of a report written by a former CIB agent named August Spencer. That's correct, I presume."

"Yes, that's correct, Mr. President."

Senator Laird could feel the accelerated stroke of his heart as he sat down in a leather chair facing the President's desk. He felt no qualms of guilt at his role in this business, whatever this business turned out to be. He was blameless, but he was also nervous, which was natural enough, for no human being of any sensitivity could be immune to the emanations of power and influence which radiated from what was literally the heartbeat of probably the mightiest nation in the world. One could call President Montrose an idiot, an incompetent, a man with a brain like a steel sieve, and while none of these things were true, one could say them with authority and impunity, and perhaps with a sense of relief, in the Senate dining room or at private parties. But at this proximity to the President, Senator Laird felt like a small child, for he had the distinct and not entirely welcome impression that he was about to become a confidante of President Montrose, and that realization created a knot of anxiety in his stomach.

The President picked up two folders from his desk and, after a perfunctory glance at the titles and classifications printed on their jackets, leaned forward and dropped them in front of Senator Laird. "You may read these after I tell you this." President Montrose leaned back in his chair and put the tips of his fingers against his temples. "The President of France is being held as a hostage in Algeria by a para-military and a para-national armed force known as the Saracen Vector. As hostage for what, we do not know. No dates have been proposed for his release, but a demand for ransom has been made. Only a handful of people in the world knows that President Barrault has been missing for five days. You are now a member of that lonely minority, Senator Laird. Perhaps you'll find this redundant, but I cannot over-emphasize the need for maximum security. I need your complete cooperation."

"Yes, of course, Mr. President." Senator Laird said.

"President Barrault attempted a reckless stroke of personal diplomacy. He apparently believed his physical presence, his widely publicized charisma, could solve the problems which exist between Egypt, Algeria and the State of Israel. He pre-taped a series of television speeches to camouflage his absence from France. Everything was impeccably planned, but there was a massive breakdown in security, which leads to the conclusion that there are treasonable elements high in the French government. Again I'll be redundant, Senator. This is a globally explosive situation. Some of Barrault's party were killed, others were taken into custody with him.

"One of Barrault's aides, Andre Leroi, apparently suspected that Barrault's excursion was dangerous. What he based his conclusions on, we don't know. We do know that he wrote to three of his former colleagues in espionage. Two Americans, one named August Spencer, the other Harry Adams. The third agent was a British subject, G.N. Wyndom Ackerley. He sent each of them two letters. One expressed his anxiety in general terms. He asked them to open the second letters only if he did not return to Paris on a given date from Barrault's country home in Foix. However, Andre Leroi, willingly or unwillingly, informed the Saracen Vector of the second, sealed, letters, which presumably outlined his suspicions in specific terms. With a lead time of several days, members of the Saracen Vector managed to collect those letters and in the process to murder Harry Adams. We've tried to find August Spencer and Wyndom Ackerley, but without success. I need your cooperation, because you were inadvertently informed that Caprifoil is missing. Caprifoil was Andre Leroi's code name in an apparatus in Germany in the sixties. If that became known, it might lead to the conclusions that Barrault also is missing."

The President nodded to the folders which he had placed on Laird's side of the desk. "Take a look at those, and you'll see what we're up against, Senator."

"May I ask a question, sir?"

"Yes, of course."

"Mr. President, is there any indication what kind of ransom these people are after?"

"Yes, they've asked for one hundred million U.S. dollars to be deposited in the National Arbitrage Bank of Tangier. The Fedayeen sent that signal to Paris. I'm aware I've been accused of playing hunches, senator, of putting my trust in gut reflexes, but deep in these old bones of mine I know they want something more than money. And that's what scares the hell out of me. One other thing they want is some kind of representation at the United Nations. I've asked Mr. Hoopes to look into it."

Senator Laird's throat was dry and he thought of going over to the bar and pouring himself a glass of water, but he decided against it. He picked up the stiff-jacketed files from the President's desk. The titles and classifications were printed in block capitals on the heavy gray bindings.

146

In the lower-right-hand corner of each jacket were printed the standard threats of fines and imprisonments which would be imposed on any unauthorized person or persons who might come into possession of these reports and read them.

"I've never seen a report from G.W.," Senator Laird said. "In fact, Mr. President, I don't know what Section G.W. is."

"Neither does the CIA, so you're in good company," President Montrose said. "G.W. is the acronym for Geopolitics West, although it could as easily mean Guess Work. Section G.W. reports only to me and General Rose."

Senator Laird opened the report.

His eyes fell on these words:

SARACEN VECTOR:

1. COMPOSITION
   Arab Nationals
2. INDIGENIZATION ANALYSIS
   hard-core Palestinians, specifically the *fedayeen* or *Fatah*, whose militant attitudes toward Israel peaked to an "action-necessary" evaluation by State in the middle '60s. Recruitments accelerated ominously in the ensuing five years. Major areas of commitment being Algeria, Saudi Arabia, Jordan, Morocco, Egypt, Lebanon and Yemen. CIA CONFIDENTIAL REPORT 91602 designates the Atlas Mountains north of Marrakesh and the desert areas fifty miles south of Algiers as the main deployment and staging areas of the Saracen Vector.
3. NUMERICAL STRENGTH
   In excess of 150,000.
4. FORCE CAPABILITY UNITS

Nine units comparable in class and weaponry to U.S. Divisional Units with Satisfactory Ratings. Five armored units comparable in class and weaponry to U.S. Divisional Units evaluated with rating Obsolete and/or Poor.

5. AIR FORCE POTENTIAL AND CAPABILITIES

Negligible. The Saracen Vector operates one airfield in the Deep Desert, north of Fort Lamy. Their Air Force consists of nine Dassaults MD 415s. (Spirale twin-engine turboprop light transports.) These aircraft are crewed by a pilot and co-pilot and can carry ten passengers. Range, 2,000 miles. Speed, in excess of 300 MPH. In addition, the Saracen Vector operates an unknown number of DC-3s on a loan-demand status from all nations in the Arab bloc.

6. THERMONUCLEAR AND/OR ATOMIC CAPABILITY UNITS

Nil

7. BASIC CAPABILITY UNITS

Indeterminate. Access to indigenous wealth in the Arab bloc of nations. Access to unspecified resources from anti-Israeli (and anti-Semitic) groups throughout the world. Among these can be included Russia and Fascist elements in France, the United Kingdom and America.

8. CDM. (CENTRAL DECISION MAKER)

Ben Gamal Hadid, age 49. Military rank: Colonel. Trained in British Army, Royal Corps. of Engineers. Nationality: Egyptian. Headquarters: Algiers.

9. VALIDATOR INDEX (CDM)

Validation of authority rooted in the fanatical support of Saracen Vector's Basic (4) and Force Capability Units (5).

10. LATITUDE INDEX (CDM)

Total.

11. OBJECTIVE: SARACEN VECTOR

Destruction of the State of Israeli by any means.

G. W.
(DESK 5)

When Senator Laird closed the file on the Saracen Vector, President Montrose said, "Would you please read the second scenario?"

Senator Laird swallowed the almost painful dryness in his throat and looked at the classification and titles printed on the second cardboard folder. They read:

SECTION: G.W.
PROBABILITY PAPER: CAPRIFOIL
CLASSIFICATION: PRESIDENT'S EYES ONLY

"Sir, do I understand that I have your explicit permission to read this report?"

"Yes. General Rose, you will witness the fact that I am hereby authorizing Senator Laird to inspect a report titled CAPRIFOIL and classified for my sole information."

"Yes, sir. I do witness that fact."

"Very well," Senator Laird said and opened the file entitled CAPRIFOIL. The report, on stiff white paper, began with the word:

CAPRIFOIL

1. In the event of a security leak which would disclose to news media that the President of France has been abducted by the Saracen Vector, it is our conclusion that the following events would occur immediately:
   a) Currencies of the world, excluding the Far East, would be devalued in panic and speculation.
   b) Control of the French government, would pass into other hands. The faction most likely to take charge of the government is that one which controls the army. Therefore, it is a reasonable assumption that leadership of the French nation would be assumed on a temporary basis by General Claude Mercier.
2. In the event there is no security leak and the United

States adopts a neutral position, we may assume the following:

a) Deep-seated, long-lasting intransigence directed at the United States by the French government and the French people.

b) It is to be assumed that France will turn to Russia for the solution of this problem. Russia cannot be expected to exterminate by thermonuclear attack her Middle Eastern allies who have embraced the Saracen Vector.

c) If Russia or France acts unilaterally against the Saracen Vector, we may expect a terminal acceleration of tensions in the Middle East.

3. Should the President of France be murdered on foreign soil, we can expect a climactic response from France. This will include thermonuclear attacks against the Middle East land masses. Should Russia attempt to frustrate or control the response of France it will be extremely difficult for the United States to maintain neutrality.

4. To insure the security defense of the United States of America, it is imperative that the President of France be safely and speedily returned to his country.

It is our conclusion that the nations of the Western Alliance are confronting what no mechanical restraints have ever been able to preclude: that is, nuclear warfare stemming from explosive national loyalties.

G.W.
(DESK 5)

Mary Donovan came into the room, and looked to General Rose.

"Sir, there's a call from Paris on your A-line. I have it at my desk."

"Excuse me, Mr. President," General Rose said.

When General Rose left the Oval Office, Senator

Laird stood and replaced the CAPRIFOIL and SARACEN VECTOR files on President Montrose's desk. He hesitated, and there was an uncharacteristic awkwardness in his manner. "I wish to assure you of my complete cooperation, Mr. President," he said. "If there is anything else you need, please count on me."

"Thank you, Senator. I won't hesitate to take you up on that."

"I'd like to ask one thing, Mr. President. Whom are we talking to in France now?"

"They've got a government stuck together with spit and hope. We're dealing with their Ambassador here, General Mercier in Paris, and the SDECE, their counter-espionage agency."

"Another question, if I may, who else is in on it?"

"Well, Mother England, of course. I've talked to Sir Dudley. Secretary Hoopes is keeping the Russians and the Chinese briefed. I sent Secretary Post to New York this morning to talk to Madame Foreign Minister of Israel. God knows, I don't envy him. Bella is the dearest woman I know, but she wants to breast-feed the entire State of Israel, and if you mention El Fatah in her presence, she comes on about as tenderly as a barracuda."

When General Rose returned to the Oval Office, he found President Montrose staring at the burning logs in the fireplace, his expression oddly distracted and withdrawn. Senator Laird was gone.

"I've just got a signal from Interpol, Mr. President."

As if he hadn't heard the general, President Montrose said: "Once you have the concept of the number four, then declaring that two and two equals four, or that three and one equals four, doesn't contribute anything to your knowledge. The fact is, three and one *is* four, and two and two *is* four." He pointed to his desk. "I was thinking about these reports. The

151

G.W. people have defined the problem, but they haven't contributed any solutions. Excuse me. You were saying?"

"I had a signal from the Interpol agent in charge of the Paris office, Theophile LeMaitre." After an almost imperceptible pause, General Rose said: "The American agent, August Spencer, was killed in Paris yesterday afternoon, their time."

"How did it happen?"

"It seems to have been an accident. He was struck by a car crossing the Place de Charles DeGaulle."

"Any news on the Britisher? What was his name? Ackerley?"

"Negative, Mr. President."

That same morning, a Secret Service detail made a sweep of two square blocks in Manhattan's upper 80s. They checked parked cars, posted agents on roof tops, and by 9:34 John Riley, the Grade 13 agent in charge, picked up Secretary Post's limousine by hand-talkie and reported that the area was about 70 percent clean. There had been no time for a check of apartments or informants.

Within minutes, of this advice, Secretary Rodman Post's limousine turned into 82nd Street and stopped in front of the Israeli Information and Administration brownstone. Flanked by two Secret Service agents, Rodman Post, a walrus of a man in his sixties, walked into the building, where an elevator was waiting to take him to Bella Daves' third-floor suite of offices.

Madame Foreign Minister was a sturdily built lady in her late thirties, with a deeply tanned complexion, a nonexistent taste in clothes, but with eyes that were surprisingly and incongruously mild and contemplative within the framework of her sharp and threatening features. Rodman Post thought, as they exchanged the briefest of greetings, that if you could infuse a scimitar with a human personality you'd have a fair likeness of Madame Minister, Bella Daves.

Bella Daves was a compulsive smoker and a constant nibbler at hard candies, which she kept in decorator bowls on her desk. The furniture in her office reflected a certain Spartan derision for creature comforts, the emphasis being on chrome and leather and highly polished woods. A single exception was a Renzo Vespignani, which illuminated a chastely white wall. The painting showed a hungry boy on a curbstone with heartbreakingly fragile wrists and enormous demanding eyes.

"In words of one syllable, what does the President expect of us?" Bella Daves asked the United States Secretary of Defense.

"He wants you in the picture, Bella," Rodman Post said. "We've agreed to pay the Saracen Vector one-hundred million dollars. Also they want to make noises at the United Nations. We're working on that."

"They're testing you," Bella Daves said. "You know, they flay prisoners and keep them alive in emulsions of salt water so their screams can be heard all through the night in the desert. They're not the people we deal with in Algeria, Jordan and Morocco. The Fedayeen are fanatics, intellectually deceived, and lusting for martyrdom. We'll play it cool, as President Montrose expects us to, unless they violate one inch of Israeli territory. Then you'll see an instant replay of our Six Day War, but we won't take that long this time."

"Goddamnit, Bella, will you stop talking like a tank commander. The People's Republic of China wants you out of business. That's a fact of life. They say you're an ethnic stink in the Middle East. Do you want to give them aces to play?"

"And may I ask who was like an elk in rut to get China into the United Nations?" They were both

153

close to shouting now. "Do you run a farm by putting welcome mats for the fox in front of the hen houses? Chiao Kuan-hua and the Egyptian delegates now have coffee and bagels, if you'll excuse the expression, on First Avenue while they talk about destroying us."

"Will you forget Sainted Mother Israel for one frigging moment? We're not talking about the cedars of Lebanon and a few square miles of thirsty real estate in the desert. We have here and now a big *magilla*, if you'll pardon the expression."

Unexpectedly, Bella Daves laughed. "Rodman, you've got a pair of brass knuckles on your tongue. You'd have made a hell of a drill sergeant."

"I consider that a compliment, Bella."

"That's how I meant it. But remember, you've never met the Fedayeen at your Rotary lunches or at Burning Tree. You can't trust them because they can't trust themselves. In my heart, I detest them and I pity them."

"Okay, I'll tell the President that your government won't make a unilateral response to the Saracen Vector. As of now, you've got a round-the-clock communications access to the Oval Office. Fair enough?"

"Yes. Please give our greetings to President Montrose."

Chapter Nine

It was dusk when Denise Morand's Jaguar stopped at her town house near Versailles. Her stocky and smiling young chauffeur, Ahmed, opened the rear door for her, and when she stepped out onto the sidewalk he gave her his usual smiling salute and salaam before climbing back into the car and driving off into the heavy traffic. He would put the car in the garage and he would be free for the evening.

Pale blue and lavender shafts of light slanted delicately through the bare trees and caused the air to shimmer and glisten with their refractions. It was at this hour of the day that Denise always felt Paris was the most exciting city in the world. She wasn't provincial, she enjoyed both London and New York, but there was something else about Paris, a childish quality of almost breathless anticipation that occurred when the blue tones of dusk faded into night.

Something exciting was about to happen. You could

almost see that feeling on the faces of people hurrying through the streets. You could sense it in their quickening smiles and carefree energy, despite the accelerating inconvenience of the city, the crowded sidewalks and the streets stuffed with cars, jammed, packed, linked together in lines that stretched as far as the eye could see.

She thought about Spencer. He had called her the day before after he left the Cathedral of St. Germaine. He had said he needed a car and would call her later. But she hadn't heard from him and she was worried. Denise shivered suddenly. She was wearing only a small black suit and a dark suede beret, but the coldness that gripped her now had nothing to do with inadequate clothing; it was fear and uncertainty that made her lips tremble.

She realized that it had been reckless to cooperate with Spencer. But it was done and she tried to stop worrying about it. She let herself into the foyer of her home and went up the short flight of stairs that led to the corridor and salon. But she stopped abruptly in the arched entrance to the salon, staring in confusion at the two men who were rising from the gold-and-green brocade sofa in front of the fireplace. They were short and stocky and their complexions were the color of old leather. They wore red fezzes and identical double-breasted black suits.

"Permit me," one of the men said in English. "I am Hamil Fatid. This is Ibrahim Abdullah. We are here to ask you certain questions."

"Questions? Are you from the police? How did you get into my house?"

"We are not from the police." The man who called himself Hamil Fatid smiled with no suggestion of humor. "We require certain information about Mr. August Spencer."

Ahmed would have parked the car in the garage by

now, she thought. In two or three minutes at the most, he would be in the room at the rear of the house, changing out of his uniform. He would hear her if she screamed. "You have no right in my house," she said coldly. "I can assure you the French police are not casual about such things."

"Mr. Spencer was here yesterday," Ibrahim Abdullah said. His voice and face registered no emotion; it was as if he hadn't heard Denise speak. "What did Mr. Spencer want of you?"

"I don't think that is any of your business," Denise said, quite angry now. She walked to the narrow rosewood desk she used for her correspondence and picked up the telephone. "Unless you leave immediately, I intend to call the police. I am serious."

They stared past her, but before she could turn a powerful hand came across her mouth, and another hand twisted her wrist suddenly and excruciatingly to a position high between her shoulder blades. The man called Ibrahim Abdullah picked up the phone she had dropped and replaced it in the cradle on the desk.

Denise twisted her head and saw that it was her chauffeur, Ahmed, who was evidently trying to break her arm.

"Ahmed will do as we tell him, Madame," Hamil Fatid said. "Please make up your mind to answer our questions. Ahmed, let her speak."

Her chauffeur removed his hand from her mouth but kept his painful grip on her wrist. She had to rise on her toes to ease the agony in her arm and shoulder. Ahmed held her close to him, and she could feel his excitement growing.

"Tell him to stop it," she said. "I won't answer your question, I'll scream."

"Ahmed!" The single word was an order from Hamil Fatid.

Ahmed released her and Denise rubbed her aching shoulder. She looked at him oddly. "Turned you on, didn't it?" she said. To the other two men, she said, "I'll try to answer your questions, but I want you to understand something. August Spencer was an agent for the American government, but I was never involved with his work."

"We'll be the judge of that," Hamil Fatid said. "What did you discuss with him yesterday?"

"He is looking for a friend of mine, Andre Leroi."

"Why did he come to you?"

"Because Andre Leroi and I have been friends for years. I saw him last about two weeks ago. Sometimes he will call me twice in one day to ask my opinion on something, and then I may not hear from him for a month or so. We have a casual relationship."

"Then why did August Spencer assume you would know where he was?"

"There was a time when my relationship with Andre Leroi was not casual."

"And what else did August Spencer talk to you about?"

"He told me he was in trouble, and that the police were after him, but he didn't tell me why." Denise felt a measure of her composure returning; like most reasonably honest people, she was comfortable with the truth, and she realized from their expressions that they believed her, and she decided to press her advantage. "He also wanted to know if I had ever done any errands in Moscow for Andre. What he meant, I gather, was whether or not Andre had ever used me as a courier. I told him not to my knowledge."

"Why did you go to the Eglise de St. Germaine yesterday?" Hamil Fatid asked her.

"I don't remember," Denise said. She felt her cheeks getting warm; as she was comfortable with the truth, she was uneasy with falsehoods and, therefore, she decided to stay as close to the facts as possible. "I had a drink late yesterday afternoon with Michele Leroi, Andre's wife, and a man named Claude Weismann. Then I stopped at the church to make a visit. Ahmed can tell you that's true. He drove me there."

"I have worked here four months," Ahmed said to Hamil Fatid. "That was the first time she asked me to drive her to church."

"I am very casual about religious observances," Denise said.

"And Madame Michele Leroi was also at the Eglise," Hamil Fatid said. "Was August Spencer there, too?"

"I didn't see him," Denise said carelessly. "I wasn't looking for him in any event."

"Why did you dress yourself as a widow?"

"You know that women like to be capricious about their clothes? May I have a cigarette?"

"It is an unbecoming habit in a woman. I will ask you to refrain from smoking," Hamil Fatid said.

"You are impertinent. What right do you have to give me orders in my home?"

"Why did you dress yourself as a widow?"

"Because I felt like it, can't you understand?"

"You have been truthful in certain areas," Hamil Fatid said. "For that I commend you."

"I don't want commendations. I want you to leave."

Hamil Fatid nodded thoughtfully. After a moment, he removed a gold watch from his pocket and examined it. Then he said something to Ibrahim Abdullah in a language Denise didn't understand. Ibrahim Abdullah inclined his head graciously and left the room. Denise heard his footsteps on the stairs leading down to the foyer, but she didn't hear him leave the house.

"But you haven't been truthful in other areas," Hamil Fatid said to Denise. He smiled and shrugged, a

159

philosopher's gesture which seemed to suggest the eventual insignificance of the entire human condition. Then he nodded to Ahmed. Denise sucked air into her lungs, but she was too late; Ahmed's hand clamped powerfully across her mouth and the scream in her throat died there.

"I will join you in fifteen minutes," Hamil Fatid said, as Ahmed dragged Denise from the salon.

A siphon of carbonated water stood on the low teakwood sideboard which Denise had set as a bar. Hamil Fatid squirted several jets of the club soda into a crystal glass and seated himself in a slim chair with green satin cushions. He lighted a thin cigar and looked out at the Avenue de Versailles. He could see the iron filigree that decorated the street lamps, and occasional cars and trucks speeding toward the Palace and Paris. The night was cold and the lights were like frost on the pavements and sidewalks.

Hamil Fatid sipped charged water and enjoyed his cigar. The tobacco was a deep brown with tiny green flecks in it, and the ash was white and firm. It was a handsome cigar, and there was time to admire it. The housekeeper was away for the night. Ahmed had arranged that. Denise Morand would tell them what they needed to know, and they would be gone before there were any interruptions.

Her defiance was undignified; it affronted him, it was a rebuke to his manhood and religion. Still, he had no wish to make her suffer; it would happen only because some cancerous additive in this Western world seemed to encourage disobedience. He could no more understand her obstinancy than he could have understood the genetic chaos which would create a two-headed camel. The harsh lands which had nourished Hamil Fatid allowed no tolerance for the whimsical insubordination of the individual. In these chang-

ing and unhappy times, good men had died because
their orders were treated as suggestions rather than
edicts, although it was clearly written that master and
slave alike obeyed the will of Allah; chance and fortune were the prerogatives of God, and only heretics
would presume to usurp those Divine rights.

A doorbell rang somewhere in the house and a little
shock of apprehension went through Hamil Fatid. He
put his glass aside and threw the cigar into the fireplace, but he did not rise. Someone from the market
or the florist. Abdullah would send him away. He
heard a murmur of voices from the foyer and the
slam of a door. Hamil Fatid stood quickly and silently
and removed an automatic hand gun from his pocket,
and with a practiced flick of his thumb moved the
safety lever to the firing position. Then he switched
off the lights in the salon and all of his movements
were cautious and silent, because Hamil Fatid possessed a talent that was superior to intelligence, and
that was the talent for survival. Standing perfectly
still, he listened with a professional lack of tension to
the silence in the house. Then he walked into the corridor and glanced down the stairs toward the dark
foyer.

He whispered Ibrahim Abdullah's name.

There was no answer. The silence was like a shroud
about the house. Hamil Fatid ran swiftly down the
steps to the foyer and found there what a thousand
years of bitter winds and the contempt of sallow foreign conquerors and the fatalism of his Moslem cul-
ture had warned him he might find, which was the
body of his friend, Ibrahim Abdullah, lying with a
broken neck on the cold tiles of the vestibule.

As surely as Allah had taken Abdullah, Hamil Fatid
now knew he would take his friend's murderer, for
whoever had killed Abdullah had entered the foyer
and must be somewhere in the dark house. Hamil Fa-

tid's vocabulary did not include the words fear or worry, but he was a brown man whose lands had often been conquered by white men, and centuries of subjection had conditioned him to accept their contemptuous estimate of him. He was born of a woman who loved water, and sired by a man who obeyed God. In his own time and place, he was easy and free, and Hamil Fatid hated only those persons who had deprived him and his religious convictions of significance. He had spent much of his mature life in tents. His home was in Palestine and the figs and myrtle of that land were bitter to him when he encountered them in foreign markets. They had come to his land with their clever minds and clever hands, and knowing nothing of water and his God had made his people a mockery in the eyes of the world.

And because his emotions were churning in anger and frustration, Hamil Fatid was tragically mismatched against what waited for him in the salon.

He went silently up the stairs toward the dark corridor and salon, prepared to shoot anything that moved, but totally unprepared for the blow that came from the darkness and broke his jaw and sent him sprawling and destroyed to the floor in front of the fireplace. The gun which he believed in, which was as sacred to him as the amulets the white devils mocked, was taken from his hand and thrust into his mouth, where the sighting tip drew blood from his tongue and throat. He was drowning in his own blood and the hand that struck his face caused an explosion of lights within his head.

August Spencer said: "Tell me where she is."

"The basement," Hamil Fatid said. He wanted to say more, he wanted to pray for the grace of submission, because Allah had a reason for everything and the virtue of man was in understanding that. These were the words that were forming in his mind when a blow caused his head to explode into blackness.

Spencer returned to the corridor. The second door he opened led to the basement of the house. He drew his gun and went silently down the stairs. A single wall lamp glowed dimly and gave him a view of a damp floor and the half-open door of a wine cellar. He saw Ahmed and Denise in the wine cellar, and he heard her soft screams, and he ran forward and fired one shot which almost surgically removed the top of the Arab's head.

The jacket of her suit and her blouse had been ripped away from her chest and a rope was attached from her wrists to the metal base of wine racks. She lay on her side and he realized from the glazed look of her eyes that she was in shock.

"My shoulder," she said, so quietly that the words were merely whispers on the air.

"Hang on," Spencer said. He wedged the side of his hand into her mouth and with his free hand twisted her shoulder powerfully, until the bone in her arm slid back into its socket with a liquid, metallic sound and, as he did this, her teeth closed on his hand like tiny, powered spikes.

In a bedroom, Spencer threw some of her things into a traveling case, stockings, underthings, toilet articles. Denise lay on the bed, her body as slack and limp as something made of silk, and watched him with dull eyes. He had given her four drops of the morphine he carried for his own migraines and she was resting without pain now, breathing slowly and evenly.

"You said I wouldn't get involved," she said in a low, trembling voice. "I was almost killed. Is that what you meant by not getting involved?"

There was no point in discussing it. "I'm taking you
163

to Foix with me," Spencer said. "Interpol has circulated a report I was killed yesterday in a traffic accident. That gives me time to find Ackerley."

"You are so goddamn clever," she said wearily. "You've smashed everything I've worked for."

"You'll be safe with me," Spencer said. "Is your passport in your handbag?"

"Where are we going?"

"After Foix, we've got to get out of France."

"I don't want to go with you," she said.

"Denise, if you don't leave now, you're likely to be killed. Will you take that on faith?"

She had always amused him with her mercurial change of moods. Now she rewarded him by managing a smile and nodding to her open closet. "Put in that beige dress, August, please."

Within twenty minutes, Spencer was driving south on the road to Foix, with Denise resting as comfortably as possible in the rear of the Jaguar. The morphine was taking effect. She was asleep long before they came to Orleans.

Chapter Ten

Andre Leroi stood at the windows of his high-ceilinged bedroom and stared down the hill toward the port town of Algiers. The villa in which he and President Barrault were quartered was situated in a barren, isolated area in the mountains above the city, and he was looking at a jumble of white plaster homes that were shining in the sunlight and covering the hillsides like pale, smooth lava. They stretched down to the sprawling city itself, which faced a dark, heavy sea, where fishing boats and trawlers stood like cutouts on the horizon. Directly in front of Andre Leroi, and directly in front of the villa, was a hardpacked, earthen courtyard that stretched out of sight to his right and to his left and surrounded this old castle, which served as headquarters for the Saracen Vector. The area, with its occasional palms and fruit trees, looked as if it needed the attention of a gardener, but the cool sunlight formed interesting

165

patterns of shadows in the crimson ropes of bougain-
villea which lay on the roofs of outbuildings and sen-
tinel shacks. Standing at the gates of the villa were
several dozen soldiers armed with rifles and wearing
the hand-me-down or improvised uniforms of the
Saracen Vector. More troops were stationed beyond
the gates at check-points on the road which led down
into the city. They also carried rifles, Kalashnikovs,
Russian-made automatics with skeletal steel stocks.

Andre Leroi pitied them, even though he realized
his emotion was misplaced; he should reserve his pity,
he thought, for his President and his country. These
Saracen Vector troops who wore the battle dress of a
dozen Arab nations and carried Russian arms were
ideally mated to the barren, difficult lands and cli-
mates they loved. They were as tough and unyielding
as the rocks themselves. The hard core of their irregu-
lar organization was comprised of Ashbal, the lion
cubs of the Palestine refugees, whose homeless and
despairing fathers had fired their minds and spirits
with but one ambition, which was to be the generation that would destroy the state of Israel and finally, in peace and honor, bring its bayonets to rest
on the shores of the Mediterranean. And having been
used, Andre Leroi thought, they would be destroyed
and swept away, lost like all martyrs and guerillas in
the black sludge of history. It was the Merciers of the
world who destroyed them all, masking treason with
words like glory and honor. But the guerillas and
martyrs not only lost their lives in the hills; they also
lost what they had fought for when the smiling nego-
tiators sat down at the bargaining tables. It was quite
simple and quite heartbreaking to understand why,
Andre Leroi thought. The majority is always wicked,
ran the French proverb, and it was demonstrable by
any head-count that martyrs and guerillas were in the
166

minority, while the majority preferred their comforts, their wines, and no long faces from their conscience.

He saw dust spinning behind a black car which was coming up the road toward the villa. Andre Leroi glanced at his watch. General Mercier was on time. The car stopped at the gates several hundred yards below the village. It was a Cadillac limousine with the flags of Algeria on its fenders. Salutes were exchanged, the gates were opened, and the limousine continued on to the entrance to the castle. Several members of Colonel Gamal's staff stood waiting to receive their distinguished visitor. Andre Leroi recognized Major Sidki of Yemen by his shining bald head and Captain Aziz of Lebanon, whose back had been broken several years ago in a barrage and who now stood and walked like a simian, his knuckles swinging below his knees.

General Mercier, in civilian clothes, stepped from the limousine and shook hands with Colonel Gamal's staff members. The general looked both handsome and distinguished with lean brown features under his skullcap of silvered hair. In public, his expression was normally stern and disciplined, but now he seemed in a relaxed mood and was smiling agreeably as he shook hands with the Arabs. It was a pleasant scene. Handsome officers, groups of self-consciously grinning soldiers, and a cold wind coming down the mountains through the olive trees. . . . Andre Leroi, like most realistic but imaginative people, was frequently deceived by appearance, and now he was philosophically puzzled by the attractive externals of treason.

He went to his dressing table and picked up a small pair of scissors and began to trim his mustache, clipping away the odd gray hairs. This seemed as sensible as anything else to do under the circumstances. History was being made and he could only watch it. General Mercier was demanding the resignation of

President Barrault. That was one condition for the safe return of Barrault to France. The Saracen Vector had imposed two more conditions, namely, a permanent forum in the U.N., and reparations from the state of Israel and its undeclared ally, the United States of America.

Andre Leroi couldn't affect the second two conditions, but he could influence the first by urging his President to stand fast against General Mercier, to call treason by its right name even if that meant a firing squad. If he hadn't believed he had this much conviction, this much sense of history, Andre Leroi could never have involved his friends. . . .

There was no knock. The door was opened by a soldier who closed it when General Mercier entered the room. "Time is crucial," the General said. "I will waste a precious moment of it and tell you your wife is well. If you have a message for her, I will be pleased to deliver it."

"I'm not amused by irrelevance," Andre Leroi said. "Your business is treason; therefore, speak of treason."

"To say you are stupid and romantic would be redundant. The words are interchangeable. Remember, Vichy called General de Gaulle a traitor. The distinction between revolution and revolt is only a matter of success."

"Spare me your rationalizations," Andre Leroi said. "I have a final answer from President Barrault. He tore the letter of resignation into a dozen pieces."

General Mercier said thoughtfully, "Andre, another letter can be prepared. In God's name, doesn't he realize I'm serious?"

"Yes, the President does not take a whimsical view of treason."

General Mercier removed his topcoat and threw it angrily onto a chair, and his fingers were trembling as he removed a silver cigarette case and lighted a cigarette. "Andre, I have watched France deteriorate morally and physically for the last three years. Our youth is spiritually bankrupt. They want to burn their universities, mock and deride all forms of discipline. I do not mean their long hair and their music," he said angrily, as he saw exasperation sharpening in Andre Leroi's expression. "No, I mean their blasphemous disrespect toward all authority, and to the symbols of our Republic. They have not earned the right to despair. They have not earned the right to disillusion. But God help me, they do have a right to mock the stupidities of President Barrault. While the dollar and the pound grow stronger, the franc grows weaker, and while the Americans and Russians are voyaging in space, our nation is putting up statues to its nine-teeth-century heroes."

"No one will ever advocate putting up a statue to you," Andre Leroi said.

Mercier held up a hand and went on, "A traitor, I submit, would support the policies of President Barrault with all cunning and force because those policies will inevitably result in the destruction of France. A patriot, I submit, must be willing to sacrifice his life and his honor to destroy President Barrault's influence. You are a reasonable man, Andre." General Mercier was pleading with him. "Can you truthfully say I am not speaking reasonably?"

"You are speaking like a Fascist," Andre Leroi said. "Your disloyalty is heinous. I almost wish to God you were insane, for then I could forgive you. But I know you are corrupt and evil and sane. Therefore, I cannot."

There were twin points of dull color in General Mercier's bronzed cheeks, but he shrugged and made a curt, dismissing gesture with his hand. "I am here neither for your approval nor for your forgiveness. I am frank with you because you still have influence

169

with President Barrault. I have none. The Americans will supply the money, one hundred million dollars. I have the impression they are removing it from a large coin purse. But what you must strive to make President Barrault understand is this: if he does not resign with honor, he will be exposed as a dangerous fool who threatened the peace of the world with his ego, with his dangerous lack of judgment, and by this criminally reckless excursion into a hostile foreign country."

"I believe he understands that, General. But in destroying himself, he will destroy you. Don't underestimate his eagerness to see you in front of a firing squad."

"My involvement couldn't be proved, Andre. The present coalition government of France has appointed me to negotiate for the President's release."

"I think it can be proven that you negotiated with the Saracen Vector before President Barrault planned this trip to Algiers. I think it can also be proved that you arranged the breakdown in security which allowed him to be taken prisoner."

"I doubt that either contention could be proven," General Mercier said. "I advised the President, and the memos are in his files, that one company of soldiers was very meager protection for a head of state. His reply was that a larger force might draw attention to his trip and thus destroy its value. But let me tell you one more thing, Andre, and I beseech you to believe me. If my part in this affair becomes known, I will not deny it. No matter if I fail, I have chosen a course I can always be proud of."

Andre Leroi said bitterly: "And those brave soldiers who were slaughtered defending their President? Did they have any choice?"

There was a look of pain in Mercier's eyes, but he said quietly, "I have acted with honor, Andre, as I have lived with honor, and as I will die with honor. I hope you can say the same of your actions in this matter. Two of the agents you involved in this affair are dead. And you are still not acting in the best interests of President Barrault."

"Who else is dead? Spencer or Ackerley?"

"August Spencer was killed yesterday afternoon in a traffic accident," General Mercier said, and walked to the door.

"Did you see the report? Do you know who signed it?" Andre Leroi spoke so rapidly that the words blurred together, for Mercier had already gone through the door into the corridor. General Mercier stopped and looked back at him, "Yes, I saw the report, Andre," he said quietly. "It was filed by Interpol and signed by Theophile LeMaitre, as I recall."

When the door closed, and the sound of Mercier's crisp footsteps had faded away, Andre Leroi began pacing, pounding a fist into his palm in a reflex of sudden hope, because he knew Theophile LeMaitre owed many things to August Spencer, one of which was his very life, and if Spencer needed a false report on his death filed by Interpol, Theophile LeMaitre could arrange it without detection and without compunction.

In a library of majestic proportions, Colonel Gamal sat at a large square table whose surface was designed as a chessboard, the squares defined in an inlay of mother-of-pearl. Colonel Gamal, who was in his late forties, was tall and deceptively slim, with an alertness and neatness in his bearing and uniform which reflected his years of professional military service. His hair was black and his skin was darkly tanned; his eyes were warm and brown under luxuriant, slightly arched eyebrows; his nose, which had been broken, looked like a rugged scimitar, and provided an incongruous, whimsical contrast to his delicate, almost feminine lips. Seated at the table with Colonel Gamal were four members of his personal staff, who also wore the uniform of the Saracen Vector, whose insignia was the Phoenix, the legendary bird consumed by fires but resurrected from its own ashes. The shoulder patches of the Saracen Vector were in colors of crimson and yellow, the bird in red with outstretched wings against desert sands. There were pots of mint tea and cigarettes and ashtrays on the table. The chair that faced Colonel Gamal from the foot of the table was empty. The library was sunken a dozen feet from the first floor of the villa, and the lower casements of its tall, narrow windows were almost eight feet from the floor. The effect was not oppressive because the proportions of the room, and an elevation created by a soaring ceiling and arched beams, gave it a sense of cool isolation. The size of the library was not deflating; on the contrary, the great space enclosed by tiled floors and vaulted ceilings seemed relaxingly intimate, which was an effect achieved by cleverly outsized rugs and furniture. The heavily fringed ends of the glowing Persian carpets were separated by almost eighty feet of casual designs in blues and greens and tans, while the ottomans, ornate in red and green leather, were almost as large as comfortable beds. Above the fireplace was a framed portrait of an elderly man with an iron-gray mustache who had been painted in the uniform of a French field marshal. From the entrance to the library, a vaulted door facing a staircase, the painting looked less than life-size, but a closer view made it apparent that the painting of the old soldier would tower at least a foot above anyone in the room.

Colonel Gamal glanced up with a smile as General Mercier appeared in the doorway above the staircase. "Please join us," Colonel Gamal said.

"Thank you," General Mercier said, and he descended the stairs to the library. He sat down in the empty chair to which he had been directed by a courteous smile from Colonel Gamal. He nodded pleasantly at the other officers at the table.

"And what is your news, General Mercier?" Colonel Gamal asked him.

The colonel spoke in English, a language in which he was proficient and eloquent; the years at Cambridge had given him a flair for the orotund and gracious phrase.

"The very best, I'm pleased to tell you. The Americans have agreed to deposit one hundred million dollars in Tangier. Secondly, through the good offices of the Americans once again, a delegation from the Saracen Vector will be invited to address the next plenary session of the United Nations."

The colonel smiled. "Would you like some tea, General? The mint is fresh from the Atlas Mountains."

"Thank you."

Colonel Gamal poured the fragrant tea into a glass which rested in a metal receptacle decorated with silver filigree. "It's pleasant to share a moment with you in this particular room." He passed the glass of tea to General Mercier. "It was your father's favorite, I understand."

"Yes, that's quite true." General Mercier smiled and sipped his tea.

"It was cleverly designed," Colonel Gamal said. "It is large but intimate. It has humor. It surprises me, because I associate such amusing deceptions with the Arabic mind rather than—." With a smiling shrug, he let the sentence trail into silence.

"Rather than the French?" General Mercier cradled the warm glass of tea in his hands and glanced up at the portrait of his father above the mantlepiece. He then looked idly at the shelves of books which rose to

173

the shadows of the vaulted ceiling and were made accessible by narrow ladders hanging at intervals against the bookcases. "But you're right, of course," he said.

General Mercier's casual manner suggested that he would be pleased to pursue this topic indefinitely and would also be delighted to explore any detours which might conceivably be encountered in the discussion. But he was not at ease and he could feel the sudden accelerated stroke of his heart. His roots were Arabic as well as French, and from experience he knew that these graceful irrelevancies were a prelude to serious bargaining. But what more was there to bargain about? Everything had been settled, both sides were in full agreement. But now General Mercier realized this wasn't so. He knew that more was to be asked of him.

General Mercier, without conscious effort, put aside his Gallic sense of logic and propriety, and prepared to submerge himself in the circling, drifting Arabic approach to the solution of problems. He smiled again at the portrait of his father. "You must understand, he had only a vague notion of what he wanted this library to be. And so he sat and talked for many afternoons in the garden with Pasha Riza Hamrin. You remember the Pasha?"

There were pleased nods from Colonel Gamal and the other officers at the table. General Mercier returned their smiles with what seemed genuine enthusiasm. "The Pasha was not an architect or a builder, but it was said of him that he was a dreamer in stone and space. The Pasha and my father didn't talk of measurements or materials. They talked of caravans and water and skies, for many afternoons, and in some fashion, the Pasha divined my father's vision of the library and the villa and its garden. Sometimes, I recall, my brother and I would interrupt their conver-

174

sation chasing a ball across the lawn. But the Pasha always tempered my father's irritation by saying, 'Never mind. We will add the sound of games and running children to the plans of your home.'"

Colonel Gamal sighed. "To spend time, to squander time in creating beauty. How wise they were, your father and the Pasha."

"Yes," General Mercier said, and waited.

"But I haven't introduced you to my staff," Colonel Gamal said.

"To delay a pleasure is only to increase it," General Mercier said.

Colonel Gamal inclined his head and smiled approvingly, but there was an irony in the gesture which informed General Mercier that his Arabic pleasantry had given the game away; they both understood now that these ritualistic civilities had served their purpose and that they would now with grace proceed to serious negotiation.

Colonel Gamal indicated the officer closest to him on his left. "Captain Basra, whose command is in the West, in Morocco. Captain Basra is of the Sunni of Palestine. His family knew the shores of the Mediterranean since the time of the Prophet, but Captain Basra has known the bitter shame of ragged tents from which he could see his stolen homeland occupied by infidels."

"May the Sunni, the partisans, know grace," General Mercier said, and inclined his head to Captain Basra.

"Thank you," Captain Basra said. "I find it rather strange but pleasant to speak with one who, while not of us, is not offensive to us."

But there was no suggestion of this pleasure in the captain's expression, General Mercier noted with clinical interest; the captain's broad face, topped by coarse black hair, only suggested the masked hostility

175

of an enemy whose passions would prevent him from striking without warning. He wouldn't be satisfied with anonymous revenge; no, this captain would want to be recognized in the dying light of his victim's eyes, to impress at last his gloating image upon that victim's fading consciousness. But you could never be sure, General Mercier thought. He never made the mistake of pretending he understood Arabs. He had grown up with them as a child, played their games, ate their food, crept as an infidel into their mosques and listened in the *medinas* to the rise and fall of the wise men's prayers. But it was a world he had never truly understood or been part of.

Colonel Gamal was speaking. "Major Othman, whose commands are in the Deep Desert, and who is familiar with artillery, engineering, and the schools of England, but also the tents outside Palestine where he worshipped as an Ismaili, a descendant of Seven."

There were no parallels in the Western world to these sects and splinters and subdivisions in the Moslem philosophy; like a thousand monoliths of faith they stood apart, hostile and unyielding in a dizzying variety of customs and convictions, but beneath the surface differences was the powerful and fundamental unity of a brotherhood bound together by their submission to the will of Allah.

"Captain Aziz from Algeria, presently of the Metwali in Lebanon."

Captain Aziz, a hunchback with scarred cheeks, and languorous, thoughtful eyes, acknowledged his introduction to General Mercier with a smile and a soft salute with his right hand.

It was remarkable, General Mercier knew, to find a Metwali, who worshipped the Twelfth Imam, and who would regard the Sunni's Seventh Imam as an impure and unworthy leader, now seated in harmony with Captain Basra in pursuit of a common goal. The disparity in religious beliefs represented at this meeting was not accidental, General Mercier decided; unless he were grossly wrong it would underscore whatever point Colonel Gamal was preparing to make.

"Major Sidki from Yemen," Colonel Gamal said. The Major, broad, stocky and with a skull so shiny and bald that it looked as if it had been sandpapered, bowed politely to General Mercier, and Colonel Gamal said: "This council represents, as you realize, most of the divergent sects who worship under the canopy of Islam."

"It is instructive to witness," General Mercier said, and waited.

"Thank you. We have learned slowly over the centuries, but I think any generous person would concede that our lack of political progress stemmed less from ignorance than from a naïve expectation of justice from our adversaries, even though they were unbelievers. But such a lack of skepticism is characteristic of the unworldly tenets of Islam."

"That is quite true," General Mercier said and waited once again; he made no attempt to anticipate what Gamal was getting at.

"How we wearied of Christian angers and violence," Colonel Gamal said, and laughed softly as if at a not wholly unpleasant memory, while his right hand raised his tea glass to his lips, and his unclean left hand moved discreetly out of sight below the table. "The Church of Rome, the Church of Alexandria, the Syrians of Antioch, the Greeks of Constantinople, all Christians worshipping the same God, but lunging like savage dogs at one another's throats, as well as at those of the believers in Islam." He sipped his tea. "I'm not presuming to lecture you, General Mercier, but certain historical facts may help you to understand a stipulation we must make with regard to the safe return of President Barrault."

177

"Please go on." It would serve no functional purpose, the General knew, to inquire now into the nature of this new stipulation; he could only wait.

"Thank you. We made the mistake of believing that such antagonisms and armed clashes resulted from religious differences. And so, when the might of Mohammed dispersed the Coptics and Jacobites and Roman Christians, the people of Islam believed it was only a religious insanity that brought the banner of the Crusaders to our land in the following centuries." Colonel Gamal smiled. "But when, after repulsing the Crusaders, the colonizers returned bearing the flags of France and England, of Belgium, Holland and Spain, of Italy, Portugal and Germany, the people of Islam understood the truth at last. It was not the conversion of Islam that the infidels wanted, but its oceans of oil and its majestic stretches of land which Allah himself devised to separate us from the infidels of the East and West."

Etiquette rather than conviction required General Mercier to dispute this point. "But Colonel, isn't it true that certain heads of state profited from these colonizers? Wasn't there, in fact, something close to a collaboration between the Pashas and Emirs of Islam and the modern proconsuls who came to your lands, not with the Imperial Eagles of Rome, but with the oil leases and pipelines of modern financial empires?"

"Yes, yes," Colonel Gamal said, and smiled at his officers, as if signalling them to take note of General Mercier's equable contention. "However, to pray five times a day in the mosque, to cleanse one's self with water, and to abominate the flesh of the pig, these observances alone cannot make a man proof against worldly temptation."

"Sadly, on occasion the foreign influences you deplore were introduced by Arab leaders," General Mercier said.

"It is prudent to examine the follies of the past," Colonel Gamal said. "We have been exploited, it is true, from within and from without. But the great and most bitter truth was not revealed until this present generation. When the Germans and the Americans and the British were fighting for domination of our lands from Alexandria to Tangier, and from the shores of the Mediterranean to the outposts below the Deep Desert in Fort Lamy and Fort Archambault, it became finally and painfully clear to the people of Islam that the infidel had chosen our subcontinent as a permanent battleground in which to settle his political and ideological differences."

The colonel paused and General Mercier sensed from the silence, and the impassive regard of Gamal's officers, an invitation for him to advance the discussion to more explicit considerations. "May I ask what additional stipulation is required before President Barrault is returned to France?"

But Colonel Gamal wasn't ready to be so explicit. "We have found, despite all our protestations and remonstrances that the infidel is prepared at any cost to maintain a status quo which can only destroy the Arab states. A foreign cell, Israel, has been forced upon the body of Islam. No healthy body can tolerate such foreign implants. The body must reject them before they proliferate in cancerous frenzy."

Etiquette required silence now, but General Mercier was compelled to say: "Colonel Gamal, if we talk of cancerous cells, doesn't it distract us from the fact that what we represent by those terms, namely states and peoples, do not obey the rules of diseases and physical bodies?"

"That is an excellent point," Colonel Gamal said. "Metaphors and symbols sometimes have a way of clouding or inflaming the thoughts of the most rational men. But would you mind if I read to you a

179

paragraph from the Balfour Declaration? You are familiar with it, of course, but would you bear with me, please? Thank you."

Colonel Gamal removed a sheet of folded paper from his pocket, opened it, and began speaking without taking his eyes from General Mercier's face.

"His Majesty's Government views with favor the establishment in Palestine of a National Home for the Jewish people, and will use their best endeavors to facilitate the achievement of this object, it being clearly understood that nothing shall be done which may prejudice the civil and religious rights of existing non-Jewish communities in Palestine or the rights and political status enjoyed by Jews in any other country."

When Colonel Gamal had read these words, he returned the sheet of paper to the inner pocket of his tunic, using for this purpose, and the significance of his act was not lost on General Mercier, his left hand, the sinister member reserved in Moslem custom for menial or unpleasant tasks.

"Please note the relative sanity of Lord Balfour," Colonel Gamal said. "Sane and courteous, although quite unacceptable. Contrast that proposal, if you will, with the present monstrous horror of a sovereign state erected in the heart of Islam, its eternal existence and ever-increasing strength guaranteed by the might of a coalition of infidels."

General Mercier thought he sensed what Colonel Gamal was leading to; to his dismay and horror, he was only partially correct.

"As the Janissaries enforced the will of the Ottoman Empire, so the Saracen Vector will enforce the will of all the Arab states." Colonel Gamal glanced around the table at his officers, touching and marking each face with the sweep of his eyes. "General Mercier, we represent in this group the secular divisions of Islam. We also represent, in the Saracen Vector, the unity

180

and brotherhood of Islam." The colonel's voice became curiously mild. "Let no man mistake apparent for real division among us. We are the cutting edge of a sword held in powerful hands by every man who worships Allah. It is our intention to bring peace, not terror, to our world. To replace insanity with sanity. We intend, therefore, to reach an agreement with the illegal state of Israel. The spurious sovereignty of Israel will be dissolved and there will be a dispersal, an ultimate Diaspora, of its army, its air force, its police, its civil officials, its customs and immigration officers; in short, what we will effect is the total dismantlement of its military and administrative systems."

General Mercier had anticipated this.

"Whether or not those goals are reasonable, I am not prepared to say," he said. "But as a practical man, I can tell you they are quite unattainable. No nation will help you to accomplish them. And in an armed conflict with Israel, you would be destroyed within a matter of hours."

Colonel Gamal smiled. "The United States aircraft carrier *Robert F. Kennedy* is presently on maneuvers in the seas north of Libya," Colonel Gamal said. "Our stipulation for the safe return of President Barrault is this: that you request the United States of America to deliver ten atomic devices of the Nevada Ten Class by aircraft to the *Robert F. Kennedy* by 0100 hours. The *Robert F. Kennedy* will steam east toward Algeria preparing to drop anchor in this port by 2400 hours tomorrow."

This was what General Mercier had not anticipated; it was pure insanity, of course, but he realized in his suddenly weary and frightened heart that his definition of sanity would never agree with that of Colonel Gamal and the Saracen Vector.

"When we are in possession of the Nevada Ten

181

devices, and when our scientists have inspected them, we will release President Barrault."

"I have been your friend, Colonel," General Mercier said. "May I, therefore, ask you this question? Your peoples and the Jews are Semites. I understand power and politics and conquest, but I cannot understand why you hate them so violently."

Captain Basra spoke for the first time. He was smiling, and his eyes were bright and clear and terrible. "Do you remember the Koran, General Mercier? It reads: 'And when ye meet those who misbelieve, then strike off the heads until ye have massacred them, and bind fast the bonds!'"

Colonel Gamal glanced at Captain Basra and said: "I did not order you to be silent because the words you quote are old and honorable. But they aren't relevant to what we are discussing.

"The State of Israel shall not be destroyed by atomic blasts, if its leaders accede to our terms." He turned to look at General Mercier. "But if they defy us, General, we will annihilate them all and reduce the land to ashes."

"Let me phrase my objections as temperately as possible," General Mercier said. "First, you have already reached an agreement with France and the United States. You have, in effect, entered into a contract with us. We will pay the stipulated monies and insure you a hearing before the United Nations. On your part, you have agreed to return President Barrault safely to France. Now you are breaking faith. My colleagues will say, what can you expect from Arabs?"

Colonel Gamal held up a hand to silence protests from his officers. Then he smiled and said, "We aren't in a personality contest, General. The first requests merely tested our strength."

"I'll point out something obvious," General Mercier

said. "Take my word for it, the United States will not give away any of its nuclear hardware. Not to France, not to England, and certainly not to the Saracen Vector. Take those American dollars, take your place in the United Nations. That is the most practical advice I can give you, Colonel."

"Thank you. I will also attempt to be practical and temperate. The United States will argue that they cannot trust us. They will argue that it would be insane for them to place such sophisticated weapons in the hands of potential enemies. Also, they will maintain that we are unstable, neurotic, emotional and all the rest of it. But, General, we have been forced to trust the United States for three anxious decades. And after that, the French and the Russians. We have prayed in our mosques that no mischance, that no emotionally disturbed young pilot would cause our lands to be destroyed in a nuclear holocaust. Now the time has come when those nations must trust us, The Arab world. We will deliver an ultimatum to Israel. If they accept it, I give you my solemn assurance there will be peace from Morocco to the easternmost tip of Saudi Arabia."

"You must realize I can only transmit your request," General Mercier said. He knew that Colonel Gamal and the Saracen Vector had reached the point of no return; they had pledged and committed their manhood and religious conviction to this cause, and they would infinitely prefer death to defeat. Having stated their terms, they would never modify them; they had been shaped like granite from the Koran, and its exhilarating promises had bred in them a lust for death. He could still remember the fear and terror their old chants had caused in him when as an infidel youth he had crept into their mosques. One in particular had always caused a shudder of paralyzing horror to run through him. It began: "The sword is the key of

183

heaven and of hell, a drop of blood shed in the cause of God, a night spent in arms is more avail than two months of fasting and prayers; whosoever falls in battle, his sins are forgiven; at the Day of Judgment his wounds shall be resplendent as vermilion and odoriferous as musk, and the loss of limbs shall be supplied by the wings of angels and cherubim."

"I will transmit your request to the appropriate officers in the White House," General Mercier said. "But I will not recommend compliance. If my life depends on it, I will not."

"Your life is of very little importance," Colonel Gamal said, and for the first time, there was a suggestion of contempt in his expression. "You will make our position known to the United States, and unless they assure us of their cooperation, we will execute President Barrault tomorrow night. Now, let us have more tea. We have talked enough of these matters. General, you will remain here in your father's villa until the negotiations are completed. We have an excellent communications network; its headquarters are located on the third floor, across from what I believe was once your nursery. You can make our demands known from here."

"Very well," General Mercier said. "May I notify my wife that I am staying here?"

"But, of course." Colonel Gamal refilled General Mercier's cup. "It would be inexcusable to alarm your good lady."

"Thank you," General Mercier said and ceremoniously concealed his left hand below the table. He smiled at Colonel Gamal and raised his glass of tea in what he knew to be his equally unclean right hand.

Chapter Eleven

     Spencer had stopped at an old inn, the Renard Rouge, on the outskirts of the city of Foix. He and Ackerley had used it as a mail drop a number of times, but the proprietor, Henri Grenoit, who was a friend of Spencer, had told him there were no calls from Ackerley.

Spencer stood at the windows of this warm high-ceilinged room and looked out across the town. The lights of Foix were fading into a pale winter's dawn, and in the hazy, translucent glow he could see the outlines of the black bulk of the railroad station and the towers of the small castle on the high ground above the city. Denise lay on the covers of a massive four-poster bed. She wore slippers and a short quilted robe, and her red hair was bright against a white pillow slip. Her face was pale and drawn and her eyes were closed, but she wasn't asleep. Spencer had helped her to change her clothes and to bathe, and had made a sling from a towel to keep the weight of her arm from her bruised shoulder.

"What kind of trouble are you in?" she asked him abruptly, without opening her eyes.

He looked at her. "Will you stop it? I'm not going to tell you. It's information you don't need."

"I'm not an idiot. I might be able to help."

"No, you can't."

She sighed. "My God, you're stubborn. You're like a mule, August. I don't understand any of this. Why must you leave France?"

Spencer smiled faintly. "You're not coming with me?"

"I'm frightened, I'm all alone, I have no money, and you say I'll be murdered if I return to Paris. What choice do I have?" She apparently forgot her injured shoulder for she attempted to shrug; the movement made her wince with pain. "Damn! Where are we going?"

Spencer sat down alongside her on the bed and began gently to massage her bruised and swollen shoulder. "I know a town in Mexico," he said. "Plenty of tourists, lots of galleries and souvenir shops. I'll learn how to make pottery. You could try your hand at weaving or something."

She pressed her cheek against the backs of his fingers. "That feels good. But your little town sounds ghastly. Why can't we go to Rio or maybe Tangier? I know people there and there are lovely shops and places to have my hair done."

"That's exactly what we don't want. San Miguel is nice and dull. We'll blend into it for a while."

"Can I have funds transferred there from Paris?"

"I'm afraid not. It wouldn't be wise."

She sighed again. "It gets worse and worse."

"Don't worry about money. I've got enough."

186

She was silent a moment. Then she said, "How much?"

"About $2,800 a month."

She looked impressed. "But do you have to pay taxes on that?"

Perhaps there was therapy in this kind of insanity, Spencer thought. If the guillotine blade was flashing toward your throat, you might just as well babble about taxes or the weather. . . .

"I pay taxes on half of it. The other half is tax-exempt income from municipals."

"How smart of you," she said, and moved her cheek again across the backs of his hands. "We'll have a lovely time in San Miguel."

Spencer smiled and shifted his position and began to massage her smooth, slim legs. When she danced, these elegant muscles were like steel springs under the velvet skin. "Did you ever tell Andre you knew me before?"

She smiled and closed her eyes. "Confidences like that are never appreciated, August." Then she laughed. "You should know that."

The phone began to ring. He picked up the receiver and said, "Yes?"

"To whom do I have the pleasure of speaking?" The voice was light and pleasant, delicately threaded with humor.

"John Carpenter," Spencer said.

"Remarkable! You sound exactly like a jolly old bugger name of August Spencer."

"Who is this?" Spencer said, although he thought he knew the answer to his question.

"It's Roger, Roger Mackay, who else? I won't waste time with amenities. Bunny Ackerley called me. He wants to meet you here at my place the soonest. I'll give you direction and ring off. I'd rather not say any more. All right?"

"Yes," Spencer said.

Spencer drove five kilometers south of Foix on the road to Perpignan, found the turn-off Mackay had told him to take and swung west into a countryside which with each kilometer became more remote and isolated; through the trees he could see only occasional lights from houses.

Mackay lived in a renovated farm house set among apple trees several hundred yards from the hard-topped road. The house was made of stone and old timbers, and the narrow leaded windows were trimmed with white paint. The early sunlight sparkled on the ice-coated limbs of the black apple trees. Spencer parked in the curved driveway, and as he went up wooden steps to the porch the massive front door was opened by Mackay, who spread his arms wide and gave Spencer the intimate, impish smile which was practically his trademark, and cried: "Steady the buffs," in his high, piping voice.

The living room with its shiny wooden floor and period furniture was a connoisseur's delight. Lowboys and ancient fruitwood chests gleamed with silver bowls and candelabra and tea services.

"When did you talk to Ackerley?"

"It was around midnight. I called the Red Fox straight away. But they weren't even expecting you. So I kept trying."

"It seems strange Ackerley didn't call me himself."

"Is there something coming loose?" Mackay asked him; there was anxiety in his voice. "It's been eight or nine years, hasn't it?"

"Something like that," Spencer said.

"I was pleased to hear from Ackerley, and pleased to relay his message to you, but I don't want to get mixed up in anything. Mind you, I'll put you up, lend you a tenner, but no tricks. Are you official, by the way?"

"No. Not for some time now."

The years had been no kinder to Mackay than they were to most people in late middle age. He was small and wiry with only a few strands of ginger-colored hair plastered across his circular baldspot. Mackay wore the gear of a country squire, cavalry twill trousers and boots, a hacking jacket of heather-shaded tweed, a tattersall vest and blocky gold cuff links shaped into horses' heads. He also had a gold tooth in the front of his mouth and this glittered as brightly as the gold cuff links when he tapped his upper teeth with the stem of a Meerschaum pipe.

Roger Mackay had left the British Intelligence Service in the early sixties. In some fashion, he had managed to accumulate money; it hadn't been by blackmail, Spencer was sure, for Mackay was too clever for that dead end.

A slim young man in yellow silk pajamas and a black cashmere robe came through the entrance to the dining alcove and smiled shyly at Spencer. Mackay clucked like a cross old hen, but his display of impatience was transparently false; he was obviously entranced by the sight of the young man, and his eyes sparkled happily in his lined but merry old face.

"There is absolutely no need for you to get up, Paul," Mackay said, rocking back and forth on his stout little boots. "You don't need your beauty sleep, heaven knows, but do you realize what an *uncivilized* hour this is?"

"I thought I would make you some coffee." The young man spoke English with a faint French accent, and continued to smile shyly at Spencer. With a theatrical sigh, Mackay said: "I don't deserve you, truly I don't. Paul, this is Mr. Spencer." The young man

189

shook hands with Spencer and bowed slightly from the waist.

He smiled. "It is a pleasure to meet you, Mr. Spencer. Would you like coffee? Or—" He glanced tentatively at Mackay. "—some whiskey, perhaps?"

"An excellent suggestion," Mackay said, beaming at the young man. "We'll both have a whiskey. Forgive me, August, but I don't remember your preference. Wait." He snapped his fingers. "It was Johnnie Walker Black Label. Right?"

"Remarkable," Spencer said, and smiled. Something was wrong here, but he couldn't even guess what it was. Why hadn't Ackerley called him? That was what worried him, because it seemed to put everything else out of focus.

Paul went gracefully to a sideboard on which there were whiskey and crystal glasses and syphon bottles, and poured drinks for Spencer and Mackay. He was in his early twenties, Spencer judged, with luxuriant dark hair and a complexion that looked as smooth and healthy as a ripe peach. Years ago, Mackay had taken to referring to himself as a retired homosexual, but his flickering, intimate smile had always implied the opposite. He had, as Paul's presence would indicate, never given up his peculiar pleasures; he had always loved young men and enjoyed them in abundance.

"Cheers!" Mackay said, looking with a fond smile after Paul. "He's such a dear boy. We met in Nice last year. I was in dreadfully low spirits. The doctors in Switzerland had been thumping and poking at me for what seemed an eternity, and I felt like a shabby old pincushion." He sipped his drink and put the glass on a table, then struck an old-fashioned kitchen match and began to light his Meerschaum. The smoke drifted in lazy spirals toward the beamed ceiling.

"He's been such a tonic," Mackay said. "I don't see how I could go on without him. I truly don't."

"Roger, are you certain it was Ackerley who called?"

"Reasonably certain." Mackay tamped tobacco in the Meerschaum with a pipe tool. "Of course, one British accent tends to sound much like another—equally absurd that is—but I've known old Bunny for years. I'd be surprised if I were mistaken."

"Exactly what did he say to you?"

"Exactly?" Mackay frowned thoughtfully and rubbed the bowl of his Meerschaum against the side of his nose. "He said: 'Roger, this is Bunny Ackerley.' I said, 'Bunny, you old devil, where are you?' He told me he was in Foix. He asked if I would do a favor for him. He asked me to call you at the Red Fox and then, and these are his exact words, he said: 'When you contact August, tell him to meet me at your place.' And that's the lot of it, August."

"This was around midnight?"

"Ten past the hour, old boy."

The phone began to ring. It was an ornate, French-style instrument with a black ebony base and a gold-trimmed receiver and cradle, and it was recessed in a bookshelf alongside a humidor and pipe racks. "Excuse me," Mackay said and walked over to the book shelves. But he didn't pick up the phone immediately. Instead, he replaced the Meerschaum in a pipe rack and lifted the lid of the humidor and removed a .38 caliber hand gun, which he pointed steadily at Spencer. The phone had stopped ringing. "I don't know what you're involved in, August, and I don't want your confidences. You carry your Browning in a spring-clip shoulder holster. Please remove it, holding it by the butt between your thumb and forefinger, and set it down on the coffee table. I was never as good as you were at this sort of thing, but remember I survived. Remember too that my nerves

191

aren't the best. Please don't do anything that might add to my present agitation."

Spencer removed the Browning and carefully placed it on the coffee table. "Get one thing clear," he said. "Ackerley and I are no threat to you."

"That's a moot point, isn't it? You see, I haven't talked to Bunny Ackerley. I talked to, or more accurately, I listened to, a large American agent named Cord, whose orders I am presently following."

"Are the Americans paying you well? Or was it the young man's baby-blue eyes that got to you?"

"Oh, for Christ's sake, it wasn't money," Mackay said. "And I was never attracted to weightlifters." His face was troubled. "Please believe me. I didn't relish adding to your problems, but they had a variety of thumbscrews to use on me. For one, Paul has a police record. And they could get messy about that. Also, I have some sources of income which won't bear, shall we say, scrutiny. They seem to know all about these things. I was in an extremely vulnerable position. As a man of advanced years, who has cultivated the arts of creative cowardice most of his life, I found I lacked the moral stamina to hold out against them." Mackay blinked his eyes rapidly. "Try to forgive me, August. I couldn't go on without Paul, and they might have taken him away from me."

Spencer heard the sound of an automobile approaching the house. More than one, he realized, two or three at least.

"Do you know how the script ends?" Spencer asked Mackay.

"Cord told me he wanted to talk to you. It was Cord who phoned just now. He said he would be here about five minutes after ringing my number."

The cars were stopping in the driveway in front of the house, their motors fading to silence. Spencer guessed that if he upended the coffee table, it might

192

deflect a bullet, and he knew that his reflexes were decades sharper than Mackay's. But he also knew that he couldn't shoot Mackay. The amiable little fag was looking out for his own, and Spencer couldn't blame him much for that. Gallant gestures were for heroes, not realists. And they were a pair of bloody realists. Spencer knew very few middle-aged liberals. And those he did know impressed him as wistful, somehow condemned types, who lived on hopes that were as brutal as lies.

There were footsteps on the porch and a knock on the door.

"Come in," Mackay said.

The door swung open and Spencer felt the astonished leap of his heart as a large, fair man wearing dark glasses came into the room.

"I'm tempted to say it's a small world," Bunny Ackerley said, and smiled.

"——they picked me up at the railway station, Cord, the big American chap, and several of his people. Absolute kid-glove treatment, they were gentle as old nannies."

Spencer and Ackerley were seated in the rear of a limousine speeding through cold sunlight on the highway that led south from Foix. In the Cadillac behind them was the American, Cord, and two other agents. One of them was the Irishman, the man who had stood on the bridge above the Seine watching Spencer and Ackerley on an afternoon that seemed eternities ago. Directly ahead of them was a Citroen with three of General Mercier's people in it. In the front seat of the limousine were two more of Cord's men, Americans, with young, impassive faces. The agent who sat beside the driver was named Clark, and he had Spencer's Browning in his hand. Cord's orders were to escort them to General Mercier's chateau, which was thirty kilometers south of Foix. He had requested their cooperation, but this was part of the charade too, since they were literally traveling with guns at their heads.

"The report that you'd been killed in a traffic accident seemed to throw a spanner into the works, but when they told me the report had been verified by LeMaitre, I gathered you were buying time."

"Has Cord told you anything except that his orders are to take us to General Mercier's?"

"No. Cord's responsibility is to collect us and deliver us. We are high-priority merchandise, August. I gather they guessed you'd come to Foix, but there were stake-outs in Paris and Ireland, and probably every other place you might conceivably have headed for."

"Who gives Cord his orders?"

"They were coming from the top like Jovean thunder bolts. From Douglas Benton. You may or may not be flattered to know that Cord's people were under orders not to draw their guns on you, even in self-defense. That's why Cord set up that hocus-pocus with Mackay."

Ackerley removed his sun glasses and looked steadily at Spencer, and his expression was cold and thoughtful, and not particularly friendly. "Do you know what this bloody row is all about?"

"Yes," Spencer said, and sighed. Then he lowered his voice and told him.

Chapter Twelve

The rain began in Washington an hour before dawn and the sleet and drizzle caused massive, nerve-shredding traffic jams as the city came awake. It fell on demonstrators on Pennsylvania Avenue and on stone monuments to patroits and into slums whose rotting deterioration had only been improved by the fires of last year's rioting, and it fell into the Potomac on the eastern seaboard from Baltimore to Roanoke.

President Montrose came into the Oval Office at 7:30 A.M. and stood for a moment looking out at the cheerless prospect of the Rose Garden. He had options now, and others would be forthcoming throughout the day. An American airborne division and three squadrons of Air Force jet fighters had been ordered to a war-readiness alert in Germany and France. The U.S. Aircraft Carrier *Robert F. Kennedy* was proceeding on an easterly course which would bring it to the approaches of the harbor at Algiers by nightfall.

The President had already briefed the National Security Council, which had met earlier that morning in the Cabinet Room. Chaired by the Vice President, the group consisted of the Secretaries of State and Defense and the director of the Office of Emergency Preparedness. They had assured him of their cooperation and confidence, and their determination to support without reservations whatever decisions he might make. They were good and loyal men, patriotic public servants, but it was obvious to the President they were relieved that he, not they, must make those final decisions.

The President's phone to General Rose rang. President Montrose pressed a button and General Rose's tired face appeared on the screen above the instrument. "We have a favorable report from Navy Engineering," General Rose said. "Since I'm not cleared for that project, the Secretary will report to you directly. Is that satisfactory, sir?"

"Yes."

At 8:30 President Montrose left the Oval Office and walked out through the White House west basement to his office in the Executive Office Building. Douglas Benton, Deputy Director of the CIA, was waiting for him there, seated beside the Theodore Roosevelt desk. Benton, a tall, rangy man with the eyes of a gunfighter, stood immediately when the President came in. "Something affirmative at last, Mr. President," Benton said. "August Spencer and Wyndom Ackerley are in custody and on their way to General Mercier's chateau."

"All I can ask for is an inspired guess," the President said. "Will they cooperate?"

Benton deliberated before replying. He frowned and ran a hand absently over his short sandy hair, and in the same distracted fashion fiddled with a button on the sleeve of his elegantly cut tweed jacket. "I don't know Wyndom Ackerley personally, Mr. President," he said at last. "I think August Spencer will cooperate. My subjective evaluation is that Ackerley will feel he's letting down the side if he doesn't go along with him."

"What makes you so sure of August Spencer?"

"I can only describe him negatively, sir. He doesn't have a death wish, and he doesn't relish being expendable. But he reacts to challenge in a way that's almost glandular."

"Interesting sort of man." The President was silent for a moment, and then, with a shrug, he dismissed the subject.

"In any event, it's one of our options."

"Mr. President, may I make two general comments?"

"Of course, Doug."

"I'm not presuming to remind you, sir, but kidnapping and terrorism have become political facts of life in the last decade. The Basques kidnapped the German Eugene Beihl, and the separatists in Quebec kidnapped and murdered a businessman who simply had the misfortune to be there with a trade commission. The same thing has happened in a half-dozen countries in South America and in Mexico, and now, because there haven't been drastic reprisals, this kind of blackmail has become common. Now we're faced with the kidnapping of the head of one of the most powerful nations in the world. I think we're going to be terribly criticized for dealing with the Saracen Vector, for negotiating with them like a sovereign state. I think we're got to put the fear of God into them, and make an example of them to the whole world."

"And your second point is?" President Montrose did not look at his watch but his manner indicated he would like to.

"It's just this, sir." Benton spoke rapidly, prodded by the impatience in President Montrose's restless eyes. "We've spent years developing close and fruitful relationships with the French government and the Sûretè. Their agents and ours work together efficiently and sensibly. But if we don't take action now, while their President is threatened, well, I'll put it this way, sir, we'll destroy their emotional confidence in the CIA."

God, what an ass, President Montrose thought, but the assessment was tempered by his realization that Benton didn't know what the Saracen Vector wanted in exchange for Barrault.

"I want to know everything that worries and concerns you, Doug," President Montrose said. "I can't make decisions in a vacuum, but understand this: when I make my decision, I don't want to hear anything more about the consequences of that decision. I'll do what I think is right, and I'll pay the price for it. Is that perfectly clear?"

"I understand, sir," Benton said.

President Montrose left the Executive Office Building and returned to the Oval Office, where General Rose and the Secretaries of State and Defense, Warren Hoopes and Rodman Post, were waiting for him. On the President's desk were four reports packaged into three-ringed red binders marked TOP SECRET. President Montrose distributed copies of this last scenario from Desk Five to General Rose and the Secretaries, and then sat down behind his desk.

"It's redundant to say I need your help. But I do need your help, gentlemen, and I need the help of God." The President looked directly into the eyes of each of the three men in his office. "The purpose of this meeting is to discuss this question: Should the United States transfer atomic devices, specifically the

Nevada Ten Class, to a para-national group called the Saracen Vector? I'd like you to read the last report from Desk Five. After that, I'd like your thinking."

The Secretaries opened the report from Desk Five and began reading. The report was captioned:

SARACEN VECTOR

1. Should the United States deliver the Atomic devices of the Nevada class to the Saracen Vector, it is the judgment of Desk Five that one of the following events would occur:
   a) President Barrault will be returned safely to France.
   b) Notwithstanding the delivery of the Nevadas, President Barrault would be executed. (It is important to note here that the Saracen Vector is a para-military and para-national organization; its members can disband and merge with total anonymity into the life stream of any Arabic nation. They can act with impunity because they know they are free from the threat of reprisal).
   c) The Saracen Vector will use the threat of atomic attack to enforce political adjustments on the State of Israel.
   d) If this fails, the Saracen Vector will employ atomic attacks in a probably successful attempt to destroy the State of Israel.
   e) In a simplistic formula, Russia will/will not support the Saracen Vector. In destroying the State of Israel, it would be transparently clear that they are choosing to commence a terminal conflict with the United States.

PRO-THINK:

1. Our continuing healthy relationship with the Republic of France demands that we exert every effort to preserve the life of President Barrault.

199

CON-THINK:

1. See paragraphs b, c, d and e above.

The President glanced at his Secretary of State. "Warren?" Warren Hoopes was fifty, a tall and deceptively slender man, whose every graceful and confident gesture somehow suggested ancestors to whom personal doubt and social insecurity would have been totally foreign concepts. And such an inference of family distinction would have been accurate. Warren Hoopes was the son of a former United States Senator and a grandson of a Governor of Virginia. The Secretary was a fox hunter, a fine shot, and had made millions in mining and shipping since his graduation from Harvard College. But these millions were no particular cause for celebration since they simply added their comfortable bulk to the fortune which had been left to him by his maternal grandparents. He spoke serviceable French and Spanish, and he had always been quietly amused by the conviction that he could have had just about any woman in the world he wanted. But his devotion to his wife of twenty-two years was a legend in the Capitol. He had three sons who were pleasant sailing companions, and a lovely and level-headed daughter who was presently studying economics at the Sorbonne. Naturally he was a snob, and naturally he pretended he wasn't. But when he appraised his endowments and accomplishments, Secretary Hoopes could only conclude that he was a remarkably gifted man. But now he felt nervous and inadequate. How could a knowledge of French and Spanish help him now? Of what value was encyclopedic information about the mining industry in Alaska, about ships beating their way around the world? He felt an uncomfortable trickle of perspiration on his ribs and realized his forehead would soon begin to blister with sweat. He envied Secretary Post's cold, hard eyes, and the steadiness in his fingers as the old boy lighted a cigarette and returned a gold Ronson to his vest pocket. Thank God, it's more his show than mine, Hoopes thought; if they committed the hardware, Defense would deliver it, and the President would have the major say in that commitment.

Secretary Hoopes crossed his legs and looked thoughtfully at the glossy tip of his slowly swinging black oxford. Bench-made, one hundred and fifty dollars, he thought with ghastly irrelevance. "Under no circumstances, Mr. President, would I recommend transferring the Nevadas to the Saracen Vector," he said. "I'd offer them grants in mining and farming equipment, subsidies——"

"Excuse me, Warren, but let's not get into alternatives. Not yet, at least. Rodman?"

Rodman Post had sat for decades on the boards of the biggest corporations in the country. His significant contribution to those corporations had been the talent and guts to make crisis decisions on an almost hourly basis, and take full responsibility for them. He was tough and blunt, and he never ducked issues. At Rubicon time, when other executives found their doodles of uncommon interest, or became entranced by the play of light on the ceiling, Post would say, "Goddamnit, yes" or "Goddamnit, no." Which usually settled the matter.

But now, Secretary Post found himself thinking rather wistfully that it would have been pleasant to have gone to Harvard like Warren Hoopes, and have the easy skill to disport himself so casually in Washington society, because if they made a mistake now, it would be the biggest goddamn mistake of the century. Hoopes could live with that, but he couldn't. Hoopes would project a mild regret, the fatalism of

201

the to-the-manor-born fuck-up, which somehow diffused criticism, but Rodman Post couldn't.

Actually, Secretary Post could only advise the President, and as he watched Montrose's serious, waiting eyes, he found himself hoping that the President had already made up his mind and would simply ask them to implement his decision. Leadership flourished through use, Post knew, and Montrose had been exercising leadership for sixteen months. He had the muscle and the guts, and like Harry Truman he knew where the buck stopped.

Secretary Post said: "Mr. President, I'd deliver those Nevadas to the Saracen Vector."

President Montrose studied him in silence. General Rose cleared his throat. Secretary Hoopes made a tent of his graceful fingers, while his eyes strayed thoughtfully to a pattern of light playing over the carpet. The silence was unnatural; something seemed to be working in it. After a pause, President Montrose said, "And?"

"Mr. President, it was my understanding you wanted a yes or a no."

"But I want the reasons. Not alternatives."

"Very well. I'd deliver the Nevadas and when Barrault was back in France, or on his way back, I'd send in three airborne divisions to seize those Nevadas. And I'd notify the government of Algeria that we were coming in. I wouldn't be put through the wringer, Mr. President, by a bunch of goddamn fanatic rag-heads, if you'll pardon the expression."

President Montrose said: "Thank you." Then he said: "Anyone want coffee?"

No one wanted coffee.

They're just as scared as I am, President Montrose thought. And they're very relieved not to be sitting on my side of the desk.

You never thought about such things when you

campaigned, when you stood with arms outstretched, smiling widely, savoring the applause and approval of the people of your giant country. You took your strength and faith from those people, but where were they now? Sleeping, driving tractors, tending their shops, knotting mufflers around the throats of children, chalking equations on blackboards . . . they were exactly where they should be, of course, living their own lives, while he was exactly where he should be, sitting behind the President's desk and trying not to betray his fears.

"General Rose?"

"No, Mr. President," General Rose said. "I wouldn't recommend transferring those Nevadas to the Saracen Vector. Not for one damn moment."

Secretary Hoopes cleared his throat. "Mr. President?"

"Yes, Warren?"

"If you don't mind my mentioning an alternative now, we could deliver disfunctional atomic devices to the Saracen Vector. I'm sure our boffins could rig them so they'd pass for the real thing."

"Well, that's one of our options, in fact," President Montrose said, "the Navy is working on it. You see, one of the Saracen Vector's conditions is that a team of scientists from the University of Beirut will inspect our Nevadas aboard the carrier *Robert F. Kennedy* prior to the release of President Barrault."

Secretary Hoopes experienced an emotion that was equally embarrassment and relief; the embarrassment stemmed from the fact that the President had bypassed him without even a token apology; the relief stemmed from the fact that the more decisions the President made, the less he was responsible for.

President Montrose picked up a slim binder from his desk, opened it and said: "Let me brief you now

203

on five options that GW has extracted from Desk Five's report." The President began reading:

A. Without evaluation of consequences, five options are implicit in the analysis of Desk Five. They are as follows:
1) To deliver the Nevadas.
2) Not to deliver the Nevadas.
3) To deliver the Nevadas and when President Barrault has been returned to France, to dispatch airborne units in sufficient strength to insure recovery of the Nevadas.
4) To deliver disarmed Nevadas with a detection lag-time flexible enough to guarantee the safe return of President Barrault to Paris.

The President rubbed the tips of his fingers against his temples; the pain there was quite severe. He continued reading:

5) Deliver to the State of Israel ten Nevada class atomic devices, thus creating a miniature nuclear stand-off in the Middle East, which would constitute a reflection of the status presently existing between the U.S.S.R. and the United States.

"Jesus Christ!" Secretary Post said. "Excuse me, sir, but are they out of their goddamn minds?"

"I asked them for options," the President said. "I can't complain if they come up with some hairy ones."

"Mr. President," General Rose said.

"Yes, General?"

General Rose's face looked suddenly tired and pale. It was as if a lifetime of rugged marches, of frozen duckblinds, of furious polo had never been. He carried his years, it seemed, with a great effort, as if his flesh were soft and his bones were brittle.

"It's hardly necessary to say I'm not anti-Semitic,"
204

the general said. "I am Jewish, of course. I hope the President will consider that in the light of the question I am going to ask. And that question is: Is the preservation of the State of Israel in its present form worth the safety of the United States of America, and the safety of her present and proven alliances in the Western world?"

"There are certain questions—" Secretary Hoopes stopped in mid-sentence. "I'm sorry, Mr. President."

"No, go ahead, Warren."

"There are certain questions of principle involved," Secretary Hoopes said. "I'm sure the General understands what they are."

"I don't need to be reminded of that, Mr. Secretary, but my question doesn't require a response in terms of principles."

Secretary Hoopes was silent, but he thought to himself, obviously not. And then he realized, with more sympathy, that someone had had to ask that particular question, and General Rose had saved them all embarrassment by asking it.

"May I make a general comment, sir?" the Secretary asked President Montrose. When the President nodded, Secretary Hoopes glanced from him to General Rose.

"In point of fact, anti-Semitism is not completely a social problem," he said. "It is not only a matter of restricted clubs and colleges quotas, and the chance epithet from ignorant people. As deplorable as these things are, they are a good deal less significant than the present tendency to equate anti-Semitism with the anti-Establishment, which is a doctrine of the Lumumba, Che Guevara and Reginald Debray advocates. The New Left, in France, in America, and in Germany in particular, where they are shouting "make the Middle East Red, and make Israel dead," these groups regard Arab terrorist tactics as a legiti-

205

mate response to the establishment of Israel, and as a concomitant they equate them with terrorist attacks by Panthers and Chicanos against the established institutions of America. I make no conclusion except to say that an abandonment of Israel may constitute support for terror tactics against the legal governments and institutions of the Western world."

"Well, fine," Secretary Post said. He had made no attempt to mask his impatience during the Secretary's speech. "That's why I'm convinced we should save the President of France, then go in with every goddamn thing that's necessary to get back those Nevadas."

"One further point, Secretary Hoopes." It was General Rose speaking. He looked as if he had recovered some of his strength; there were points of color in his cheeks. "Herbert Marcuse, the guru of the New Left you're talking about, also lived through the Nazi tyranny. And he doesn't dismiss anti-Semitism as either a social problem or a philosophical toy of terrorists. He identifies it for what it is, a virulent, killing disease."

President Montrose was staring absently at the surface of his desk, and it would have been difficult to judge from his expression whether or not he had been listening to his advisors. After a moment, he got up and looked out at the gardens. The Secretaries and General Rose stood and watched him in silence. From his attitude, it seemed likely that he had something more to say to them, or something more to ask of them, but at last he turned and smiled faintly and dismissed them by saying: "Thank you very much, gentlemen."

When he was alone, President Montrose walked to the windows and looked out across the Rose Garden, feeling every hour of his fifty-seven years. The rain had stopped and the trees were wet and black in the cold sunlight. Within hours, he must make a decision, and no one could help him do that, not State, not Defense, not the fatalists who worked in GW and at Desk Five. The world was so sweet and so many men and women loved it, that it seemed a design of vicious gods to insist that one man make the decision which could place it in jeopardy.

The President took a coin from his pocket and flipped it in the air. Catching it with his right hand, he slapped the coin down on his muscular wrist, and when he raised his hand, he found himself looking down at the profile of John F. Kennedy, the blend of toughness and warmth caught in miniature on the shining half-dollar.

"I'd take your Bay of Pigs any day, Jack," President Montrose said, and dropped the coin back into his pocket.

Chapter Thirteen

The chateau and estates of General Mercier were north of Foix on the road to Bordeaux. A curving approach to the massive old house, whose stones were like lavender in the afternoon light, twisted through columns of sycamores, each graceful turn marked by clusters of topiary figures. Their driver parked the limousine under a portecochere, and the cars that had escorted them from Foix stopped behind them. The American agent, Cord, joined Spencer and Ackerley at the foot of broad marble steps which rose to double mahogany doors brightened by shining brass hinges.

"We'll wait here," Cord said to them. He had been joined by a half-dozen French and American agents who stood in a loose semicircle behind him. "We're not functional now. It seems to be your show."

In Cord's smile there was a suggestion of malice, Spencer thought, but as he attempted to understand this, he realized he was wrong, for a shifting ray of late sunlight revealed nothing in the big American's expression but a sense of puzzled complicity.

"We'd like our guns," Spencer said.

"Later, Mr. Spencer. Those are my orders."

Spencer shrugged and glanced at Ackerley. Ackerley also shrugged, and they went up the broad steps to the double mahogany doors, which were opened by a butler who was obviously expecting them. The butler escorted them through a cool, dim corridor to a drawing room with bay windows which gave them views of fruit trees and gardens, and lighted hangars and a runway which stretched off to the horizon. The butler, who was elderly and grave but walked with spritely steps, told them he would inform Madame Mercier of their arrival and withdrew.

Ackerley stretched out in a deep chair and ran a hand tiredly over his fair rumpled hair. "No point wondering what they want, I expect," he said.

"Not much," Spencer said. He glanced around, feeling the stillness and quietness of the house. If there was anything going on, if roses were being snipped by a gardner, or shallots chopped up for dinner, it was all going on at a respectful distance from the drawing room.

There was nothing mysterious about it, he decided; it was just wealth at work, silently and discreetly. There was wealth everywhere in the room, Gobelin tapestries, glowing old highboys supporting porcelain vases in Bremen blue, marble-topped tables with curling gold-leaf legs, a panelled and vaulted ceiling laced with fretworks of landscapes and equestrian figures.

The old butler returned silently pushing a cart of whiskey and open-faced sandwiches and tea things. Madame Mercier sent her compliments, he said, and would be pleased to join them shortly. The lights bordering the runway had been turned on, and the blue and red markers gleamed against the glowing darkness and stretched south to infinity.

Spencer made two large whiskies and gave one of them to Ackerley. He wasn't hungry, but Ackerley helped himself to bread and paté and gherkins. Spencer sipped his drink and studied the fireplace and the delicate marble inlay of the mantlepiece. In the leaded glass of a bookcase, he caught a blurred reflection of himself, his black hair needing combing, his broad, hard face framed by the upturned collar of his duffle coat.

He heard a sound and turned. A woman he assumed to be Madame Mercier entered the drawing room in a wheelchair. The sound which had alerted him was the faint hum of its motor.

She was younger than he had guessed she would be, in her middle or late thirties. She wore gold bracelets on her wrists and a loose silken robe belted at the waist. Her hair was thick and dark and combed loosely down to her shoulders. Her small head was supported on a slim white neck and her features were both elegant and fragile. She projected to Spencer the privileged look of the ill and beautiful—an orchid in a hothouse, regal and vulnerable. But then, as she drew nearer to them, he saw the pain in her eyes and the effort she was making to smile.

"I'm August Spencer," he said. "This is Mr. Wyndom Ackerley."

"They told me to expect you. I'm Madame Mercier." She pressed a button which stopped the motor of her wheelchair, and again the silence became pervasive. Her smile was cooler now, and the glance she directed at Ackerley seemed to make him uncomfortably aware that he was standing at tea time with a large whiskey in one hand and a sandwich of paté in the other. "You know my husband, I believe."

Ackerley swallowed and said, "I haven't had that pleasure, ma'am."

"I know your husband," Spencer said.

"Then you understand, you may understand, that is——" Madame Mercier made a small, dismissing gesture with her pale hand as if to intimate that Spencer's opinion didn't particularly matter after all. Or, more accurately, Spencer thought, she was implying that he wasn't qualified to have an opinion one way or the other. "What you must realize," Madame Mercier continued, "is that what my husband did, or whatever he did, would only reflect his own certain honor and his own certain values. It couldn't be otherwise. Do you understand that, Mr. Spencer?"

He realized with surprise that his answer would be desperately important to her, but her cool, superior smile pretended it didn't matter at all. In a woman who rode and hunted and danced, that response would have been transparent and uninteresting, but Spencer was conscious only of her wasted limbs under the silken robe and the agony in her eyes.

"A certain honor, certain values," Spencer said. "Yes, I can understand."

She smiled at the backs of her hands and then asked him if he would pour her a glass of sherry. Which, Spencer thought, was as close as Madame Mercier could come to saying thank you.

After she sipped the sherry she said: "It has been an eventful day. I've talked to your people in Washington and to my husband. I've been busy, and useful, which was pleasant."

"Excuse me," Spencer said and put his glass down and walked over to the bay window which faced the runway. Ackerley joined him and removed his sunglasses and looked thoughtfully up at the dark sky. They listened to the helicopter, and when it settled into the lights at the hangar, its rotary blades sending up clouds of dust, Spencer recognized it as a Bell 204-B, the commercial version of the Bell Iroquois.

From the shadowed room behind them, Madame Mercier said, "I expect that's your people now."

As they came into the drawing room, Spencer recognized General Rose from press pictures. The stiff white crew-cut hair, the heavy chest and shoulders, the rolling cavalryman's stride were all well-publicized trademarks. He said hello to Benton, with whom he had worked before, and introduced him to Ackerley. Spencer sensed a hostility in Benton, a resentment in this cool and predictably unemotional man, and he wondered at it.

After the introductions were complete, and the butler had offered drinks which were refused, Madame Mercier said, to the group in general: "Will you excuse me, please? I am quite tired."

"Yes, of course," General Rose said.

She pressed the button on the arm of the wheelchair and the motor hummed faintly. In the arched doorway of the drawing room, she turned and looked back at them, her small head silhouetted strangely by the flashing red and blue lights from the runway.

"My husband is a brave man," she said. "He has faced the enemies of France all his life with courage. I know he will be able to face his conscience."

When the wheelchair had carried her smoothly from the room, General Rose looked at Ackerley and Spencer. His manner had changed abruptly, and the change was not casual or subtle; the general looked baffled and anxious and angry. "Gentlemen, I don't have much time. Maybe none of us do. I'm going to give you this once, and then I want an immediate yes or no. Madame Mercier has relayed one condition to her husband, who passed it on to Colonel Gamal, who is in charge of the Saracen Vector. The condition is that two of our people take a look at President Barrault and fingerprint him to make goddamn sure he *is* Barrault."

Spencer decided he needed another drink. He poured himself a mild one and lit a cigarette. Ackerley was staring at the ceiling. The silence in the house was inviolate and enveloping.

"Two men," he said. "You mean Ackerley and me."

"Obviously," Benton said. "You're both in the picture. If we have to brief anyone else, we broaden the security base and shorten the odds on maintaining cover."

The general was staring at Ackerley. "London told us you did a year of pre-med at Birmingham University. In addition to identifying Barrault, we want assurance he's not in a terminal condition."

"I can check his blood pressure and pulse, but if he's under sedation, which is likely, he could be a vegetable for all I could tell."

"My orders are from President Montrose," the general said. "He asked me to get a yes or no, and fast. So what is it going to be?"

"Don't waste any more time," Benton said. "There's damn little left."

Ackerley removed his sunglasses and regarded Benton coolly and appraisingly. There was a suggestion of humor in his eyes, but Spencer knew Ackerley saw nothing amusing in any of this. In fact, Spencer surmised, Ackerley had also become aware of Benton's hostility, and had identified it; they had both, he realized, arrived at the same cheerless conclusion.

"Is Andre Leroi alive?" Spencer asked Benton.

"You go in, you'll find out. We don't know."

They know us so well, Spencer thought, our unexamined loyalties, our unrealistic gallantries.

He glanced at Ackerley and they were silent for as long as fifteen to twenty seconds, and then Ackerley answered the question in Spencer's eyes with a casual nod.

"We'll go in," Spencer said.

General Rose's instructions were simple: Spencer and Ackerley would return immediately to Orly with Benton and Rose in the Bell 204-B. Spencer and Ackerley would transplane to a waiting C-58, which would take off immediately for Algiers. It was the same aircraft which had brought Benton and Rose from Washington to Paris, and it was capable of speeds approaching Mach. 2.5. On the plane was a dossier of President Barrault which included photographs, fingerprints and descriptions of distinguishing physical characterestics. Also, medical and fingerprint equipment. The C-58 would be met at Algiers by General Mercier and Major Sidki, Colonel Ben Gamal's Chief of Staff. When the identification and medical examination of Barrault were completed, Spencer would report to General Rose at the American Embassy in Paris on a radio frequency which had already been assigned to Colonel Gamal.

The code would be based on personal questions and answers, neither known to Spencer in advance. Spencer would report, defining himself in three words: "I am Spencer." Authentication by voiceprint would take one second, then General Rose would ask Spencer two questions, personal questions only Spencer could know the answers to. If Spencer failed to answer correctly within three seconds, the connection would be broken in Paris, and it would be presumed that President Barrault was dead.

"Make that radio report to the American Embassy as close as possible to one-o'clock tomorrow morning," General Rose said, "0100 hours."

Spencer finished his drink and put it aside. But the whiskey didn't help much. He was cold all over, but it

214

was not an unpleasant feeling. It was like the simple frenzy of H-hour. "There's a timetable then," he said to General Rose.

"I've outlined your responsibilities. I can't tell you anything else."

Then Spencer began to understand the mixture of hostility and resentment he had noticed in Benton's expression. When a man decided that another man was expendable, and went on to implement that decision, he sometimes envied the man he was reducing to a statistic. And envy usually led to hatred.

Spencer smiled. "Something's coming in at one-o'clock then, General. Are we part of it?"

For an instant that stretched unnaturally in time, General Rose looked at Spencer and Ackerley with cold, appraising eyes, and his impersonal, dispassionate expression was a model of those worn by all commanders since men began to fight wars. But then a curious thing happened; the general turned away from them and rubbed his forehead, and his strength seemed to leave him, and in that instant, he became less or more than a soldier, and instead a worried and lonely human being. "I won't bore you with nonsense," he said in a voice that was empty and weary. "We've told ourselves for so long that all men are created equal that we've stopped believing it. While we proclaim it, we don't mean it and we don't act on it. The brutal fact we have accepted is that President Barrault is worth whatever human and physical price we have to pay for him."

General Rose glanced with what seemed to be irrelevant anxiety at the service chart and then at the red and blue runway lights flashing against the bay windows. "Would you gentlemen have a drink with me before we leave? I'd like it if you did."

In a second-floor bedroom which faced a small formal park and meadow, Madame Mercier lay fully

215

clothed on the coverlet of her bed, with only a light cashmere blanket across her thin and forever useless legs. The graceful bulk of the chateau stood between her little park and the hangars and runways, but she could see a reflection of the gaudy runway flares in her windows, so strange and charming that they put her in mind of things she had loved as a child. Circuses and Punch and Judy shows and ponies in the Bois de Bologne. She heard the helicopter take off, and after a moment the sound of its motors faded away toward Paris. . . .

Her maid came in with a tray on which there was a single glass and a carafe of water. The carafe was from Waterford and the slim square glass was from Limoges. The maid placed the tray on a bedside table within reach of Madame Mercier's hand and when Madame thanked her with a small smile, the maid went softly away and closed the door.

The sound of the helicopter was gone, gone away toward Paris, and the silence in the chateau was thick and smooth as velvet, so smooth and thick she could almost feel it.

Madame Mercier uncapped a tiny bottle of pills and poured them one by one into the palm of her hand. She usually took one of these if she planned to read for half an hour or so, and two if she wanted to go straight into a sleep that would last until the morning light was spilling across the bed. She had been warned never to take a third pill, that is, unless some crisis had stretched her nerves to the point of hysteria. Madame Mercier swallowed ten of the pills, one by one, following each with a small sip of water from the sturdy Limoges glass.

She strained to hear the sound of the helicopter. She thought she heard it, but she was already too drowsy to be sure. Or maybe it was something else she heard. But she couldn't be sure about that either.

He had said that he understood her and she had asked him for sherry. He would tell him then. He would tell her husband what she had said about him.

Madame Mercier realized that the rigid rules of caste no longer applied to her; she could do exactly as she pleased now, there was no more need for the straight back to support the broken heart, no reason at all to endure pain with dry eyes and dismissing smiles. She was like a little girl in a garden on an idle summer day, a little girl who could do or be anything she wanted, anything at all. And so, released at last and free, Madame Mercier did what she had wanted to do for so very long. She wept, but only for a little while.

At 2100 hours minus 6 minutes, the U.S. Aircraft Carrier *Robert F. Kennedy* steamed at maximum cruising speed in a southwesterly direction toward the port of Algiers. The towering sprays cast aside by her soaring bow were coated in shimmering, sparkling colors from erratic moonlight drifting through layers of thin clouds. Bizerte and Bougie lay far behind the *Robert F. Kennedy*. North and east of the aircraft carrier were the Balearics, Minorca, Ibiza and Majorica.

General Quarters had sounded when the aircraft carrier came within 2,500 yards of the range of Algerian coastal batteries. Fire control officers were at stations scanning radar screens and computers which fed data to automatic cannons. On the flight deck pilots stood on ten-second alerts to scramble their A-4-Ds and Crusader F-8-U-2NEs, which were armed with Sidewinders.

In his private quarters, the skipper of the *Robert F. Kennedy*, Rear Admiral Marcus Burkholder, stood watching the second hand of the chronometer on his desk. When the hand swept past 2100 hours, Admiral

Burkholder opened the sealed envelope he was holding. After reading his instructions, which came from the Secretary himself, he picked up a telephone and punched a button at its base. He required no conscious effort of will to keep his voice crisp and steady, since thirty-odd years of taking orders without hesitation or even reflection had honed his reactions to the mechanical efficiency of a computer. "Send the following signal at five-minute intervals," he told his dispatcher, and then relayed the first phase of the Secretary's orders.

Those orders would alert the officers in command of the port of Algiers that the *R.F.K.* would be standing off the approaches to the harbor in approximately ninety minutes. . . .

Admiral Burkholder was a tall, slender man in his early fifties with cold, searching eyes, thinning wheat-colored hair, and almost classically chiseled features which were saved from routine harmony by a nose which had been broken twice in the ring in college and a scar which furrowed his forehead and gave his expression, even when he was in a good humor, a suggestion of ferocious intensity. Presently, he wore suntans, and the collar of his shirt was open, the points pulled down by the weight of his four stars, but even so, and despite the efficient air-conditioning of the ship, there was sweat on his forehead and dark patches of it staining the underarms of his shirt.

Admiral Burkholder didn't like his orders and he didn't like obeying them. But that thought was like an act of treason in itself. He had been raised as a boy in the traditions of Halsey and King and Nimitz, and he was totally and painfully at a loss in a world of Pueblos and U-2 flights, and timorous guidelines from Navy as to the treatment of enemy aliens who sought sanctuary on American ships. Admiral Burkholder was not a romantic man, not given to daydreams, but

218

occasionally he had thought wistfully of the opportunity to look across the gunsights of his carrier at an enemy ship demanding the right to board him. . . .

He went over to his desk and took out his private log and began to write an account of the curious and improbable events which had taken place in the last few hours aboard the aircraft carrier. He dated the page, and made a note of the time, and began with:

My orders were delivered by courier, Commander Frank Killorgan, who came aboard by Navy helicopter—a Bell HU-L One—at 1700 hours and 30 minutes. The Commander carried two sets of sealed orders, one from the Secretary of the Navy, one from the President of the United States.

Prior to this, I had been instructed in code by Washington to receive aboard my ship ten atomic devices of the Nevada Class. These were delivered from a disfunctional NATO base at Rota, Spain, by two U.S. Marine helicopters, Class HH53.

The atomic devices were crated in plastic containers approximately three feet square and six feet long (the Nevadas, as is generally known, are compact, sophisticated, twelfth-generation atomic warheads).

The ten crates were dispatched to a hold at a maximum distance from the nuclear reactors of the R.F.K. I was further instructed by radio code from Washington to receive aboard my ship a four-man team which would inspect the Nevadas. In a Sud-Aviation S.E. 3130, Alouette Two, this team arrived at approximately 1800 hours. The pilot stayed on the flight deck and the four men went below to inspect the Nevadas. They uncrated the devices, and, using the lead shields which are part of our ship's complement to protect themselves, they removed the fuse housings from the Nevadas and applied Geiger counters to the sub-critical masses of U-235 within the warheads. They seemed satisfied that the Nevadas were functional, and, after replacing the fuse housings, they used our short-wave radio to transmit coded messages on frequencies our monitors have detected in use in Morocco and Algeria. The inspection team has remained aboard the ship, maintaining a guard in the hold where the Nevadas are stored. The devices have been re-crated. (The members of the inspection team are small in stature, dark of complexion and in my judgment, are Lebanese or Egyptian—Arabs, in any case.)

Admiral Burkholder closed the log and began pacing once again, his eyes fixed on the chronometer on his desk. When the second hand touched 2300 hours and 30 minutes, Admiral Burkholder opened sealed orders from the President of the United States.

Chapter Fourteen

General Mercier and Major Sidki, Colonel Ben Gamal's Chief of Staff, arrived at the military airport in the environs of Algiers at 2300 hours. They said little of consequence to one another until they had cleared military checkpoints and were standing together in the enclosure which faced the airport's secondary landing strip. Red landing lights stretched away from them to the horizon, and high above them a beacon on top of the control tower cut rhythmic and brilliant slashes through the darkness.

"The values we assign to human life are very whimsical," Major Sidki said then. He wore a heavy brown overcoat which dropped almost to his ankles, and a woolen cap under his visored cap. With his bald head covered, his features seemed more animated and youthful. "In warfare a nation will sacrifice a generation of its finest young men, while in another instance, teams of doctors and nurses will exercise their devotion and skill to save the life of one small child. As now you have the spectacle of America and France hastening to do our bidding, simply to save the life of an old man whose only value is that he is the President of a sovereign state."

"Kings were always ransomed," General Mercier said. His hands and feet were cold and numb. In the last three days, a fear and self-revulsion had been growing in him like a devouring cancer, eroding whatever had been the source of his pride and dignity.

"You're right," Major Sidki said. "The kings were ransomed while common soldiers were bred for oblivion." He glanced at his watch. "We were assured that the American and British agents would arrive at 2300 hours."

"You must consider factors we can't control," General Mercier said.

"I'm afraid you don't understand us," Major Sidki said. He smiled. "You've read the Koran, you know the divisions in Islam, but you don't understand the dynamics of our strength. Pure terror is that which stems from actions devoid of self-interest. That is what we are capable of, and that is our strength."

"Let me say I don't believe you. Your acts of terror are not without self-interest, they are practical and political," General Mercier said.

"I won't concede that," Major Sidki said. He stamped his stoutly-booted feet against the numbing cold. "We might chop logic for hours, but for that we need a warm fire and mint tea. But, let me ask you this: why do you think we didn't ask the Russians to ransom President Barrault?"

"Because, in the language of the gutter, they would have told you to fuck off."

Major Sidki smiled. "Yes. It's interesting, isn't it? The Russians are crude, but they understand power.

The Americans are also crude, but they don't understand power. Consider Cuba."

Consider Hiroshima and consider Nagasaki, General Mercier thought, but he said nothing, for Major Sidki was smiling and pointing toward the horizon where the lights of a distant aircraft were probing the darkness. They heard the sound of its jets then like a faint rumble of thunder and saw the identification lights on its wings and tail assemblage blinking on and off in rhythmic patterns.

The C-58 raced down the mile-long runway, seeming too huge to have ever been airborne, and as its jets reversed with a thundering roar of protest, the air and the very earth began to vibrate with hysterical intensity. But when the pilot flamed out his jets and depressed his flaps to maximum breaking pitch, the sounds and tremors gradually faded away, and the aircraft, like something gentled and reassured, taxied smoothly toward a hard-standing where ground crews brought it to a stop with flashing torches.

A companionway was pushed into place. Doors opened in the bay of the aircraft, and Spencer and Ackerley came down the steps, briefcases in hand, and walked through the darkness to join General Mercier and Major Sidki.

They were driven from the airfield to the chateau in the hills high above the port of Algiers. Colonel Ben Gamal received them in the massively proportioned library, seated at the head of a table which Spencer noted was surfaced with mother-of-pearl and designed to function as a huge chessboard. With Colonel Gamal were two other officers, a hunchback with a scarred face, and a thick-shouldered man with coarse black hair which almost merged with his bushy eyebrows. Colonel Gamal introduced them to Spencer

223

and Ackerley as Captain Aziz of Lebanon and Captain Basra of Morocco. They had already had the pleasure of meeting Major Sidki, who now stood alongside Ben Gamal, the bright overhead lights gleaming erratically on his immense bald head.

General Mercier stood apart from Spencer and Ackerley, as if attempting to disassociate himself equally from them and the Arab captains at the table. The General's face, Spencer had noticed, was tired and lined, but it lacked the candid honor of a battered shield; instead, the weariness, the deadened, withdrawn eyes suggested something used and useless and about to be discarded without regret or compunction.

The mood of the Arabs was one of bland euphoria. It was as if they were deliberately and sensually savoring this moment, curbing their triumphant excitement in an attempt to prolong a moment of exquisite gratification. Colonel Gamal, white teeth shining against his strong olive features, puffed complacently on an Upmann, and settled back in his chair to regard Spencer and Ackerley with what seemed to be amiable interest.

"It's rather a shame that Andre Leroi sent you those letters," Colonel Ben Gamal said.

Ackerley cleared his throat and said, "If he could cast a vote, I rather imagine Harry Adams would share your views."

"As I say, it's a shame, but we are at war. We can look at it in no other way." Colonel Gamal smiled faintly at Spencer. "You knew that Caprifoil was missing of course. That information was in Leroi's first letter. But tell me, please, how did you learn that President Barrault was missing?"

Spencer realized he must tell a reasonable lie; he could not disclose that it was Andre Leroi's wife, Michele, who had told him about Barrault. He frowned at Colonel Gamal, pretending not to understand, stalling.

"Do you mean, when did I find out he was missing?"

"Allah preserve us from the ignorant," Colonel Gamal murmured, and smiled at his officers, who responded to him with approving smiles and nods.

Spencer couldn't help understanding and sympathizing in a small way with Colonel Gamal and his captains, for they had been kicked in the ass so long and their noses had been rubbed in dirt so long, that they lacked the sophistication to accept victory with the suggestion of mild regret, which the British had learned to do in centuries of conquest by armies and clubs and guns. Colonel Gamal was honestly and frankly gloating at his triumph, and at their helplessness. And his captains were savoring each rewarding and annealing moment of it.

"Mr. Spencer, I am not impatient of honest ignorance or honest mistakes," Colonel Gamal said. "But I am impatient of inexactitude and deception. Let me put my question to you again. How, not *when*, did you learn that President Barrault was being held hostage?"

"I learned that from an Interpol agent, Theophile LeMaitre."

"How did he have access to this information?"

"I don't know," Spencer said.

Colonel Gamal glanced at General Mercier. "Does that sound reasonable? Could Interpol have had this information?"

"It's possible," General Mercier said. "Interpol has close contacts at Quai D'Orsay. Theophile LeMaitre is a highly placed officer; it's likely he was briefed."

Colonel Gamal turned his attention again to Spencer and Ackerley. He smiled. "And you are here now to identify President Barrault, to determine that

225

he is healthy, to determine that we are not returning an impostor or a corpse to France."

"Those are our orders," Spencer said.

Colonel Gamal blew a fat but lopsided smoke ring into the air, and then placed his cigar in an ashtray. "Assuming that you find Barrault to be the genuine article, do you know what the Americans are prepared to give us in exchange for him?"

"No, sir, I do not," Spencer said. "Our orders are to fingerprint and examine President Barrault, and report our findings to General Rose in Paris."

Colonel Gamal seemed to be amused; his smile was bright and kindly. "You are then simply good soldiers, loyal to your superiors, blindly carrying out their orders. Is that correct?"

"You could say that, sir," Spencer said.

"Then it follows, as a corollary, that to question those orders would be disloyal. Is that correct?"

It was Ackerley who answered him. "That's not part of our job, sir."

"Let me ask you a question then," Colonel Gamal said, and his tone was so idle and incurious that his audience anticipated additional significance from whatever he was getting at. "Do you realize that your blind acceptance of these orders has placed you both in a very dangerous position?"

"I don't understand, sir," Spencer said.

"It's obvious enough, I should think. Regardless of what your examination of President Barrault indicates, we can make you tell General Rose anything we want." Colonel Gamal smiled pleasantly. "Now, can't we?"

"Not true," Spencer said. "The exchange between General Rose and me will be authenticated by a personal question-and-answer code, which means the General will ask me two questions relating to my personal life. I don't know what the questions are, but I am the only one who can know the answers. If I do not reply accurately within three seconds, the connection will be broken in Paris, and it will be presumed that the President of France is dead."

Colonel Gamal nodded thoughtfully. "And you believe that's foolproof?"

"I'm sure of it, sir," Spencer said. "May I?" Without waiting for a reply, he picked up Colonel Gamal's smouldering cigar and held it between thumb and forefinger above the back of his hand. "Would you mind counting to three, sir?" he said, and lowered the tip of the cigar to his wrist.

Colonel Gamal smiled. "An interesting demonstration," he said, and glanced at Captain Basra. "One." He nodded thoughtfully and looked at Major Sidki. "Two." He was still smiling, but there was a suggestion of confusion in his expression as his eyes went to Captain Aziz, the hunchback from Lebanon. "Three."

Spencer released his breath and dropped Colonel Gamal's cigar in the ashtray. "You see, sir, there is nothing you could do in three seconds that would make me falsify a report of any kind."

Colonel Gamal laughed and glanced at his captains. "And they call us devious and tricky," he said. But his manner had changed; he seemed more relaxed and friendly. He came around the table and patted Spencer on the shoulder. "That was effective, but unnecessary, as you'll see. Do you want something for that burn?"

"No, it's all right," Spencer said.

"Then let's go upstairs." Colonel Gamal patted Spencer on the shoulder again, a diffident respect in his manner, and said, "I think I can trust you. I hope so. At any rate, will you and Mr. Ackerley give your sidearms to Major Sidki?"

Spencer and Ackerley removed their hand guns from their holsters and extended them butt first to the

Major, who removed the clips and placed them on the table and then dropped the guns into the pockets of his tunic.

The group left the library and went up a wide, spiralling staircase to the second floor, where troops of the Saracen Vector stood at regular intervals along the corridors. Out of habit, Spencer attempted a head-count but gave up when he reached a hundred. It was a pointless exercise; there was no knowing how many men there were outside the villa, and on the road leading down to Algiers. He had seen hundreds on the ride up from the airport.

Colonel Gamal and Spencer walked abreast, with Ackerley and Mercier behind them and Gamal's captains in the rear, casually returning the salutes of the soldiers posted at ten-foot intervals along the corridors.

The time was 2400 hours and 28 minutes, Spencer knew. There were now thirty-two minutes left to meet the timetable imposed upon him by General Rose.

Colonel Gamal was saying, "You are a simple soldier, but I don't think that's so simple. We may disagree, I don't know. But obedience is not a small virtue. It seems to us that when an order is given, and when that order is executed faithfully, a third grace is created by the merger of these two things. Like the Holy Spirit that exists only between the intraction of God the Father and God the Son in the Christian belief. Tell me, do you have sons?"

"I have a son," Spencer said.

"I am pleased for you." Colonel Gamal sounded gloomy. "I have only two daughters, and to say that daughters are a delight——" The Colonel shrugged. "I don't know. It's like saying roses are fragrant, that birds sing at nightfall."

They turned a corner into a wider corridor and

228

walked past lines of soldiers whose evidence of rank indicated to Spencer that they were approaching more significant security areas. On the sleeves and tunics of the squat dark soldiers were haphazard displays of chevrons, pips and hash marks, representing commissioned and non-commissioned insignia from French and British and even American uniforms. At the end of the corridor were double doors standing open, and beyond them a large drawing room or library with soldiers and officers of the Saracen Vector standing at casual attention.

As they entered the room, Spencer rapidly noted details. Double French windows, giving on balconies, with a courtyard below, six soldiers on guard, seeming more alert than those he had seen in the corridors. Three wore sidearms, two carried antiquated M-3s which fired .45 caliber ammo, but the sixth man, a British Captain if his pips meant anything, had an AR-18 slung over his shoulder, and Spencer wondered how this new and beautiful American weapon with its folding stock and formidable rate of fire had got halfway around the world from the battlefields of Vietnam to this improbable villa in Algeria.

Colonel Gamal pointed to an adjoining bedroom and said: "Gentlemen, the President of France. You may begin your examination."

In the bedroom, which was separated from the library drawing room by an archway and a short corridor and carved doors which stood open, President Barrault was sleeping in a double bed under a coverlet of heavily embroidered silk, breathing slowly and evenly, his snowy hair spread against a pillow to form a corona about his massive head.

"He is under mild sedation," Colonel Gamal said. "Considering his age and temperament, we thought that advisable. Correct, Mercier?" Colonel Gamal did

229

not snap his fingers at the General, but the gesture was suggested in the sharpness of his voice. "Right?"

"Yes," General Mercier said. He sat down on a chair that faced the windows and the courtyard and at last the shining sea. He looked weary and confused and the military spring was gone from his carriage. He held his body together with an effort, as if it were a clumsy, loosely tied package which he was afraid might any minute slip from his hands.

Spencer and Ackerley went into the bedroom and began their examination of President Barrault. Colonel Gamal stood watching them from the corridor that connected the bedroom and the library.

It was then at the stroke of the half hour; thirty minutes from deadline. It would have been an easy matter to stall, to provoke delays, if President Barrault had been conscious; they could have asked ineptly phrased questions, insisted on an interpreter and pretended not to understand what the old man was saying, but under the present circumstances, none of these tactics was available to them and their examination under the careful eye of Colonel Gamal progressed with frightening efficiency. Spencer rolled the fingertips and thumb of the old man across an ink-pad and then applied them to papers which he examined with a magnifying glass, and checked against the official prints given him by General Rose. Ackerley took the President's pulse and blood pressure and found them within the upper reaches of normal. He looked into his eyes and placed a stethoscope against his chest, and while he was making note of these results on a medical chart, Spencer rolled up the President's shirt sleeve and looked at a scar that traversed his tricep, a result of a shrapnel wound he had received at the Maginot Line during World War II, and as he did this, the old man stirred unexpectedly and opened his large gray eyes and stared

230

straight at Spencer. He murmured something in French which Spencer didn't understand, but hearing the question in President Barrault's voice, Spencer made a guess and said: "I'm an American. My name is Spencer. It's all right, sir."

Colonel Gamal walked into the room, looking suspiciously at Spencer, but by then, the old man had closed his eyes and Spencer shrugged and said, "He asked me who I was. I thought it best to answer him."

"Are you satisfied, then?" Gamal said.

"Yes," Spencer said. The examination had taken only five minutes; the remaining twenty-five stretched off to eternity.

But to Spencer's relief, when Colonel Gamal glanced at Ackerley, Ackerley looped the stethoscope about his neck and said: "Well, I'm not satisfied, not by half." He walked past Colonel Gamal into the library, shaking his head decisively.

Gamal ran after him and shouted: "What do you mean, you are not satisfied? Do you think you are in command here?"

Ackerley turned and threw his head back and looked down his long nose at Colonel Gamal, a large, fair and confident man who might have been standing in his own club regarding an inept servant with only mild interest. "You've asked me to examine this old gentleman, but I've no way of knowing if you're sincere," he said. "I'll confess I never understood you chaps. Dare say, I never tried. But you can't expect me, as a medical man and a British subject, to make an examination without some immediate medical history. I mean, how do I know he hasn't been tampered with?" Ackerley's well-bred tones suggested something gross. Spencer knew what Ackerley was doing, and it was a charade he himself could never have managed. He could have ripped the AR-18 from the young soldier with the captain's pips and broken his face with it, but he couldn't stand as Ackerley was standing and remind Gamal by his very presence and being that he came from a race of men who venerated fair ladies with the mists of Devon in their hair and who had shamed the lesser breeds out of their lands and rights by a force of arms and the way they wore their dinner clothes. How many times had Ackerley's people found starving Arabs stealing from their kitchens and flogged them for it, and how many times had Arab servants been booted in the backside for failing to bring the proper shine to polo boots?

"What more do you want?" Gamal cried angrily. "We have taken care of him, given him everything."

"That's very well to say, but I'd like to see someone who's been in contact with him this last week. I'd like to know what drugs he's been given, that sort of thing." Ackerley abruptly pointed a finger at Spencer. "And please, let's hear no Yank talk about expediency, is that quite clear? I'm not sure I understand you people either."

Colonel Gamal furiously snapped an order at one of his soldiers and when the man hurried from the room, he said to Ackerley, "I think we can satisfy your medical sense of propriety."

"Do you now, really," Ackerley said, and the idle dismissing question further widened the distance between them and forever placed Colonel Gamal in the company of wandering Arabs crossing deserts without purpose on stinking camels.

When the soldier returned to the room, he was accompanied by Andre Leroi. Colonel Gamal said, "Caprifoil is no longer missing," but because his confidence was splintered and he was roiling with timeless, bitter angers, the phrase lacked the irony and significance he hoped to give it.

There was a moment of silence as Ackerley and
232

Spencer and Leroi stared at one another and then Ackerley cleared his throat and said, "Hello, Andre."

"Hello, Bunny. Hello, August," Andre Leroi said.

"Were you expecting us?" Spencer asked him.

"No." Andre Leroi glanced at General Mercier, who sat staring out the window toward the sea. A tic pulled rhythmically at the corner of the general's lower lip and gave the impression that he was smiling in a mechanical and programmed fashion, like a robot. "Mercier didn't tell me you were joining us," Andre Leroi said.

Spencer marvelled at his aplomb and poise. In a formal black suit, without a hair out of place, Andre looked as casual and relaxed as if he had encountered them by chance in a Paris café. Andre Leroi came from the race that had effortlessly dominated Morocco and Algeria, from a race of poets and logicians, and from soldiers who called their troops to attention to salute choice vineyards in the Medoc, and some of this was in his cool regard of Colonel Gamal.

"Tell him," Colonel Gamal shouted at Leroi, while jabbing his finger at Ackerley. "Tell him your President is in excellent health. Tell him we have done nothing to him, we have given him no drugs, only a sleeping potion to let him rest. He thinks we are dogs, he thinks we are savages. Tell him we have protected your President."

Colonel Gamal's mercurial angers had infected his captains, and Captain Basra was muttering bitterly to himself, while Major Sidki's eyes were rolling in his head like a stallion scenting smoke and fire in a barn.

"Yes, I will explain the matter to him," Andre Leroi said.

With an abrupt and unsettling change of pace, Ackerley said, "Well, I wish you'd get on with it, Andre, and stop wasting our bloody time. Colonel Gamal's been decent about all this, I must say. Damned patient with us."

It was a cue and Andre didn't miss it. Hurry-up meant slow-down....

"Of course, we must cooperate with Colonel Gamal," Andre Leroi said. "But what is it precisely you wish to know?"

"You've been with him every day?"

"Yes."

"And he seemed quite lucid?"

"I beg your pardon. I didn't mean to imply that I was with the President throughout the day. I usually saw him for a brief time in the morning and again in the afternoon."

"But on those occasions he seemed quite lucid?"

"Yes, quite lucid."

"And he's been given no drugs, except a sleeping pill?"

"As far as I know, yes."

"What's that supposed to mean? As far as you know?"

Colonel Gamal was watching them with growing suspicion and Spencer realized they were stretching the game past safe limits. He said: "I think it's clear enough what he means, Ackerley."

"Well, I rather expected that from you," Ackerley said. "Get the job done, one way or another." His sigh absolved himself from shoddy expediency. "Very well, I'll concede. I've done all I can."

But he hadn't done enough, Spencer knew, as he left the library with Colonel Gamal, to report to General Rose.

It was still eight minutes from the one o'clock deadline....

The story had always disturbed and haunted Admiral Marcus Burkholder, because he had never consciously or unconsciously been tempted by the Manichean heresy. On the contrary, he believed as effortlessly as he breathed air in and out of his lungs, that God must always triumph over the devil, the good must always overcome evil, and that the United States of America must always vanquish her enemies, foreign and domestic, in the present and in the future. It was repugnant to him to think of the conflict between God and the devil as a toss-up, a stand-off, an inconclusive battle to be decided by a referee or the flip of a coin. He could not understand treason, although to his credit he had tried to. But he could no more embrace the concept of being a disloyal American than he could embrace the concept of not being alive. It was a simple credo, but it had given him the privilege of serving his God and country with stubborn intensity and affection.

And for these reasons, the story of the cruiser *Indianapolis* had always haunted him. The *Indianapolis* had delivered the atom bombs to the Mariannas Command three decades ago and those weapons had surely been used on the side of God, for they had brought an end to the most savage war in the history of the world. But more significantly, they had saved the lives of probably a million American soldiers who might have died had it been necessary to invade Japan.

And yet on its homing course, the *Indianapolis* had been sunk in the Philippine Sea with a loss of 880 American lives. There had been a communications foul-up; radio signals had been garbled, and the *Indianapolis*, her flanks unprotected, had steamed into the path of a Japanese submarine, whose officers had sighted along a lance of moonlight, and had ripped open her starboard side with six torpedoes.

The story haunted the Admiral, for if ever a ship

and her crew deserved a safe trip home under gentle winds, it had been the cruiser *Indianapolis*.

He paced the floor of his quarters aware unconsciously of the lessening roll of his ship, the orders from President Montrose in one hand, and his other anxiously rubbing the permanent furrow in his forehead.

The admiral had been ordered to steam into the Port of Algiers on a course and at a speed given him by the Harbor Master at Algiers. He had been ordered to place the *Robert F. Kennedy* under the temporary command of the Harbor Master, and to allow a work party of Algerians to board his ship and remove the ten atomic devices of the Nevada Class.

His first reaction had been an oath and a vow that he would not do it. He had knelt and prayed for strength, but had found no peace.

He wanted help from without or within, but there was nothing to buttress him, nothing to support him, nothing but the orders in his hand signed by the President of his country, and he knew in sudden loneliness that he would obey them without ever knowing whether he was doing right or wrong.

He strode rapidly to the phone on his desk, knowing that delays were the seeds of mutiny, and snapped a switch and gave his orders to the bridge.

An incredulous officer said: "*What!*"

As flustered and uncertain as a midshipman, the admiral shouted, "Tack a *sir* on that, Mister," and broke the connection.

"Thank you," Spencer said to Colonel Gamal, and nodded his appreciation to the corpsman who had applied a salve and a bandage to the burn on his wrist.

"That is the penalty of heroics," Colonel Gamal said. "We pay for them in private."

They stood at the end of the corridor facing a large

room which had been converted into a communications center. Soldiers of the Saracen Vector in their motley uniforms stood at intervals up and down the long corridor, which stretched between the communications center and the library where Spencer had left Ackerley and Andre Leroi. In an attempt to gain time, Spencer had pretended that the discomfort of his burn was acute, and Colonel Gamal had insisted on summoning a corpsman to treat him. Spencer casually adjusted the bandage on his wrist and checked his watch; it was three minutes of one.

"It's more comfortable?" Colonel Gamal asked him.

"Yes. It's fine," Spencer said. The Colonel seemed relaxed and at ease with him, Spencer thought; at least, he apparently preferred his company, and their straightforward, almost friendly exchanges, to the psychological hazings he had suffered from Ackerley and Andre Leroi.

The communications center was as large as the outsized downstairs library, and brilliantly illuminated by overhead tubes of fluorescent lighting. Five uniformed operators sat facing what Spencer surmised to be 5,000-watt Single Sight Band V.F.O. transmitters. They wore earphones and faced standing mikes and telegraph keys and panels with rheostats to tune desired frequencies. Monitors were emplaced in the walls above the transmitters. On another wall were large maps of Europe and North Africa. In the middle of the room were two hydraulically operated antenna towers, whose tapering columns fitted snugly through apertures in the ceiling. At an order from Colonel Gamal, a radio operator threw a switch, and one of the six-inch metal columns moved swiftly upward to elevate the exterior antenna. The stationary column, Spencer guessed, was one-dimensional, while the column that had been activated was probably

237

omni-directional, with a tuning potential to refine its signal to any given point on the compass.

"Five hundred and forty kilocycles," Colonel Gamal said to the radio operator nearest him, and the soldier nodded and turned the rheostat to the prescribed frequency. Colonel Gamal picked up a microphone and handed it to Spencer. "It's the old-fashioned, push-talk, release-listen system. You're familiar with it, I imagine."

"Yes, I'm familiar with it," Spencer said.

Colonel Gamal glanced at the loudspeakers above the transmitters. "We will monitor your conversation, you understand."

"Yes, of course," Spencer said, his voice steady, almost casual, but he could feel the heavy stroke of his heart as Colonel Gamal gave an order in Arabic to the radio operators, who began to complete their connections to the American Embassy in Paris. But before contact was made, one of the operators turned and beckoned to Colonel Gamal. Gamal walked over to the operator, who removed his earphone and gave them to the Colonel. Static filled the room, abrasive splinters of noise, cracking and reverberating as if someone were shredding tinfoil in front of a microphone, but distantly through these interruptions Spencer could hear General Rose's voice, tiny and indistinct, the sense of the words smothered in erratic electronic currents.

Major Sidki came into the communications center. He was smiling widely and the shine of his teeth matched the shine of the overhead lights on his bald head. Colonel Gamal gave the earphones back to the operator and turned and grinned at Major Sidki. In their expressions Spencer saw more than pleasure and satisfaction; their smiles were blissful and radiant. They embraced and pounded one another on the shoulders and backs. Their laughter became so festive
238

that the radio operators turned in their chairs and smiled at them like children watching a sudden bizarre performance by adults.

"It's done, it's done!" Colonel Gamal shouted happily.

The static faded away and General Rose's voice sounded from the monitoring loudspeakers above the transmitters.

"I'm answering your signal on a frequency of 540 from Paris. This is General Rose. I will speak to August Spencer."

Colonel Gamal turned from Major Sidki and gripped Spencer's arm. "You heard. It's done. The *Robert F. Kennedy* is at anchor in the Port of Algiers. When you assure General Rose that President Barrault is alive and healthy, our working parties will board the carrier. Make your report."

Spencer depressed the button on the hand of his microphone and said what he had been told to say: "I am Spencer."

There was silence. Everyone in the communications center stared up at the speakers. Then General Rose's voice sounded again: "We have authenticated your voice, Spencer. Here are the questions you will have three seconds to answer: Your foster father, Colonel Andrew Bradford, once gave you a pony on your birthday. The questions are: What did you name that pony? How old were you on the birthday? Reply immediately."

"I named the pony Bellflower. I was fifteen."

"Please report, Spencer."

Colonel Gamal sighed and smiled and patted Spencer awkwardly and affectionately on the shoulder.

"I have fingerprinted President Barrault and checked his scar against the description of it in his service records. The man I examined is, without any

239

doubt, President Barrault. His pulse and blood pressure are normal and, although he is under sedation, Wyndom Ackerley states that his general health is good."

Static erupted from the loudspeakers, and Colonel Gamal and Major Sidki glanced at them curiously. Then the static faded away and they heard a man's voice speaking in French, but the words blurred together so rapidly that Spencer caught only a few of them. He heard the word "alert" and the word "mutiny" and the words "Nord-Atlas" and the word "Bordeaux," but when he glanced uncertainly at Colonel Gamal, Spencer realized that the Colonel had understood all of the message and didn't like it. His expression was one of thoughtful appraisal, but while he seemed to be making an effort to restrain his anger, his eyes looked hot with confusion and suspicion.

The speakers were abruptly silent. Then General Rose's voice came in again. "Spencer, can you hear me?"

"Yes, sir."

"Is Colonel Gamal with you?"

"Yes, sir."

"Then please ask the colonel to listen to me." General Rose's voice was quite calm and steady, but this laconic, matter-of-fact tone was one that Spencer had heard on battlefields, and it suggested only one thing to him, the suppression of panic by an act of will. "We just received this alert from the commander of the French air squadron at Bordeaux. They've had a mutiny. Several platoons of General Mercier's paratroops have taken off without orders. Coastal radar plots their course due south to Algiers. We don't know what it means yet, but it's an unauthorized mission and the officers commanding it are in direct violation of orders. Spencer, is Colonel Gamal monitoring us?"

"Yes, sir."

240

"I want to talk to him. Will you put him on?"

Spencer glanced at Colonel Gamal, who looked without expression at Major Sidki and then shook his head with slow finality.

"Negative, sir," Spencer said.

"Goddamnit, he's got to understand—"

The speakers went silent; a radio operator had broken the connection at a nod from Colonel Gamal. The stillness in the room seemed close and unnatural to Spencer. The radio operators sat rigidly in front of their transmitters, and Major Sidki was staring as silently and expectantly at Colonel Gamal as an attack-trained guard dog.

The colonel walked to the windows and pulled back the heavy draperies, and beyond him Spencer could see the lights of the port on the horizon.

"It's a question of how much we are to believe," Colonel Gamal said, and he turned from the windows to look at the wall maps. He took a gold pencil from the pocket of his tunic and walked to a map and drew a line from the city of Bordeaux down across the sea to Algiers.

"I have several questions for the general," Colonel Gamal said, studying the map. Without turning, he snapped his fingers at the radio operators. "Make the connection to Paris." To Spencer he said: "Ask the general for the exact time the French aircraft left Bordeaux, and the number of troops involved in this mission."

When the connection was reestablished and Spencer had repeated these questions, General Rose's voice, edged now with tension, filled the communications center.

"At two-three-zero-zero-minus-eight. Approximately two hours and fifteen minutes ago. The commander's body-count indicates there are seventy-four paratroops, including non-coms, and eight officers airborne

241

at 23 minus 8, in a pair of Nord-Atlas 250-8s. You've got to make him understand this is a fanatic and suicidal—"

Again the speakers were silent; again Colonel Gamal had ordered the operators to break the connection to Paris. Colonel Gamal studied the map and the pencil line he had drawn from Bordeaux to Algiers, and made an x on the line somewhere south of the Balearic Islands. Then he murmured a few words in Arabic to Major Sidki, who nodded and left the communications center. Colonel Gamal made a last inspection of the map, and then turned to Spencer. "Well, what do you think?" He was smiling, and he seemed pleased with himself. "Is this a French-American trick? One more kick in the ass for the poor Arabs? Or do you believe your General Rose?"

"Loyalty isn't a very logical emotion," Spencer said. "If Mercier's troops want to commit suicide, how can you talk them out of it?"

"Ask General Rose what steps they are taking in Paris to abort this mission."

This time the radio operators reestablished contact without waiting for orders from the colonel, and when Spencer repeated his question, General Rose said: "We've scrambled two Ranger Battalions in the fastest equipment we've got, and our projection is that we can intercept the Nord-Atlases before they reach the coast of Africa. If Colonel Gamal will maintain security, we can eliminate the French paratroops."

Colonel Gamal laughed unexpectedly and when Spencer turned to him, he saw that the Colonel's eyes were warm and lively and expectant, and he wondered then, without bitterness or much interest, if there was hope for any of them, any hope for the world, for in the Colonel's expression was the masked lust he had seen at times in the eyes of Ackerley and Harry Adams and other friends and other enemies over the years—the need for challenge, sacrifice and death, the exultant gratitude at the opportunity to obey unexamined orders, to worship dubious flags or altars. . . . It was dignity of race, pride in manhood, that was shining in Colonel Gamal's eyes.

The colonel laughed again and said: "Tell your general we'll protect the President of France. The kick-ass Arabs, a race of men casually referred to as rats by the French, those sordid, thieving bastards—" Colonel Gamal's voice rose emotionally. "Tell them we will destroy Mercier's lunatics and conclude our agreements with France and America in honor. But tell him also, if this is a deception, I will blow their President's brains out myself."

Spencer and the colonel left the communications center and walked back along the corridor to the second-floor library. Only a half-dozen soldiers were still on duty, and Spencer surmised from the shouts and running footsteps he could hear outside the villa that the bulk of the Saracen Vector's troops were being deployed down the road toward the port and in a perimeter defense of the villa. Above them was a sudden thunder of jets. They were flying low, rupturing the air, and Spencer could feel the floor tremble beneath him. From the high ceilings flecks of paint and plaster fell and swirled around them in erratic patterns. When they entered the library, Spencer noted the tension in the expressions of the soldiers guarding Ackerley and Mercier and Andre Leroi. One of them, the stocky soldier with the captain's pips and the AR-18 slung over his shoulder, stood at the window staring apprehensively into the darkness, where they could hear the explosive and crescendoing wail of jet aircraft.

A phone on a table rang and Colonel Gamal answered it. He listened and said, "I don't know who they are," and his voice was hoarse.

243

Captain Aziz, the hunchback from Lebanon, came sidling into the room like a giant crab, knuckles swinging below his knees, his face a rigid mask of anxiety. "The aircraft are from the *Robert F. Kennedy*," he said to Colonel Gamal. "We have a signal from the captain of the ship, an Admiral Burkholder, who reports he has orders from Washington to keep his aircraft in the air during the transfer."

Gamal pounded a fist angrily on the table. "Tell him to send his aircraft out to sea and south of Bizerte. They are destroying our radar cover."

"Admiral Burkholder reports there are Russian trawlers escorted by naval units steaming south from Corsica."

Colonel Gamal rubbed his jaw in a nervous gesture, and looked at General Mercier. "Have you had any reports of Russian naval activity so far west of Sicily?"

General Mercier still sat slumped in a chair facing the windows, but he seemed oblivious to the darkness in front of him, and equally oblivious to the men in the room. "I don't know," he said to Colonel Gamal. "It's probable."

Colonel Gamal looked in fuming exasperation at Captain Aziz. "What class of aircraft is assigned to the *Robert F. Kennedy?*"

"I don't know," Captain Aziz said.

"Damn! Didn't you ask?"

Captain Aziz sighed. "There is interference. We lost our signal to the carrier."

Major Sidki hurried into the library from the corridor, the bright overhead light splintering on the sweat of his bald head. "We have secured the road and all approaches to the villa," he said to Colonel Gamal. But he was obviously holding something back; in his expression was the hang-dog look of a messenger who wants credit for bearing good news before confessing disasters.

244

Interpreting this, Colonel Gamal said sharply, "And?"

"Our radar equipment is useless, sir."

Colonel Gamal nodded thoughtfully. Curiously, Spencer decided, the Colonel seemed to accept the information with dour satisfaction. He glanced at Spencer and then he turned and looked toward the open doors of the bedroom where President Barrault lay motionless under a light coverlet.

"I trust you made my intentions clear to your General Rose," he said.

"As emphatically as I could, sir."

The air above the villa was turbulent with the sound of the streaking jets, and Spencer sensed a betrayal in the winds that shook the old floors and created a humming vibration in the leaded window panes. And he sensed the colonel was aware of it. He was more comfortable in defeat than he would have been in victory, Spencer realized, and this made him even more dangerous. In some fashion, he knew he had been betrayed by the clever white man who had raped his race and land for centuries. He must have known all along that would happen; deep in his unconscious, he had known they would destroy him. But secure in his timeless role of victim, the colonel had been bred to fight hopeless battles without fear of consequences.

When Colonel Gamal, with a deliberate and ritualistic gesture, unbuttoned the flap of his holster, Spencer shot a glance at Ackerley and said, "Colonel, can I make a suggestion?"

"Please do."

"The planes flying off the *Kennedy* are Navy A-4-Ds," Spencer said. "Your gunners can identify the Nord-Atlas planes by sound, because they're twin-prop jobs with twin tail-booms. They can also identify

245

them by their speed because compared to the A-4-Ds, the Nord-Atlas 250-8s seem to be standing still."

"That's valid," Andre Leroi said. "You don't need radar, Colonel." Andre Leroi seemed unaware of the subtle but steadily accelerating tensions in the room; the angle of his narrow head, the way he stroked his small dark mustache, even the casual tone of his voice suggested a civilized disengagement from impending crisis. But Spencer wasn't fooled by his seemingly detached attitude.

"Yes, that's quite true," Ackerley said, and strolled with apparent aimlessness toward a soldier who was watching Colonal Gamal. "But Spencer, doesn't the *Kennedy* have a complement of Crusaders?"

"Yes, of course," Spencer said. "They have Crusaders."

"What are they?" Colonel Gamal asked him.

"F-8-Us, Navy fighters; they're armed with Sidewinders. But there's no way to mistake one for a Nord-Atlas, they're one-third the size. . . ."

The colonel's composure was deserting him, and he seemed tense and agitated again as they prodded him from the inbred security of defeat toward victory.

Shots sounded below them in the garden, and a man screamed in agony. Machine guns were firing from the road, each burst stingingly clear and isolated in the silence. Over the constant wail of the jets there was a crash of pounding footsteps from the first floor of the villa.

Suddenly the room blazed with light. The panes of the single undraped window seemed coated with a pale and brilliant fire. Major Sidki ran to the double French doors, his eyes bright with panic, and jerked aside the heavy velvet draperies. He recoiled from a sky as white and blazing as a sun-bleached desert. Flares were falling on the road and in the gardens and high in the hills, changing the black night to high

246

noon, and in this terrible radiance, soldiers of the Saracen Vector ran like fleeting shadows, stumbling and falling, while bursts of machine-gun fire crashed like exclamation points above the thunder of circling planes. And through the unnatural light, descending on the villa as if to smother it, came waves of parachutes and paratroopers. Not seventy-odd of Mercier's fanatics, not a strike by mutinous, suicidal soldiers, but an attack in force by the regular French army.

Colonel Gamal screamed in a spasm of rage. He pulled an automatic from his holster and ran toward the bedroom, but General Mercier leaped after him and caught his arm, pleading with him in words that were lost in the noise of the jets. When Colonel Gamal threw him aside, and fired two shots that tore the general's face apart, Spencer spun and kicked the soldier with the captain's pips in the stomach and ripped the AR-18 from his limp hands. The gun was not on automatic, it was not even on semi-automatic, it was on safe, and Spencer thought they never had a chance, not one goddamn chance, as he flipped the safe-lever to automatic and fired a burst that almost cut Colonel Gamal in two and knocked him sprawling into the corridor between the library and the bed-room.

Soldiers of the Saracen Vector, a ragged squad of four, ran in terror along the corridor and into the li-brary, and Spencer, on his knees, and in profile to them, fired a second burst that piled their lifeless bodies in a heap in the doorway. Andre Leroi put a knee into Captain Aziz' face, sending the hunchback to the floor, and Ackerley leaped up from the soldier he had half-throttled and ran toward Major Sidki, but it was a futile charge, as gallant as flags in a stiff wind, but futile nonetheless, for Major Sidki's gun was in his hands by then, and he fired three shots

247

that struck Ackerley with the impact of powerful fists. He stumbled to his knees and then collapsed and fell to the floor, choking out his life. Too late, a lifetime too late, Andre Leroi struck Major Sidki from behind, and kicked the gun from his hand. There were tears of anger in his eyes as he looked beyond Ackerley's fallen body, beyond the destruction of General Mercier, to the bedroom where President Barrault was snoring gently in his sleep.

When the first French paratroopers burst into the library, their blood up, eager to kill anything that moved, Andre Leroi checked them with an unraised hand and pointed toward the President of France. Then he knelt beside Spencer, who had turned Ackerley on his back.

Ackerley was alive and he was trying to say something, and while the words were clear enough, they made no sense to Spencer. It was something about another battle, or another war, something about the XV Corps, the Fricourt Woods.

"What is it, Bunny?" Spencer said very quietly. "What is it?"

Ackerley died before he could tell Spencer the rest of it.

Chapter Fifteen

The call came into the Oval Office a few minutes past eight o'clock on a line that had been cleared direct to Paris for the previous sixteen hours.

"Shall I take it, sir?" General Rose asked the President.

"No, if it's bad, I want it first-hand."

The President and General Rose had slept only fitfully during the night; they had kept the long vigil with coffee and aspirin, and they were both in need of shaves and rest and clean linen. President Montrose put a hand on the telephone, picked up the receiver and said: "Yes?"

Within seconds, he was grinning broadly, and General Rose, knowing the dangerous gamble had been won, let out his breath slowly, and sat down in the leather chair facing the President's desk. He was trembling with exhaustion, but he was smiling at the President, who was saying, "Please extend my personal congratulations to every member of your staff, to everyone at the Embassy, Jack. They've done a magnificent job. Also, I want you to call on President Barrault as soon as possible, and give him my kindest personal regards."

President Montrose replaced the receiver and glanced at General Rose.

"It's over," he said. "President Barrault is back in Paris."

"I don't think it's over, sir. I don't see how they can keep a lid on it."

"It's their house, General, and they'll have to clean it up. There will be rumors, but they will be officially denied. With luck, they may get away with it."

"I believe they'll need more than luck, sir. They can camouflage General Mercier's death in a dozen-odd ways, I'm sure, but everything will come unglued if Algeria makes an official protest to the French government."

"Take my word for it, they won't," President Montrose said. "We knew in advance the welcome mat was out. Unofficially, the Algerian government was pleased to have the French Army do a job on the Saracen Vector. It would have been political suicide for any responsible Arab leader to denounce the Saracen Vector, but most of them not only feared it, they despised it."

"President Montrose, I think I have been as close to you as any man in your administration," General Rose said. "I mention that because I want to ask you a question I know is out of line."

"Well, fire away," President Montrose smiled and fingered the tiny golden dragon which adorned his watch chain. "But I can't promise I'll answer it."

"I understand that. But if this story ever breaks, this is a question which may be asked by millions."

General Rose hesitated, and President Montrose
250

broke the uneasy silence by saying: "I told you, fire away."

"It's this, sir: were you committed to delivering those ten atomic devices to the Saracen Vector?"

President Montrose looked thoughtfully at the tiny dragon he was toying with. One of its ruby eyes was sparkling in the faint sunlight that was now drifting through the fog above the city. He was mildly irritated by General Rose's question, but he tried not to show it and considered how best to answer it.

He had promised the provisional French government three things, and three things only: number one, he had promised to make a convincing pretense of acceding to the demands of the Saracen Vector. But he had made it bluntly clear that he would send only disfunctional atomic devices to the *Robert F. Kennedy*. Navy Engineering had removed the subcritical masses of U-235 from ten Nevadas and had replaced them with comparable amounts of non-fissionable U-238. These elements had then been thinly coated with sufficient U-235 to activate Gieger counters and to pass reasonable inspection. Number two, he had assumed the responsibility of determining that President Barrault was, in fact, alive, and had coordinated that information with the French plan to attack the villa in Algiers with regiments of paratroopers. Number three, he had ordered Admiral Burkholder to scramble his aircraft to disrupt the Saracen Vector's radar screens, thus allowing the French airborne units to approach the villa undetected.

"I'll answer your question this way," President Montrose said. "I assured the French spokesmen, that is, their counter-espionage people, that we would establish a convincing charade in the Mediterranean. I told them we'd appear to have our hands on the trigger, with all elements at a war-strike basis. But I couldn't make any further commitments. We determined that

Barrault was alive at Zero Hour. We got that signal through August Spencer, and the Britisher who was killed, Wyndom Ackerley. We put up one hell of a smokescreen by jamming all radar on that coast. The Nord-Atlas strike, Mercier's fanatic troops, that was part of the charade. You weren't briefed so your reaction was sufficiently uptight to be plausible. But we were never even close to fail-safe. General, I am going to let you in on a well-kept secret. I have a small ketch in Tulagi Harbor which allows me to assume at any hour of the day that the sun is under the yard-arm. What's your pleasure?"

Shortly before noon, an elderly waiter carried a tray of coffee and croissants along the pleasantly shabby corridor of the Hotel Angleterre in Paris. He rapped lightly on a door and when a voice answered he went into the small bedroom. Spencer was at a dresser topped by an oblong mirror, brushing his hair. He wasn't wearing a shirt and the muscles in his big arms and shoulders flexed as he used the brush. His Browning was under a towel on top of the dresser, and Spencer watched the waiter in the mirror as he placed the tray and a folded newspaper on a bedside table. Spencer gave the old man a few coins and locked the door when he left.

He drank a cup of the hot, bitter coffee and studied the picture of General Mercier which was on the first page of *Le Monde*. The accompanying story, which he scanned quickly, didn't surprise him. "The nation mourns ... the loss of its great centurion ... training accident ... a tragic crash in the Deep Desert ... a routine flight ... paratroop maneuvers...."

There was nothing about Ackerley, of course. The British press would have a paragraph or two on that, a puzzling and sordid casualty in a cheap bar or brothel....

252

The phone began to ring. It was a long-distance call, and after the usual electronic noises and interruptions by overseas operators, Spencer heard Denise's voice.

"August, can you hear me?"

"Yes, go ahead. It's fine."

"Well, I hear odd buzzings. I think it's the connection."

"I can hear you," Spencer said.

The trouble might not be the overseas operators or distant, far-flung relay points; the trouble could be downstairs at the switchboard of the Angleterre, where an operator might be monitoring their conversation.

"When did you arrive?"

"Just an hour or so ago. It's marvelous, but it's cold, August. I've already had a hot bath and I'm sipping a little cognac."

"Just be as comfortable as you can. I'll be there in a few days."

"A few days!" Denise's voice was surprised and unhappy. "Why so long?"

"I've got some business matters to settle, the usual loose ends." He couldn't go straight to Denise, he would have to zigzag until he was certain he wasn't under surveillance.

"Will you cable me when you're arriving? I want to meet your flight."

"Don't worry. I'll let you know."

When he rang off, Spencer finished dressing, packed a single bag and went downstairs to find a cab to take him to Andre Leroi's apartment in the Sixteenth.

He wasn't sure whether anyone followed him on the trip across the river and through the heavy traffic on the boulevards. When the cab stopped at Andre's,

253

Spencer left his luggage in the rear seat and asked the driver to wait for him.

Andre was standing in the open door of his apartment, and there was a sadness and resignation in his manner, which Spencer realized reflected his own emotions at what must be a reluctant and not quite honorable farewell.

"I left my things in the cab," Spencer said.

"Good. If anyone is interested in you, that should nail them down for a while. My car is downstairs in the garage. I'll drive you to the airport. Michele wants to see you. What do you think?"

"Let's skip that," Spencer said.

"I think you're wise."

... Spencer and Andre Leroi had returned from Algiers to Paris the night before with President Barrault in the Presidential plane, a converted Caravelle SE-210. The French paratroopers had accomplished their mission, and when the carnage was over, there were cars to take Spencer, Andre Leroi and President Barrault to the airport. The Caravelle was waiting and they were airborne within minutes, President Barrault asleep in his private quarters and Spencer and Andre Leroi in a compartment ahead of the large cabin used by the radio operators.

Spencer and Andre Leroi had been silent for what seemed a very long time. There was a disquieting sense of betrayal between them and it stemmed from the appeals Andre had sent to Spencer and Harry Adams and Ackerley. "You knew we'd look for you," Spencer said at last, but it was a simple statement without bitterness.

"That wasn't why I sent the letters." Andre Leroi had glanced at Spencer then in the dim light of the compartment, and there had been lines of weariness and tension around his eyes. "When the treachery I suspected did, in fact, occur, I showed Mercier copies
254

of my letters to you, to Adams, to Ackerley. I thought the fear of exposure would make him change course. But I hadn't anticipated his moral myopia. He gave those letters to Major Sidki, who dispatched assassins to retrieve the originals."

"They didn't do too badly," Spencer had said. Again it was a simple statement without bitterness. "Two out of three is pretty good. Tell me, Andre: do you think your people can sweep all this under the rug?"

"We must," Andre Leroi said quietly. "The alternatives are too disastrous to think of."

When they had landed at Orly, and Spencer had made his way through the discreet cordons of security police, he had phoned Denise to give her instructions. . . .

The night's sleep had refreshed Andre Leroi. His cheeks were fresh and pink and he wore a dark suit with white piping on the vest, but still there was something somber and haunted in his eyes. They descended to the garage in the basement of Andre Leroi's apartment building.

"I urge you not to come back to Paris, August. Do you understand?"

"Sure. I'm not coming back. But do you still think you can keep this story covered up?"

"As I told you on the plane, we have no alternative."

Spencer nodded. "Which would mean destroying every official record, every written order to Army staffs, and even every person who might be a security risk."

"It can come to that, yes." Andre Leroi looked steadily at Spencer. "That's why I'm driving you to the airport. If there's any trouble, I can handle it."

"Don't get involved on my account, Andre."

Spencer hadn't intended to be sarcastic but he saw a faint touch of color rise in Andre's cheeks.

"I didn't mean it to end this way," Andre said. "If I'd known that Harry Adams and Ackerley were going to die, I'm not sure what course I'd have taken."

"You'd have done the same damn thing," Spencer said. "You wouldn't have hesitated a second. Neither would I."

"That helps a little," Andre said. "What are your plans?"

"I haven't any," Spencer said. "Let's go."

Spencer trusted in his talents for survival. Experience had engrained in him the simplistic truth that it was exceedingly difficult to kill a man if you didn't know where he was. . . .

To his complete surprise and to his definite chagrin Spencer was paged in the terminal building of the Dublin airport, six hours after his flight had departed from Paris. For a moment he considered not answering it. But he had a fair notion of who was on the phone, and he knew that if he didn't take the call now, it would be waiting for him inevitably wherever he chose to go.

It was Douglas Benton, CIA. He said: "Got a line on you through LeMaitre. What are your plans?"

"Nothing that would interest you, Doug."

"No forwarding address? Relax, I don't want it. There'll never be anything in writing, but the man in the Oval Office wants me to send you his thanks. End of conversation, August. Good luck."

Spencer smiled and replaced the phone on its cradle. He felt suddenly clean and free, and very eager to join Denise. There was just time for a pot of tea before he had to board the Pan American 747, whose flight plan would take it soaring over Atlantic time zones to land in tomorrow's sunshine in Mexico City.